DARK HEART FOREVER

Other books by Hodder Children's Books

BEAUTIFUL DEAD
Eden Maguire
Jonas
Arizona
Summer
Phoenix

VAMPIRE DIARIES
L.J. Smith
Volume I: The Awakening and The Struggle
Volume II: The Fury and The Reunion
The Return: Nightfall
The Return: Shadow Souls

NIGHT WORLD
L.J. Smith
Volume I: Secret Vampire, Daughters of Darkness
and Enchantress
Volume II: Dark Angel, The Chosen and Soulmate
Volume III: Huntress, Black Dawn and Witchlight

SECRET CIRCLE
L.J. Smith
Volume I: The Captive and The Initiation Part I
Volume II: The Initiation Part II and The Power

DARK
HEART
FOREVER

LEE MONROE

*Hodder
Children's
Books*

A division of Hachette Children's Books

Typeset in Berkeley Book by Avon DataSet Ltd,
Bidford on Avon, Warwickshire

Printed and bound in Great Britain by
CPI Bookmarque Ltd, Croydon, Surrey

The paper and board used in this paperback by Hodder Children's Books
are natural recyclable products made from wood grown in
sustainable forests. The manufacturing processes conform to the
environmental regulations of the country of origin.

Hodder Children's Books
a division of Hachette Children's Books
338 Euston Road, London NW1 3BH
An Hachette UK company
www.hachette.co.uk

For Molly R.

Branches whipped my face as I ran and my cheek stung where it had been lashed. I pushed forward, warm blood on my lips, my heart thudding faster in my chest. Above me, the night clouds slid uneasily over the pale moon. Beyond me I heard the crunch of boots on snow and glimpsed the dark figure winding through the dense trees. I was so close I could cry, but he slipped quickly out of sight. I should have called out. But the unknown kept me silent.

As I reached the clearing, a spot I knew well at the base of the hill, I heard the sound of a truck groaning slightly along the mountain road. I came to a halt and then stood, panting, to see nothing but the black curving tarmac and the half-moon in the sky.

Whoever he was, he had disappeared.

Suddenly the energy, the force that had kept me

running through the woods evaporated. I stood, freezing and defeated, and tilted my head back to look up at the sky. Midnight blue. No clouds now. Just a bitter, unforgiving night.

A sound behind me – the snap of a twig – made me jerk. But as I turned to look, something heavy gripped my shoulder and I stopped. My face was still but my eyes darted down to see long pale fingers resting on my collarbone.

'Don't move,' someone whispered. 'And don't be frightened.' The owner of the hand gently turned me to look at him. Large eyes, wide mouth, short brown hair. I knew him. I knew this boy.

But we had never met.

'Jane,' said the boy, his hand, surprisingly warm, holding mine. 'Please. I would never hurt you.'

'Who are you?' As I spoke my breath clouded in the cold. 'What am I doing here?' I had no recollection of why I had come into these woods.

'You followed me. You have been dreaming about me for a long time and now you know I'm real . . . Well,' he gave a dry laugh, 'almost real.'

'Please,' I said weakly, as though I had not been in pursuit of him. 'Just let me go home.'

'Jane. You are home.' He let go of my hand and put

both of his around my face, drawing it closer to him.

Green eyes, and skin like a child's, but the bones in his cheeks belonged to a man. His face was gentle, though in his pupils there was something alert and wild. I was so cold I couldn't move, except for my hands shaking and my heart thumping.

Watching my confusion, he stroked my cheeks with his fingertips, and my head lolled, soothed all of a sudden. Then gradually I felt aware of the rest of my body, my legs, my hips, my breasts.

'This is where your story begins,' he whispered. 'With me, in this place.'

And as I listened I knew that here, in this moment, it was true.

Today was my sixteenth birthday, and my story had begun.

CHAPTER ONE

'Jane?'

Something was shaking me.

'Jane. Wake up!'

I jerked awake. Opening my eyes, I saw golden plaits and gingham pyjamas.

'Dot,' I said grumpily, 'what day is it?'

My nine-year-old sister tilted her head, her large, blue eyes regarding me seriously. She wrinkled her nose. 'Saturday, stupid. Your birthday!' She put both hands on my bed and levered herself up to perch next to me. 'They're talking about you downstairs.'

'Already?' I said, still sleepy. 'What are they saying today?'

Dot sighed a little melodramatically. 'Mum is worried about you getting up in the night, opening windows and doors.' She nestled in close to me. 'Last night you left footprints on the carpet in the hall.'

'Oh.' I rested my head back. 'I sleepwalked.'

Dot nodded happily. 'I think it's cool.' She fiddled with the silver chain on my wrist. 'Where do you go, Jane? Aren't you scared?'

'I don't know and I don't know,' I said, pressing my cheek against her blonde head. 'I'm kind of asleep . . . you know?'

Dot giggled. 'Well, I think you're brave,' she said. 'Don't listen to them.'

'What else does Mum say?' I asked casually.

'That maybe you should go to boarding school,' Dot replied sadly. 'Because you're too insolar.'

'What?' I prodded Dot's arm. '*Insolar?*'

'You don't have enough friends.' Dot turned to face me. She slid her arms around my waist and kissed my cheek. 'But I told her you've got me.'

'Right.' I smiled. 'I think the word is *insular*.'

'Like I said.' Dot buried her face in my chest. 'Insolar.'

'I'm sixteen. I don't have to go to school any more. Not if I don't want to.'

'You're lucky.' Dot scrambled to sit up. She examined my face. 'What's that?' She pointed at my cheek, pushing my hair to the side. 'You've got a scratch. It wasn't there yesterday.'

I stared at her and put my hand up to my face, feeling the rough, puckered skin.

'I must have done it in my sleep,' I said cautiously, remembering the trees and intense cold and then … warmth like I'd never felt before. And someone—

'You'd better cover it up.' Dot broke my thoughts, pulling my dark, curly hair over my face, covering the wound. 'Or Mum will start locking your bedroom door at night.'

'She fusses too much.' I said, half wishing that I could be locked away. For the few weeks leading up to my birthday I'd been having these dreams. At first I'd had no real memory of what happened in them, but lately . . . lately I had been remembering more, waking exhausted and sometimes finding inexplicable bruises and scratches.

'I'm hungry.' Dot slithered off the bed. 'Breakfast time!'

Downstairs it was a typically unceremonious Jonas birthday breakfast. My mother doesn't believe in spoiling. She and Dad were buying me a car for my seventeenth, so this year was some money in a bank account. Dot, bless her, had bought me a book token and Dad had kissed me on the cheek and got back to tapping out numbers on his calculator. Hot topic of the day I was not. The mood this morning was sober.

'Happy birthday to me,' I muttered, pushing rabbit food around in a bowl.

'Old Murray's cancelled his commission,' said my father, to no one in particular.

'Oh God.' My mother sighed, pushing away her unfinished yoghurt and banana. 'Not another one.'

Dad nodded, brushing his beard with a napkin. 'But we'll be fine, Anna. I have Mrs Benjamin's kitchen table and Pete's staircase. We won't starve.'

Mum picked up her bowl and pushed her chair back, shooing our Irish wolfhound, Bobby, out of the way. She walked into the kitchen. 'But it's drying up, Jack,' she called back. 'No one's got any money, and they're not coming up this far.' She started putting on rubber gloves. 'Mrs Caffrey in the post office says everyone thinks this little mountain is cursed.'

My dad winked at my sister and me. 'I'm a carpenter,' he said. 'I'll always get work.'

My mother, who never fails to look on the dark side of life, grunted and began wrestling with the bin liner. 'We need to prepare ourselves for the worst, is all I'm saying.'

'What's a curse?' asked Dot, plunging a soldier into her

boiled egg. I watched queasily as the yolk trickled on to the shell.

'It's made up, is what it is,' I told her. 'There are no such things as curses.'

'Like what they say about magic?' Dot stared, interested.

'That doesn't exist either,' I said, rolling my eyes. 'It's what Grandma Jonas used to call *claptrap*.' I looked up and met my mother's eyes as she stood, one hand clutching a bag full of rubbish, in the doorway.

'We need to talk about your education for the next few years, Jane,' she said abruptly. 'I can't go on teaching you at home. I need to get a job.'

'Fine. I'll go to college.' I drank the rest of my tea. 'There's one in Hassock. And it's only five miles away.' I smiled at Dot. 'I can go by bike.'

'No,' said Mum quickly. 'Not here.'

'Boarding school.' Dot poked my arm. 'I told you, Jane.'

'I'm too old,' I said. 'It's ridiculous.'

Mum put down the rubbish. 'Not boarding school. God knows we can't afford that. But somewhere you can mix with girls your own age. It's not healthy for you to be stuck up here all day.' She sighed. 'A fresh start. Right, Jack?'

My dad rubbed his forehead awkwardly. 'I don't know, Anna . . . is it really necessary?' He looked over at me. 'Your mother just wants you to be happy – after what those girls . . . I mean, a new school might help you forget.'

Mum tried smiling at me. 'It'll be good for you, Jane. You'll make proper friends.'

I winced. 'I don't need to make friends. It's my birthday and you're spoiling it. I'm fine as I am.'

My parents exchanged a look that said *We'll see*.

You won't, I thought defiantly.

'I'm going out for a bike ride,' I said, scraping back my chair and walking to the back door. As I pulled my hair into an untidy ponytail my hand knocked against the scratch on my face.

'Ow.' I grabbed at the door handle, flustered.

'Jane?' called my mother.

'I'm fine.' I snapped. 'Stop fussing.'

'Wrap up warm, sweetheart,' she said limply.

I ignored her and pulled my hood up.

'Be back by twelve,' she said. 'We need to do Maths today.'

I stepped outside without answering, immediately regretting not taking a coat.

I don't need change, I thought angrily as I wheeled

my bike out of the shed. I don't need friends. I closed my eyes, thinking of a year ago, when I had walked out of school for the last time. I'd had no friends, Sarah had seen to that. Queen Bee, Sarah Emerson, she who ruled the school and cast a poisonous spell over everyone in it.

'You're a freak, Jonas,' she told me, over and over again. 'You look like a boy. You dress like a tramp.' For Sarah, who never wore the same thing twice, who learned the word 'materialistic' before 'mama', I was incomprehensible.

I took the rugged hill path down towards the town. It seemed right that my journey was uncomfortable, jolting over the stones as I curved down our piece of the mountain. After days of grey sky that had sealed us in, this morning it was a beautiful bright day. A day of escape. The crispness of the air pecked satisfyingly at my cheeks as I rode and I began to warm up as I pushed hard on the pedals. To my left was the wood, pines with a frosting of snow. It was dense and eerie, not somewhere you'd want to be at night.

I was there last night.

I shook my head, suddenly anxious, and found myself braking. I put one foot down on the ground and thought I heard someone call my name. Something in the trees. I swallowed and dropped my bike where it was. As the wheel spun behind me I trod through the gorse to take a closer look. I reached the outskirts of the wood and saw nothing. No one. I had turned away when I heard it again, a soft sound that could almost have been the wind. '*Jane*.'

'Jane!'

I dropped my hand and jerked round. My sister was crouched down by my bike, spinning the wheel with one hand as she looked over at me.

'You ran all this way?' I asked her.

'I want to come too,' she said in a wheedling voice. 'Mum and Dad are arguing again.'

'Fine. But I'm taking the painful route,' I told her.

Dot nodded furiously. 'I don't mind the stones,' she said brightly. 'It's fun.'

'Strange child.' But I smiled at her all the same. As she struggled with getting the bike upright again I turned back to take one more look at the dense trees, listening.

Nothing.

'What are you doing?' Dot called, jigging from foot to foot. 'Let's go.'

I did a final examination of the trees before walking back to the path. Disappointed.

CHAPTER TWO

Our nearest town, Bale, was only a mile from the house, but Dot moaning in front of me meant it took forever. When we finally got on to the main street – what my mother called 'civilisation' – Dot's bottom was aching.

'Told you it was the painful route.' I grinned at her. 'Was that fun for you?'

Dot screwed up her nose and stuck her tongue out. 'We need a milkshake,' she said, looking hopefully down the street.

Bale was a bit like one of those towns you see in old Wild West films starring Clint Eastwood. Just one wide road, flanked by mismatched buildings. No supermarket. No fancy shops. Just the essentials. A local grocer's, selling everything from needle and thread to caviar; a cobbler's, a tiny junk shop – optimistically known as the Town Antiques Emporium – a tiny post office and a café:

13

Fabio's. It used to belong to an Italian family, who'd disappeared before I was born, but Eileen and her husband Greg had kept the name. It was a friendly, old-fashioned place, laid out like a diner. I'd been coming to Fabio's since I was able to pronounce 'vanilla chocolate'. I'd outgrown the milkshake now, but it was Dot's favourite place in the world.

She rushed along the pavement towards it, leaving me locking up the bike by the defunct petrol station. As I straightened up again, a figure crossing the road caught my eye. Tall, checked shirt and long legs in dark blue jeans. He was about my age, maybe a little older, with a tanned face and sun-streaked, short, messy hair. Even from this distance I could see he was one of those intimidating, good-looking, alpha-male types, and we didn't get many of those round here. I saw him glance my way and I sniffed, indifferently, and moved to follow Dot into the café.

I watched as the boy reached the entrance of Fabio's at the same time as my sister and performed a comical bow, holding the door open for her. I heard her shriek, delighted, and slowed right down. Suddenly I wished I'd worn something less androgynous than my shabby old grey hoodie and ancient dungarees that were too short for me.

'Do you have to dress like a ragamuffin, Jane?' was my mother's familiar refrain. 'You're a young woman, not a car mechanic.'

Just for today I conceded, she had a point.

I quickly unzipped my hoodie and tied it round my waist. As I passed the windows to get to the door and glimpsed my reflection I realised this was not an improvement. Irritated, I untied it and bunched it under one arm.

As I walked into the café I saw that Dot was already perched on a stool by the counter. The boy was sitting next to her, still making her laugh. I dug my purse out of my front pocket and stood at the other end of the counter.

Eileen sashayed over, beaming at me. 'She's already got her order in,' she said, cocking her head in Dot's direction. 'And she's got an admirer.'

'Who is that boy?' I asked casually, emptying my change on to the counter. 'Never seen him before.'

'Evan?' She shrugged, then leaned closer to me. 'He's got family around here apparently – step-family, I think.' She pursed her lips in concentration. 'He was the one in the paper . . . you know. The boy who went missing in Australia – turned up on his dad's doorstep. I can't for the life of me think of his surname.'

'I don't remember that.' I frowned.

Eileen shook her head. 'You must walk round with a blindfold on and earplugs in,' she said, with a smile. 'That boy was the talk of the town a few weeks ago.'

'Interesting,' I said, sneaking a look over at him.

'Very interesting,' she said with a wink. 'And a looker too.'

'Hmm.' I wrinkled my nose and pushed over seven pounds in coins. 'Guess I'd better rescue him from Dot. She's the clingy type.'

Eileen chuckled. 'She's adorable and you know it,' she said, waving away the money. 'Which is why you girls get your milkshakes on the house.'

'Thanks, Eileen,' I said gruffly. 'I think I'll have a coffee today.'

Even though I hate coffee.

'Okey-dokey.' Eileen winked at me. 'Much more sophisticated.'

I blushed what must have been crimson pink and shuffled over to Dot and Evan.

'This is Evan,' announced Dot, as I approached. 'He's looking for some company. Evan, this is Jane.'

Evan turned, smiling. His eyes were incredibly blue. And though they were bright and friendly, there was something else there too. Something sharp, clever.

16

'Hi Jane.' His voice was deep, but quiet.

I nodded rudely, looking away quickly. Up close he was unnervingly beautiful. Every feature moulded to perfection. Practically inhuman.

We need to leave as soon as possible, I told myself. I couldn't hold a conversation with anyone my own age, let alone this vision.

'We haven't got much time,' I told Dot, who narrowed her eyes.

'We've only just got here,' she said, kicking her legs out and catching Evan's knee with her boot. He smiled gracefully.

'I've got Maths, remember?' I picked up the menu, to occupy my awkward hands.

Dot threw a look over at the Beautiful One.

'Jane is home-schooled,' she told him matter-of-factly.

'You don't go to school?' he asked, and I was forced to engage with him.

'Yeah . . . No . . . I used to . . .' His mouth tilted into a half-smile, puzzled. 'But – it's a long story.' I looked at Dot, willing her to keep her mouth shut, and her eyes grew big. But Eileen was setting down a cup and saucer and Dot's milkshake, and my sister swivelled round to pick it up, taking a long, noisy slurp through the straw. I rolled my eyes and caught Evan's and then we were both smiling.

'You can tell me all about your secret past another time, then,' he said, studying my face. 'You look like a girl with a story to tell.'

'Not me,' I said. 'Nothing much goes on in my life.'

Unlike yours, I wanted to add. But didn't. Because I am socially retarded.

'Eileen said you had family here?' I said instead.

Evan picked up a napkin from the box and started folding it. 'Yep,' he said. 'My dad. Bill Forrest and his family. I was living with my mum in Australia for a long time.'

As I tried to think of who Bill was – the surname seemed familiar – Evan's fingers were moving quickly and my eyes fell on what he was doing. Origami?

'I'm staying with Dad over the summer – maybe longer,' he went on, and he looked up at me through his eyelashes, 'if I can find something to keep me busy.' He dropped his head again to concentrate on folding quickly. All of a sudden, there in his hands was a white, tissue swan.

'Cool!' said Dot, pushing away her drink and grabbing hold of it.

'Dot, don't break it,' I said quickly. I looked at Evan. 'You realise you have to teach her how to do that now?'

'Any time,' he said, winking at my sister. 'Told you I need to make myself useful.'

'Can you do odd jobs?' asked Dot, putting the swan in her pocket before scraping the last of her shake out of her glass with a long spoon. 'My dad needs someone for odd jobs.'

'No he doesn't,' I said. 'When did he say that?'

She shook her head. 'I heard him telling Mum.' She poked Evan's arm. 'How old are you?'

'Eighteen,' said Evan. 'Just.'

'It's Jane's birthday today,' Dot told him proudly. 'She's sixteen.'

'Is that right?' I noticed his taut cheekbones and his eyes flicker over me subtly as a slow grin spread across his face. 'Sweet sixteen.'

Before I had a chance to colour up, Eileen called from across the room.

'Sixteen already.' She shook her head and put two clean cups back on the shelf above the coffee machine. 'I'm getting old.' She smiled at the three of us. 'You've got yourself a little party at least. Happy birthday.'

'Thanks, Eileen.' I took a sip of my drink, feeling Evan's eyes on me.

'So,' he said, adding some sugar to his coffee. 'What's the birthday girl doing to celebrate?'

'Oh, nothing.' I finally looked across at him. 'It's no big deal.'

'We're playing Scrabble later,' Dot said, fiddling with her straw. 'And Mum will cook a special dinner.'

I nodded at Evan. 'Sadly, she's right. We don't make a fuss in our house.'

'What about your friends?' Evan drank some coffee, not taking his eyes off me.

'I . . .'

'She doesn't have any,' Dot supplied. 'She likes her own company.'

There was a small silence, as I fought the urge to strangle my sister.

Evan finished his coffee and smiled at me. 'Well, I bet it's excellent company,' he said.

This time the blush crept into my cheeks and though I tried to smile back, I ended up grimacing weirdly.

'I'm sure you could come for dinner,' Dot told him. 'Mum always makes too much food.'

'Don't be silly,' I said quickly, a little sharply. 'He's not interested in coming to dinner with a bunch of strangers.'

'How do you know?'

Dot wouldn't let up, so I shot her a warning look.

'We've got to get going. It'll take us half an hour and it's uphill.'

20

Evan looked from one to the other of us. 'Where do you two live anyway?'

'Up the road—' I began.

'We live on the mountain,' Dot interrupted me. 'The house nearest the top. You can't miss it.'

'Come on.' I dragged her off the stool and smiled tightly at Evan. 'Nice meeting you. See you around.'

'Hope so.' He was staring at me, and as he lifted his head I noticed a small, faint, disc-shaped scar on one side of his neck. 'I'll be here tomorrow.'

'Right.'

'At the same time.'

'OK.' I started pushing Dot towards the door before she could answer on my behalf. 'Bye, Eileen,' I called, and she waved a cloth at me.

As we reached the door, I glanced back quickly to see Evan watching.

'He's cuuuuttte,' said Dot, dancing about on the pavement.

'Shut up.'

'I don't think he really noticed your weird dungarees either,' she went on, tugging at them. 'He was too desperately in love.'

I grunted and made to wallop her. 'You're insane, you know that.'

21

'You should see him again,' she said, ignoring me. 'He's very good-looking.'

'Stop right there, Dorothea Jonas. It's not your business and I'm not interested in having a boyfriend.' I gave her a stern look. 'Besides. He's not someone Mum would approve of.'

'Why?' She frowned.

'Because . . . because he's been in trouble.' I paused before deciding to go on. 'He was in the paper apparently . . . He went missing in Australia and turned up here months later.'

'He's *that* boy!?' Dot was saucer-eyed. 'Dad was talking about him the other day. Mum went all soppy over it.'

'Yup. So he must be pretty mixed-up.'

'They're the cute ones. That's what Cassidy's sister says. The mixed-up ones are always the ones girls want.'

'Yeah, well,' I said, rolling my eyes. 'Cassidy's sister doesn't know everything.'

Dot gave me one of her shrewd, appraising looks.

'By the way, we're walking home,' I said. 'Or Mum will send out a search party.'

I'd read enough bad romances to know that boys flirt and it doesn't mean a thing. And it was only a matter of time before Evan would find out that I was the freak around here. The girl who dressed like a boy and had no friends.

But as I wheeled the bike home, with Dot chattering to me perched on the saddle, I couldn't help feeling that something had rolled away from in front of me.

Everything was a little brighter now.

CHAPTER THREE

I didn't want to go to sleep that night. I couldn't. Thoughts were tumbling around in my head, all mixed up. But I was also afraid of what I would dream. I was tired of waking every morning with a headache and the kind of fatigue I used to get on cross-country runs at school.

I propped myself up on pillows and watched the not-quite-full moon as it sat, serene, in the sky. A clear night, the tops of the trees just visible through the window. I shivered, realising that the window was slightly open, and got out of bed to shut it.

As I approached the ledge a sound – the sound of boots on snow – stopped me dead. Dad?

Putting one hand to my chest I tiptoed over and reached out to pull the window closed, but before I could a voice came, clear, from outside.

'Jane.'

Heart thumping, I leaned forward and looked down. *He* was there, dressed in a black coat, long enough to reach his ankles. Dark hair flopping over his face. He wasn't exactly good-looking, he had more of an interesting face. Fine-boned, pale. Though even from this distance I could see his eyes were extraordinary, large and kind of almond-shaped. The colour was like moss on a pebble in a stream.

'I came to find you today.' His voice was surprisingly deep, assured.

'You called my name,' I heard myself say. 'And then you disappeared.'

He smiled. 'I saw your sister. I wanted to see you alone.'

I leaned further out of the window. 'This is a dream too, then. It must be.'

'Is it?' He stepped back quietly. 'How do you know?'

I gave a short laugh. 'Because in my waking life I don't get visited by strangers in the middle of the night.'

'And what about today?' he said. 'When I called your name. Was that a dream?'

'No.' I bit my lip. 'I don't know. I could have imagined it.'

There was a silence. He regarded me seriously.

'OK.' Resting my elbows on the window ledge, I

put my face in my hands. 'There is something familiar about you.'

He laughed. 'Tell me my name.'

'Luca,' I said without thinking.

'See.' He hugged himself. 'You do know me.'

'I don't know how. Why is this happening?'

'Don't look for logical answers.' He pushed his hands deeper in his pockets. 'It won't make sense, any of it. But it will, in time. You'll see.'

'Wait there.' I stepped back from the window and grabbed my socks and boots and the thick woollen poncho that belonged to my grandmother. Passing the wardrobe mirror I grimaced at my bizarre reflection before moving to the staircase and down to the back door.

He was standing right in front of me when I opened it.

'Nice poncho.' He tugged at the fringe.

I stepped outside, pulling the door nearly shut behind me. 'Look,' I whispered. 'I don't know who you are. I just know I'm tired of dreaming about you.' I glared at him. 'I don't need this.'

He said nothing, but leaned forward and put his arms around me, holding me gently in the moonlight. I didn't try and stop him, or pull away. It felt right somehow. He smelled of wood, a little smoky. He was warm.

'It's so good to be with you at last,' he said, his head resting against mine. Though I thought I should struggle or scream, I only felt soothed and comfortable. I let him hold me for a minute longer before putting my arms around him. He was slender but solid.

Luca leaned back and took my head in his hands. 'Do you think you can stretch the boundaries of your reality?'

'What?'

'Well.' He paused. 'Imagine for a moment that the world you know is not the only one.'

I rolled my eyes, pulling away from him. 'Listen, Gandalf, I'm not into parallel worlds and all that supernatural bullshit. If this is some kind of joke—'

I wondered suddenly whether this was some prank of Sarah's. She must have been so bored this past year with no one to torment. Was this Stage Two of her plan to break me for good?

As we stood, something scratched at the door behind me and Bobby's head pushed through my legs, sniffing at the ground. I put one hand down to stroke his silkiness but a rough predatory growl stopped me. Bobby was crouching back on his hind legs, staring up at Luca, snarling, teeth bared.

'Easy.' I bent to be level with the dog. 'What's up, boy?' But Bobby continued to growl and he was shaking too.

I looked up at Luca, who had stepped back. 'It's OK,' I told him. 'He really won't hurt you.'

'He wants to,' Luca said, wiping his face with his sleeve.

I rubbed the dog's soft ears. 'Bobby's not like that. He's a friendly dog, aren't you, boy?'

'No, I mean . . .' Luca hesitated. 'He can sense that I'm . . .' He stopped, swallowing. 'I'm not from here.'

'Me and him both,' I said dryly. 'Because you're not.'

Luca looked up at the sky, up at the almost-perfectly-round moon. 'I want to tell you all about me, but you don't trust me yet and it will sound . . . ridiculous,' he said. 'I wish there was more time. Tomorrow I . . .'

'Tomorrow you what?'

I got to my feet and moved towards him, Bobby still whining behind me.

Luca reached out to take hold of my hands but then stopped, putting his back in his pockets. 'You won't understand. It will scare you.'

'Like you're not scaring me now?'

'Is that really how you feel?' he asked. 'Scared?'

I realised I felt nothing but calm, which in itself was worrying.

'No. This is just a dream. Like the others . . .'

'Or does it feel as though it's really happening?'
Luca stared at me, unblinking.

I held his eye.

'It feels . . . real,' I answered, eventually.

'Then it is,' he said simply. 'That scratch on your face.
You got that in a dream?'

I swallowed. I knew where I had got it.

'You have nothing to fear. Not from me,' he said softly.
'I would never hurt you.'

'I know,' I whispered, because somehow I did.

And then I felt his lips on my forehead, the softest
kiss, and the smell of him. It made me want to nestle
against his body and I felt my own responding. I lifted my
head to meet his lips, suddenly knowing what to do, and
what I wanted, but he remained still, sad-eyed now.

'We are friends,' he said, touching the wound on
my face. Then he took my hand and twined his fingers
through mine.

I closed my eyes, weary all of a sudden and muddled.

'Evan,' I said, 'what do you want?'

My eyes snapped open as Luca jerked away from me.
When he spoke his voice was a little hostile.

'Who's Evan?'

The next day I felt shattered. I spent as long as I could

lying in bed, before my mother's angry clattering downstairs forced me to get up and dressed.

Another fashion triumph, I told myself as I studied my reflection in the wardrobe mirror. Combat trousers, so old the knee was ripped and the belt hooks had gone. A thick, striped, wool jumper my dad's mum had knitted me before she died two years ago. And on my feet, the slipper-socks I'd got for Christmas last year.

My hair had grown long and was probably the best thing about me. I pulled it down, wondering what it would look like straight and sleek. I should actually start doing something about my appearance. Two mysterious boys had suddenly appeared on the scene. The least I could do was make myself more presentable.

'Down here, now,' came my mother's voice, cranky and impatient. 'This is not a doss-house.'

Dot gave me a warning look as I arrived in the kitchen, then, grabbing hold of Bobby's collar, she disappeared out of the back door to see my father, who was working outside.

Mum's eyes slid down to my snug jumper. 'You should give that to Dot,' she said, staring at my chest which, like my hair, had grown some over the past few months.

'We need to get you some new clothes, you're getting bigger.' My mother flapped out a tea towel and folded it over the handle on the oven door. 'A proper bra.' She had her back to me, so didn't see my eyes rolling up at the ceiling. 'You need more than a vest these days.'

'Fine,' I said without interest. I pulled out a chair, pouring cereal into a bowl.

Mum stopped pottering and stood watching me as I ate.

'You went outside last night again?' She gripped the back of a chair with her hands. 'I heard you, talking to yourself.'

I swallowed a mouthful of cereal before answering. 'I don't remember.'

My mother sat down opposite me. 'It's not good. It's unsettling us all.'

'Really?' I hadn't noticed Dot or my father being remotely bothered. Just her.

'Do you not remember anything, Jane?' she said, rubbing at a spot on the table. 'Nothing at all?'

'No,' I said firmly. As if she would believe me if I did tell her. 'Nothing.'

'Look at you, you look exhausted. I think we need to take you to the doctor . . .'

'There's nothing wrong with me. It's just a phase or something . . .' I pushed my bowl away. 'Why are you getting so worked up about it?'

'I worry about you, sweetheart,' she said, softly now. 'You're growing up, and things are changing – you know, with your body. Hormones . . .' She trailed off awkwardly.

'So, that's the explanation. It's just me being hormonal.' I smiled falsely. 'And then they'll settle down and everything will be fine.'

'Maybe.' But her face was anxious. 'Perhaps that is all it is.'

I glanced out of the window, hearing Dad and Dot chatting outside. 'Am I free to go outside now?' I asked in a dry tone. 'Or will that upset you, too?'

'Go on . . .' She got up and watched me as I went to get my hiking boots from the hall.

As I opened the back door I glanced at her observing me, fearfully almost. And I felt a twinge of guilt. I was being a brat.

'I'll be fine, Mum,' I told her softly. 'Don't worry.'

'Bobby, what is it with you?' I said, pushing him off my lap as I sat in front of my computer. 'You won't leave me alone today.'

It was four in the afternoon and I had finally got down to homework, or 'work', since I didn't actually go to school. I'd been assigned the Tudors as my History topic by my mother for this term. Normally I loved History, for me it was like escaping into another world, discovering a life I could hardly imagine. But today I wasn't concentrating, even though I was desperate for a diversion. What had happened to me last night was, for the first time, clear in practically every detail. No wonder the antics of Henry and his poor wives had lost interest for me. My own life had taken on a whole new and unsettling dimension. I wondered briefly if I had some kind of mental disorder, something that had lain dormant for years until now. I was seeing things that weren't there, imagining green-eyed boys singling me out for nocturnal visits. It would make sense, I thought, to invent a situation that would never happen. Never happen to *me*, anyway.

Bobby gave me his most winning look and pawed my leg. 'Dottie!' I called. 'Take the dog out, would you? He's all over me.'

Dot appeared in the doorway. 'Here, boy . . .' She bent down and opened her arms out to embrace the dog, but he remained, indifferent, beside me.

'Silly dog.' She straightened up and walked over to look at my screen. 'Ugh. History homework. Poor Jane.' She put her arm around my shoulders, and I turned my face up to hers and smiled.

'Your scratch has gone,' she said, touching the place where it had been.

I put my hand up and felt only smooth skin.

'Janey, you look like you've seen a ghost or something.'

Not a ghost, I thought, calmly. But something just as unreal.

'Anyway, Mum wants you to go with Dad to the shops before they shut. She's run out of "ladies' things". He's leaving right now.'

On cue, we both heard the sound of Dad starting the engine in his truck. I looked down at my combats and dolly jumper. 'I need to change,' I told Dot, shutting down the computer. 'Tell Dad five minutes.'

'You're changing to go to the shops with Dad?' Dot raised an eyebrow.

'So? I can't go out like this.'

Dot twirled maddeningly around the chair then abruptly stopped. 'Put on a skirt. You might bump into you-know-who . . .'

Evan. I had almost forgotten about him. Boys are obviously like buses – just when you've given up waiting, two of them come round the corner.

'Forget it,' I told Dot as I walked towards the stairs. 'And I don't even have a skirt.'

'Borrow one of Mother's,' my sister called as I climbed up to my bedroom. 'She won't mind . . .'

I huffed as I threw sweatshirts, shorts, jeans and leggings out of my drawers. It was true. I didn't have a single item of feminine clothing. The only girly thing about me was my hair. Thick, dark and unfashionably curly. I studied my face in the wardrobe mirror. My eyes were OK, big and a dark grey-blue colour, but my skin was a nightmare. Pale and sickly. There was no hope for me.

'Jane, hurry up,' called Dad from outside. 'What are you doing up there?'

Quickly I put on a little eyeliner I'd stolen from Mum once. It was an improvement, I realised as I checked out my eyes in the mirror. I rubbed in a dab of red lipstick to give my cheeks some colour. Then I ran my fingers through my hair, which at least was glossy. What do you think you're doing? I asked myself. Evan can't possibly be interested in you.

Still, I carefully chose my newest, dark, straight-legged jeans and a T-shirt that usually made me self-conscious because it was too tight over my chest, but today I somehow didn't mind. I cast around the room to find something warm to put over it. My eyes fell on the poncho on my chair. I'd take it off if I saw Evan, I told myself.

Even if it meant freezing to death.

Stop it. You're not going to see him.

My dad tooted his horn loudly.

'OK, OK.' I moved towards the rumpled poncho and pulled it over my head. 'I'm coming.'

I had the strangest feeling as I pulled it down, a feeling of foreboding. Out of the window, I could see my father waiting patiently by the truck. I smiled, trying to shrug off dark thoughts. I always loved going places with my dad. He'd turn on the radio and sing, and I'd always feign embarrassment. Secretly, though, I loved him singing as we drove. It made me feel safe, protected.

Dad looked up at my window and waved.

'You look beautiful, Janey,' he said. 'Now hurry up or your mother will make both of our lives miserable.'

I grabbed my purse and ran down the stairs, foreboding gone.

Almost.

CHAPTER FOUR

'Damn, this old thing is getting crankier every day,' said Dad as the engine sputtered unhealthily on the road down to Bale. He changed gear, deafening us both with the noise.

'You need a new one,' I said, as he pressed his foot down on the accelerator. The truck swerved unhelpfully towards the side of the road and then swung out again.

'Dad?' I said, alarmed. 'This feels dangerous.'

'It's fine.' I wasn't reassured. 'It's the cold weather lately. She's telling me she's had enough.' We were coming to the bottom of the hill. Dad tried to get a station on the radio but it crackled unhelpfully and he gave up. I put my feet up on the dashboard and leaned back.

As I looked through my window, I saw the sky turning rapidly from bright to overcast. A huge black cloud appeared from nowhere and the light dimmed to near-darkness.

'Great.' Dad reached into the glove compartment for his glasses. 'Can't see a thing. Janey, can you . . . ?'

But a shape coming out of the patch of trees to the right diverted my attention. An animal, the biggest dog I had ever seen, hurtled powerfully into the road in front of us. As the animal sped past, it leaped.

A snarling head, teeth bared, the red of its angry gums visible. I saw its eyes, black as night, hateful. I dropped my feet from the dashboard.

'Dad!' I heard myself scream. 'Stop!'

'Jesus!' I turned to see my father's face ashen and frightened. 'I can't . . .' With enormous effort he gripped the steering wheel and turned it to swerve out of the creature's way, and the truck seemed to gain momentum, careering towards the wire fence holding back the mountain trees. Panicking, I put my hands to my eyes, unable to look, registering only that I had my seatbelt on. All I could hear was the buzzing of the engine and then the massive jolt as it drove into the fence and the low stone wall behind it. I kept my hands over my eyes, waiting for it to be over.

We had stopped moving, but the engine was going mad, humming maniacally like the most powerful chainsaw you've ever heard.

My heart still thumping, I took my hands from my eyes and turned to my father. He lay slumped over the wheel, his forehead streaked with blood. Not moving.

'Dad?' I gasped, moving cautiously in my seat. I didn't seem to be hurt. Snapping out of my seatbelt, I scooched over to him, leaning forward to see if his eyes were open. They weren't. I swallowed, feeling frightened tears coming.

Don't panic, Jane, I told myself, but I had no idea what to do. I didn't even own a mobile phone because I had no one to ring – but Dad did. I frantically dug around in the pockets of his coat – but nothing, he must have left it behind today. I closed my eyes, willing another car to come past and see us, but there was only silence. I knew very well that this stretch of road had no drive-throughs. It led up to our house and nothing else. Nobody would come up this far.

I let out a small moan and sat back, trying to think. I'd left the Girl Guides the week I'd joined, typically antisocial. If I'd stayed, I might have some clue about what to do in this kind of emergency.

Selfish idiot.

I wound down the window and let the freezing air calm me. I had a feeling, Girl Guides or not, that you were supposed to keep warm if you were in shock – but it felt like the right thing. Above me the dark clouds dispersed, revealing a full moon.

I stared at it, perfect and round up there in the sky, as though it would provide some vital inspiration. Then, knowing that I was wasting time, I shut my eyes, willing myself to be strong, to think.

Think, Jane.

And then there was just stillness, and I emptied my head of every other thought but what I wanted, really wanted. Help him. Help him. Help him. I chanted it in my mind, over and over.

In my head I saw my father on a trolley in the A&E in Hassock, rushing through corridors to where a doctor and two nurses were standing. And then the frantic administering of drugs, a heart monitor, the beeping of machines, someone shouting out orders, and a hand on my arm, rubbing it, a soft, female voice, talking to me.

'Is he going to be OK?'

I opened my eyes, startling myself with the sound of my voice.

A woman in scrubs, with small, birdlike features, was smiling at me.

'He's going to be OK.' She studied me. 'Are you sure

you weren't hurt? I think we need to check you out.'

'I thought he was . . .' I stopped, relief making me shake.

'He's concussed and lost consciousness for a while and he's got nasty head and neck injuries,' said the nurse. 'But you got him here quickly.'

'How did I . . . ?' I began. How had we got here? It didn't make sense.

'Never seen anything like it,' she said, shining a thin torch into my eyes. 'Your friend just walking in, carrying your dad in his arms. Quite the hero.' She clicked off the light. 'And you seem in good shape. You're very lucky.'

'My friend?' Could this day get any more surreal?

'He's back in the visitors' room,' she said, picking up a clipboard and writing something down. 'And he's causing quite a stir.' She winked at me. 'Lucky girl.'

I smiled weakly. 'I'll be right back. If you could just tell me where the visitors' room is?'

She pointed down the corridor. 'Keep walking and first left.'

I walked slowly, unable to catch my breath. Who was I going to find in that room?

I knew only two boys, and one of them was technically a figment of my imagination.

As I rounded the corner I looked down at myself. My poncho, my jeans, my T-shirt were perfectly intact, even my green Converse were without a mark. I hadn't got a scratch.

A large sign saying VISITORS' ROOM sat above a glass door with a Venetian blind hanging behind it. I took hold of the handle and held my breath. Slowly I turned it and the door opened to reveal an almost-empty room. Empty but for a figure in a familiar dark coat, hunched in a seat, his long legs resting on a low table in front of him. His face looked paler than ever, but the sight of it, and his soft, green eyes regarding me where I stood, made me curiously calm again.

'You helped us . . .' I whispered, tears coming quietly. 'Thank you.'

'You're welcome.' He gave me a weak smile, keeping his arms wrapped around him, his hands lost in the folds of his coat. I moved to sit next to him, but he shook his head.

'No . . . Jane,' he said, his voice strained. 'Now is not the time. I will explain this to you. I promise.' I noticed he was trembling.

'What's the matter with you?' I looked down, noticing the whole of his body seemed to be in spasm.

'I . . . I'll explain that, too . . .' Luca's voice juddered.

'But you have to leave now, you understand. Go back to your father.'

'But I . . .' I took another step closer, reluctant to leave him like this.

'Please leave,' he said. And his tone was hard now, his eyes growing wide and aggressive. I stepped back, shocked, and Luca swallowed, speaking again with effort. 'Believe me, this will be too much for you. Go.'

I nodded, turning back – and then I heard it. A sound, low and hoarse, behind me. I swallowed and ran through the door, shutting it firmly. Then, not wanting to hear what was happening inside, I walked quickly back to where I needed to be.

CHAPTER FIVE

Greek myths and legends, I'd studied them. I'd drawn the parallels with feelings and behaviour and all the dilemmas and challenges people face today. But elves and goblins, complicated labyrinthine worlds where dragons speak and quests are embarked on? I'd never taken them seriously. I knew that it was strange, given my alienation from a world full of social networks and fashion magazines and cliques, that I hadn't lost myself in these worlds, loved them and believed in them – but I hadn't. My dad always said I was born seeing black and white and nothing in between, but I didn't think that was true. I guess deep down, I never dared believe that magic existed. Until the day Dad ended up in hospital.

I picked up the box of cereal I'd been staring at for five minutes and added it to my basket. I checked Mum's list.

Soap, dog food and a copy of the local newspaper.

I found the soap further along. Unperfumed. Typical of my mother.

Then I moved up the second aisle in our cramped little grocer's, picking up two tins of fancy dog food. Again, typical. Bobby was the only recipient of luxury in our family.

The papers and magazines were kept in front of the counter and as I headed towards them I could see the headline of the *Hassock Gazette*. You couldn't miss it. *WHERE DID THE MYSTERIOUS HERO GO?*

I took a sharp breath, frowning. I couldn't think about this any more.

Him.

Nearly a month had passed since the accident. I'd spent weeks going over every detail, and I still couldn't make sense of it. I'd just stayed in my room, reading old historical romances of my mother's and moping about with Dot. The whole family was in shock as Dad convalesced at home, slow and fragile. He was getting better now, but it had shaken us all up. My mother had stopped going on about sending me to school, at least. But she seemed permanently stressed, snapping at me and Dot over the slightest thing, telling us to get out from under her feet. But I didn't want to go anywhere. My dreams had stopped.

Luca had gone. And though I should have been relieved, all I felt was let down. Crazy. I didn't know him.

Taking a copy of the paper and dumping my basket on the counter, I nodded at the boy working the till. He'd been at my school, a couple of years above me. Eric. One of the few people at Hassock Academy who hadn't bothered to torment me. He was nice enough . . . maybe a little dim. Eric glanced up at me once and started adding up the items. When he got to the *Gazette* he paused, taking in the headline.

'So cool,' he said, looking up at me. 'That guy. Like some kind of superhero.'

'Superheroes don't exist,' I said witheringly, grabbing the paper and stuffing it in my rucksack. 'They're for little boys.'

Eric straightened up. 'I know that,' he said defensively. 'It's just, you know, pretty weird how he was kind of "wandering around" a mountain road.' He put the rest of the stuff into a plastic bag. 'You have to admit it.'

I shrugged. 'No, I don't.' I took the bag from him and handed him a ten-pound note. As he counted out the change, he kept looking up at me. I put the money in my purse and smiled tightly at him.

'Hey?' he said, recognition finally coming. 'You're Jane Jonas!' He banged his hand triumphantly on the counter.

I closed my eyes, hoping that when I opened them again he'd have disappeared. But he was still there.

'Jane Jonas . . .' He jiggled about on the spot. 'You're the girl from the accident.'

'I'd appreciate it if you'd just shut up,' I said coldly. 'I don't want to talk about it.'

'Jane – Jane Jonas,' he chanted, before his eye caught something behind me and he stopped.

'She told you to shut up,' said a voice I vaguely recognised. 'So do it, moron.'

There was a silence as I turned to take in my rescuer. Tall, blond, smiling at me now, tiny little creases around pool-blue eyes. I swallowed, realising once again that I wasn't exactly dressed for the occasion.

'Hi Evan,' I said, willing my face not to burst into flames. 'It's OK. I can handle it.'

Evan moved swiftly and confidently towards me and reached out his hand.

'Let me take that,' he said, grabbing the plastic bag. 'And that,' he slipped my rucksack off my shoulder. 'You must be a little shaken up still . . . after what happened.'

'I don't—' I started, as he pushed a stray curl off my face and tucked it behind my ear.

'I know,' he said softly. 'You don't want to talk about it.'

I nodded, all the feisty draining out of me.

'I'll give you a lift back home.'

'It's OK. I've got my bike.'

'And I've got a car.' He opened the door to let me through. 'So I win.'

Evan drove slowly up back to the house. I hadn't said a word walking to his car, and now that I was sitting in the front seat next to him, I just concentrated on not looking at him. I didn't look at his long, muscular legs, I didn't look at his strong, steady hands holding the steering wheel. I definitely didn't look at his perfect, straight nose and his streaked, messy hair. But I didn't have to – I had committed every part of him to memory in the entire half-hour I'd spent in his company since we'd met.

I stared ahead of me as we pulled off the main road and focused on keeping my heart rate down. I should have been asking questions. Making conversation; something like, 'Hey, I hear you ran away and lived like a vagrant for six months and caused your family no end of heartache and worry.' But I couldn't. His physical presence made me shyer than ever.

It was a little like avoiding the elephant in the room.

'You ever play pool?' asked Evan eventually.

'Pool?' I shook my head. 'There's nowhere you can play pool here. Not for miles.'

'I know a place.' He glanced at me. 'It's a way out of here, but it's a good place to hang out.' I nodded, both hoping and dreading that his next question would be 'Want to come sometime?' When nothing came I stared out of the passenger window and studied the roadside bushes. Evan changed gear as we began the ascent up the mountain road and my heart beat more quickly. In a couple of minutes we'd be there, where that *thing* had forced Dad off the road.

I felt Evan's eyes on me. 'You OK?' he asked softly.

I exhaled, determined not to see the crushed fence on the other side of the road. 'I'm fine.' I smiled at him. 'Really.' Through the trees I could see the lights on in our house a mile or so up. 'You can drop me where the rough track begins. I can walk from there.'

'Whatever you want. But I'd be happy to take you all the way.'

'No need.' I started gathering up my bags. 'If you could help me get the bike out . . .'

As Evan shut the boot of his car, I stood awkwardly holding my bike, rucksack on one shoulder, the other hand swinging my bag like a silly little girl.

He pushed his hands through his hair, then stuck them

in his jeans pockets, his eyes on me.

'You make me nervous, Jane,' he said, grinning. 'And I never get nervous.'

'Really?'

'Yeah. I mean, I like that you're serious. You know, not shallow like a lot of girls. You don't talk just to fill a silence.' He paused. 'But that does make it more difficult to ask you to come out with me. You know, on a date, because ... I have no idea what you think of me.' And even in the dark I could see he was holding his breath.

I smiled, shivering slightly, though it definitely wasn't the cold.

'That would be nice,' was all I could come out with.

'That's a yes?'

'It's a yes.' I looked back up at the house. 'But I really have to go.'

'That's cool.' He stepped towards me and, before I could think about it, leaned down to kiss my cheek. I felt the stubble on his chin and his hair brushing against my face. 'Tomorrow night?'

'OK,' I said, dazed. 'Tomorrow night.'

'Great. I'll pick you up.'

'No,' I said quickly, thinking of the sheer excruciation. 'I'll meet you in the town.'

He grinned. 'Of course. Outside the old petrol station

at six? We can take it from there.'

'Fine,' I waved the shopping at him again. 'See you at six.'

I watched as his car reversed away and turned to go down the mountain road towards the town. When I finally resumed walking up the track to our house, I couldn't keep the goofy smile off my face. I slung my rucksack and the shopping over the handlebars of my bike and trudged forwards in a daze. A rustling in the bushes halted me, making me turn to the side of the track.

'Who's there?' I said loudly.

'Jane.' A voice came from my left, low but intense. I caught my breath and stopped, squinting in the half-light, already knowing who the voice belonged to.

A shape emerged from the long foliage by the track. A dark coat, green eyes. I lost my grip on the bike and it crashed to the ground, two tins of dog food rolling into the undergrowth.

'You?' I said, trying to catch my breath. 'You came back.'

He looked weary, the dark shadows accentuated by his white skin. He moved slowly towards me.

'I came to explain.' He licked his lips, and I saw his eyes were hooded, evasive.

I put out my hand to touch him and, though he kept

his own hands by his side, he smiled. 'Your father – he's OK?'

I nodded. 'What happened to you that night? Why did you send me away?'

'Long story.' He took his hands out of his pockets and rubbed his eyes, then looked back down the track. 'Can we walk somewhere? Just for a bit.'

I glanced at my bike on the ground then back at him. He bent and picked up the dog food from where it had rolled, examining the labels. 'Mr Chow's Chow Time,' he said, raising an eyebrow.

I snatched the tins from him, my mouth twitching. 'Dogs. No class.'

He watched as I stuffed the tins back into the plastic bag.

'There's a path around the hill.' I indicated a small opening in the trees across the track. 'But I have to be back in twenty minutes or Dot will start fretting.'

'Ah. Dot.' Luca smiled. 'She's very protective of you.'

I frowned. 'How do you know that?' I said sharply. 'Have you been spying on us?'

'No.' He laughed. 'I'm just . . . perceptive.'

'Hmm.' I walked over to my bike and dropped the shopping down next to it. 'Come on, let's walk.'

Luca and I trod without speaking along the damp

path that circled our side of the mountain. I came here a lot in the summer, with the dog, and sometimes with Dot. When the sun was out the view down to the small town and the surrounding landscape was spectacular. It was a peaceful place.

'So,' I said eventually. 'Explain to me why you've suddenly appeared in my life?' I glanced at him. 'In my waking life . . . Because those dreams have stopped.'

Luca stopped and walked to the edge of the path, looking down at the trees. He cleared his throat.

'Remember what I told you before . . . About stretching the bound—'

'The boundaries of my reality,' I finished for him. 'Yes. I remember.'

'Well . . .' He hesitated. 'This is going to sound . . . fantastical. But imagine that there is a place like this, where . . . living things, beings with hearts and minds and . . . longings . . . exist.' He tried to smile. 'Where somebody like you grows up feeling as though they don't fit in with everyone else. Like there is a part of them missing. And even though they know they should stay where they are, be happy without that missing part, they can't. They are only aware of that empty space.'

I stared at him: flashes of my childhood. Of the birthday parties, year after year, where local kids had come,

53

under duress, because I didn't know how to play with them; of the times I had hidden when relatives visited; of the need I had always had to sit, reading, thinking by myself. None of the people around me understood me, and I wanted to be understood. I loved Dot more than anything, but she didn't understand.

'I can imagine that,' I said, holding his gaze, waiting for him to elaborate. When he didn't I focused on something else he'd said.

'You said "living things".'

He took a deep breath before answering. 'I am human, in most ways,' he said finally. 'Except I can live forever, if I want to.'

'My God.' I stared at him and then my eyes narrowed. 'Don't tell me, you're really two hundred years old?'

'No.' He grinned now. 'I'm seventeen. But I will stop ageing when I reach fifty.'

'Seriously?' I wrapped my arms around myself, dumbfounded, and examined Luca's face. Not a hint of a smile. 'You're not kidding, are you?'

He shook his head.

I breathed out heavily. 'So . . . where do I come into all this?'

'You're the one,' Luca said simply. 'The one I've had in my dreams for a long time. My missing part.'

I stared at him, not knowing whether to laugh. Whether this was some kind of surreal joke. But at the back of my mind I felt recognition too. I know I did. It was just I couldn't articulate that. Because it didn't make sense. Yet.

'God. I'm flattered and everything but—'

'And I am *your* missing part,' Luca interrupted me. 'Hence . . . your dreams.'

I frowned a little. 'You mean, even though I didn't know you existed, I have been missing you?'

'Yes, I'm sure of it.'

I shivered. 'Let's keep walking. There's a clearing a few metres ahead and a little bench. My dad made it.'

We continued until we reached a circular patch, clear of trees and bushes, where my father's carved bench nestled back against the wood. I sat down and, after a pause, Luca joined me. I rubbed my hands together, not looking at him.

'So. What you're saying is kind of . . . insane.'

He laughed and his face lit up. Lovely moss-green eyes shining in the dimming light. 'I know.' He turned his face up to the sky. 'But where I come from, we have the dubious privilege of pursuing the insane. We know no real boundaries – though we are advised not to exploit that.'

A heavy movement behind us made me jump. Luca

put his hand on my arm, reassuring. 'It's an owl,' he said, calmly. 'Nothing to be frightened of.' And then there it was, the soft call of an owl behind us. I relaxed.

'How did you know I needed help,' I asked quietly, 'that day?'

'I just knew,' was all he said, not meeting my eyes.

I rubbed at my knees. 'I'm not going to ask why you sent me away – from the waiting room.' I paused. 'I thought I heard—'

'It's complicated,' Luca cut in. 'I wish I could tell you in some way that wouldn't freak you out, but you need to trust me first . . .' He trailed off. I continued looking down at my legs. And we sat for a minute or two, not speaking.

'I've got something for you.' He rummaged in his pocket, drawing out a battered-looking notebook. 'A long time ago I went to my favourite place in the whole world and . . .' He paused for some reason, as though thinking out his next sentence. 'Well, let's just say I found, buried under some rocks by a river we call the Water Path, a book.' He held out the notebook. 'This book.'

I took it from him, turning it over in my hands. It was covered in faded pencil sketches; ethereal, abstract loops and curls. I looked at Luca questioningly.

'Whoever wrote in this book was going through some awful turmoil. They were in love, but something had gone

56

wrong. Or got in the way. The bond was breaking.'
He stopped for a moment. 'If you read it, you'll see.' He
touched my arm. 'I want you to keep it.'

'Why are you giving this to me?'

'Because something about this book has led me to you,
Jane. I don't know how, but I know it is connected with
you, and me.'

I frowned, but I too had the strangest sensation as I
held the journal. The same feeling I had when Luca
touched me. A feeling of warmth and safety, of home.

'OK.' I slipped the book into my coat pocket,
remembering the shopping and that I was late. 'I have to
get back . . . My mother will be worried.'

He smiled. 'Of course. But I will see you again soon.'

'I hope so,' I said, meaning it. I got up from the bench
and started down the path. I glanced back to see Luca
still seated. 'You're staying here?'

'Yes. I'll get home from here,' he said. 'But I'll come
again . . . tomorrow, or . . .'

I remembered Evan. 'Oh . . . tomorrow . . . I have a
thing,' I said awkwardly.

'Right,' he said, getting up to stand, his back to the
wood. 'We'll find a way.'

And as he slowly moved backwards towards the trees
he seemed to merge into them. And then suddenly he was

gone, leaving me to make my way home.

When I got back to my bike and my mother's shopping, I slipped the notebook into the pocket of my hoodie before picking the bike up and continued up the track to the house.

If it hadn't been for the weight of Luca's present in my pocket, I still wouldn't have believed he existed. But not only did I now know this for sure, I also knew that when I was with him, I felt more real than I'd ever felt in my life.

I was relieved to see Dot and my mother watching TV when I walked into the living room. Our remote home means Dot relies on me for company. But Dad's accident had zapped some of the pluck and curiosity out of her. Instead of following me around the house like an eager puppy, these past few weeks she had switched allegiance to Mum, and become timid and clingy. It unsettled me. I relied on Dot to be the life to my soul. She encouraged me to take risks and, though I'd never thanked her to her face, I knew that without her I would be a whole lot lonelier and more 'insolar' than I already was.

'Hey, kiddo.' I ruffled her untidy blonde curls. 'Wassup?'

Dot looked up. 'Can I sleep in your bed tonight?' She

glanced uneasily at my mother, who returned one of mock disapproval. 'Just one more night,' Dot pleaded. 'Please?'

'If it's OK with Jane, then I suppose . . .' Mum smiled at me. 'One more night?'

What I really wanted was to curl up on my bed and unpick the unbelievable events of the past hour. I needed to rationalise. Convince myself I was a normal sixteen-year-old girl. But I had never been 'normal', and what was happening in my life now, though it should surprise me, kind of didn't. I also needed to get to the bottom of why Luca freaked me out less than Evan did. With Dot next to me, I wouldn't get the chance.

'Sure,' I said. 'One more night.'

'Thank you, sweetie,' Mum said, getting up to go into the kitchen. 'I'll make us something to eat.'

'You're brave,' Dot said, winding melted cheese round her fork. 'Don't you feel brave?'

Dad was asleep upstairs and Mum had made us all cheese on toast. I couldn't eat mine. I was still too churned up inside. Dot was morbidly obsessed, as she had been for the past few weeks, with the night of the accident.

'Not really,' I muttered. 'I didn't do anything.'

'I wouldn't say that. You ran to get help.' She squeezed a large dollop of tomato sauce on to her plate. 'In the

59

freezing darkness. You must have been terrified.' She shook her head. 'Thank goodness for that boy. It's such a shame he ran off before we could thank him.'

'Yeah,' I said, looking down at my plate.

'Makes me shudder to think we have wolves around here,' she went on.

Dot's eyes were wide, her hands still clutching her knife and fork.

'Do wolves eat people?' she asked anxiously.

Mum and I exchanged a look.

'They're predators, sweetie,' Mum told her. 'But they're very rare.' She glanced at me. 'We just have to make sure we don't go wandering into the woods at night. Alone. Then we'll be OK.'

I lowered my head, feeling her eyes still on me. Did she know?

'Did you see its face?' Dot couldn't stop asking questions.

'Think so . . .' I had a flash of those black eyes, the red mouth, the teeth, the huge, vaulting body. I got up abruptly. 'I'm going to be sick.'

'Jane?' Mum stood up too, hovering awkwardly over me. 'Sweetheart . . .'

I ran, nearly tripping over the sleeping dog, to the bathroom downstairs. After I'd been sick I stayed, crouched over, a mixture of fear and disbelief coursing through me.

I'd waited sixteen years for something to happen in my life, for a sign that I fitted in somewhere . . . with someone. Was my destiny a strange, skinny boy in a black overcoat? A boy who came to me in my dreams, who'd never die. Who came from a world straight out of Tolkien, but with whom I felt no fear.

And what about Evan, a mysterious human boy in my waking life, who made my hair stand on end just by being next to me?

I shook my head, trying to empty some of the thoughts out. What was this all supposed to mean?

'What's happening to me?' I said out loud.

The sound of footsteps outside the door made me look up. My mother stood, holding a dishcloth in her hands. She was looking at me, not smiling.

'I made you some hot chocolate,' she said, her eyes dropping away from mine. 'It'll make everything seem normal.'

'Normal?' I said quietly.

'It's important to get back to normal.' She half turned to go back to the kitchen but stopped. 'Back to what you know.'

'I'm not sure if that's possible,' I told her, stupidly

melodramatic. 'Stuff has happened—'

'I know, and you have been very brave.' But her tone was abrupt, hostile even. 'And now you have to try very hard to move on.' She turned round again and there was warning in her eyes. 'To leave it behind.' She stepped out into the hallway and shouted to Dot to finish her meal, leaving me baffled. What was she getting so riled about?

I waited until Dot was asleep before I slipped out of bed and padded as quietly as possible to my hoodie. I took the notebook out of the pocket and, glancing quickly back at my sleeping sister, pushed the rest of my crumpled clothes off the chair and curled up on it.

I opened the book to the first page.

To my dearest darling,
I don't know if I will ever see you again, it's getting harder to come to you. I am needed at home. I know that soon I will have to choose between you and my family, and it is SO hard. I love you. I didn't think it was possible to love a boy so much. But . . .

The page was torn and I skipped to the next page to find a clearer entry.

I saw you today and we lay in our favourite spot, listening to the babbling, spitting brook, and I had my head on your chest and felt your heartbeat so strong, and wanted never to come home. But real life is intervening, sweetest. I am lying on my bed, knowing that soon I will need to go to my mother and tell her I will never leave her, and always look after her because I am all she has got. She won't live forever. That is clearer to me now than it ever has been.

I turned the page to see a drawing of a river and some trees. It wasn't good, it was naïve and out of proportion, and in the corner there was a crudely drawn pair of wings with the words *My Angel* written underneath. I felt as though I was intruding and I wondered who she was, this love-struck girl. And how on earth Luca had come to have her diary.

Real life is intervening . . . What did she mean?

I shut the book, saving the rest for another time, and got back into bed, gently shifting Dot over as she slept.

I didn't dream that night, I fell into a peaceful sleep. But my last thought was of a rushing stream, beside which a girl and a boy lay blissfully in each other's arms.

CHAPTER SIX

'You need to relax your shoulders,' Evan told me as I bent, cue in hands, over the table. 'Just let them flop.'

I tried to do as he said, but it was difficult to relax with a demi-god beside me. Evan laughed. 'You'll get the hang of it,' he said, picking up his bottle of beer and taking a swig.

I trained the wooden cue to line up with the white ball. I knew I needed to hit it against the red ball so that it rolled into the corner pocket. I took a clumsy shot and the ball bounced off the side of the table and on to the floor. I grunted impatiently.

'I'm a most unsatisfactory pool partner.' I looked apologetically at Evan. 'I should have warned you that I'm not the most coordinated person in the world.' I went over to pick up the ball and as I straightened up, caught him watching me carefully.

'Feel free to play with someone else.'

'I don't want to play with anyone else,' he said, smoothly. He finished his beer. 'But I'll get us another drink and we can have a break.'

'Great.' As Evan walked over to the bar to get himself another beer and a Coke for me, I looked around the crowded room to find somewhere to sit. Against a wall was a soft leather couch, unoccupied and inviting. I headed for it, sat down and curled up with my legs tucked under me.

We'd driven out a few miles to this pool hall. It was mostly men, boys. A few girlfriends stood around, looking bored and swigging at bottles of Bacardi Breezer or whatever, dressed up to the nines on a Saturday night. I'd spent two hours hurling my dismal clothing around my bedroom. Eventually I'd cut the sleeves off an old tight black T-shirt and turned it into a mini-skirt over black tights and newly washed white Converse plimsolls. Then I'd ironed a white cotton shirt and put that on top. I washed my hair and let it dry in big glossy curls. Looking in the mirror, I was relieved to see that I didn't look a complete mess. At least my legs were long and the shirt disguised my burgeoning chest. The last thing I wanted was to look like I was showing off my body. I didn't like it enough to do that.

'You look great,' Evan had said, when I'd arrived to meet him five minutes early. Amazingly my mother had been pleased I was going out. With a boy. Dot had obviously convinced her he wasn't an axe-murderer and when I'd finally got the courage to tell her and Dad I had 'a sort-of date' she'd not batted an eyelid. Dad had muttered something about the years flying faster than a rat out of a trap. But Mum had shushed him, telling him he should be glad I was just doing what all sixteen-year-olds do.

She'd insisted on giving me a lift in her car as far as the main street, leaving too much time to get there of course. I was pretty sure she'd spy on us for a while before driving off again. But I was too grateful for her good mood to mind if she did. It made a nice change from the gloom and doom she'd be spreading lately.

'It's good to see you have legs,' she said, giving one of them a pat. 'Great legs, too.' She'd smiled wistfully. 'Your grandmother had a great pair of pins.'

'You think there's too much leg?' I said, worried, pulling down my skirt.

'At your age, there's no such thing.' She leaned forward and kissed me on the cheek. 'Have fun. And tell this Evan we'd like to meet him sometime.'

'Mother.' I rolled my eyes. 'Are you trying to get rid

66

of him already? 'Cause he's kind of got a history of running away.'

She laughed. 'I'm sure that's all behind him now.'

We had pulled up just behind the main road, in accordance with my specific instructions.

'Go on. And I'll see you back home by eleven. OK?'

'OK.' I opened the car door, nerves gripping my stomach. 'But don't be surprised if I'm back in half an hour.'

As I shut the door, I left Mum shaking her head, smiling, waiting a bit before she started the engine. I wished I shared her confidence about the evening. Honestly. I was terrified.

And sitting curled up on the leather sofa, looking at these other girls, I felt immature and clueless. What the hell does he see in me? I thought, watching as Evan joked with the barman and collected our drinks.

He smiled as he came over and handed me a drink. Sitting back with his legs apart, he took a mouthful of beer and then turned to me.

'I'm not much of a people person either,' he said, quietly. 'I spent a lot of my childhood in Australia messing about by myself on the beach, playing alone.' He drummed his bottle with one finger. 'I never felt like

I connected with anyone.'

'Like an outsider?' I took a drink. 'Like everyone else was in on some private joke and you didn't get it?'

He laughed. 'Something like that.' He scrunched up his eyes, thinking. 'My mother was always on at me to get out and play football, hang out with people I went to school with. But the things they talked about . . . didn't interest me. I sometimes felt I had more in common with our dog than boys my age.'

'Oh me too.' I leaned my head back. 'I still feel like that . . . Well, I did.' I looked across at him.

'So, what happened?' I said boldly. 'Why did you run away?'

For a split second his expression was sharp, defensive.

'Stuff,' he said, putting the bottle to his lips. 'I just felt trapped. There were places I wanted to go . . . It was complicated.' He looked awkward. 'Let's just say I had to get away. I wasn't getting on too well with my mum.' He shrugged. 'I could have handled it better, I guess . . .'

'I can understand,' I said, though the explanation seemed a bit flimsy to me. He obviously didn't want to tell me the whole story.

Evan rolled the beer bottle in his palms, more animated now.

'When I was fifteen, I looked on a map of the world, and I saw it all out there.' He sat forward. 'And I thought, there are so many different kinds of people, and cultures, and beliefs in all these countries.' He looked across at me. 'It's like you can be whatever you want, wherever you happen to be, make up your own story.'

I said nothing for a minute, thinking. 'You mean, write your own life script?'

'I guess.' He smiled at my thoughtful expression and then leaned back in his seat.

'When did your parents split up?' I asked, feeling more confident.

I watched him shut down a little again, his lips pressing together firmly. 'When I was five,' he said, without emotion. 'He's remarried now. She's in between relationships.' His tone told me he wasn't willing to elaborate on that.

'Oh.' My eyes darted about the room, trying to find inspiration to change the subject and failing. I felt him watching me as he took another swig of beer.

'And what about you, Jane?' he said finally.

'What about me?' I pulled my skirt down self-consciously.

'Am I allowed to ask why you gave up school?'

I had expected the question and had decided I would

tell the truth, leaving out some of the more pathetic details. 'I didn't get on with the other kids.' I scratched at my glass Coke bottle. 'One in particular . . .' I stopped, remembering that time in my life, recalling Sarah's pinched, mean face, as she stood blocking the toilet door one day at break-time, watching coldly as I scrabbled around on the cubicle floor, trying to rescue my recently flushed belongings. Her two minions, Jennifer Gibson and Mariella Hoult, had formed a blockade. When I'd tried to push my way past them and out of the girls' toilets, Mariella's heel had ground into my foot.

'Where d'you think you're going, bitch?' Sarah had snarled. 'Did I say you could leave?' She'd grabbed my bag and upturned it again. I'd watched helplessly, knowing this, or something like it, was going to happen the next day and the day after that.

'Girls can be vicious.' Evan interrupted my thoughts. He coughed quickly. 'I mean, I assume it was a girl?'

I nodded, exhaling loudly. 'Well, she had the face and body of a girl.' I put the Coke bottle to my lips and then pulled it away again, adding, 'But she was more like a monster.'

He laughed softly, picking at the label on his bottle. 'She made your life hell, then,' he said, looking down, 'this monster?'

'Yep. Every single day, there was always something. Some way in which I had to be punished.'

'She was jealous,' he said looking across at me. 'Obviously.'

Heat flooded my cheeks. 'Obviously.' I smirked to cover my embarrassment.

'She did quite a job on you, hey?' Evan held eye contact. 'You really believe you're a freak?'

I prickled at the sound of that word, one I hadn't yet used with him. It was as though he had read my mind. I wasn't sure whether this made me feel comforted or exposed.

I smiled weakly, suddenly feeling I was saying too much, to someone I hardly knew. I wasn't sure I was ready for this. Or for a boy like him telling me these things about myself. It was all too fast.

'You OK? Jane?'

'I need to go home,' I said quickly, putting my bottle down on the table in front of us. 'I've had a great time, but . . .' I paused. 'I'm sorry.'

Evan jumped to his feet. 'Of course,' he said kindly. 'Whatever you want.'

As we drove back, I sat, silently as usual, hating myself for not handling the evening as I'd wanted to. Evan turned the radio on to some country music station. It soothed me. Country music is all about stories. I concentrated on Dolly Parton bemoaning her rival Jolene and looked straight ahead of me. I'd ruined the night because I was a lonely freak who couldn't get over Sarah Emerson and didn't trust anyone outside of my family. I closed my eyes, thinking that maybe that wasn't quite true. After what had happened the night of the accident, I trusted Luca. But could I really trust someone I didn't know?

I came out of my thoughts, guiltily. It was Evan sitting next to me, not Luca. One outlandish situation at a time, I told myself. Just be in the moment, Jane.

The sound of Evan clearing his throat brought me back down to earth.

'I wish I'd known you back then,' he said out of the blue, changing gear. 'I'd have put that little witch in her place.'

I sighed. 'It's done now.' I shifted in my seat. 'I just want to forget about her.'

'Makes me mad,' he went on, as though he hadn't heard me. 'How people get away with hurting others like that.'

I looked over at him, his face taut as he drove. 'Well maybe they don't in the end,' I told him. 'Maybe things even out?'

'Hope so.' He chewed his lip then, realising I was staring at him, relaxed his face and smiled at me.

'You hungry? We could get a burger or something?' We were approaching Fabio's, where the lights were on. On Saturday nights, Eileen stayed open later than usual. I spotted her through the windows, laughing with a customer by the bar.

I realised I was starving. 'Can we stop here?' I said, needing to be somewhere familiar and friendly. 'Eileen does a mean cheeseburger and fries.'

'Sure.' Evan slowed down and looked for somewhere to park. 'Whatever you want.'

I smiled. How many times had he said that? *Whatever you want.* He was a truly nice person. I felt bad for feeling uncomfortable. Evan was on my side.

'Just prepare yourself for an almighty fuss,' I warned him, gesturing at Eileen. 'We're going to be a big news item in there. Eileen's usual clientele is a bunch of geriatrics and bored, loner teenagers buying their little sister milkshakes.'

'Hey,' said Evan, nudging my arm and grinning as he locked up his car. 'I'm going to make sure you're never bored . . . or lonely while I'm around. OK?'

I laughed, glad that the evening had turned around. 'OK.' I even linked my arm through his, and as we walked into Fabio's I met Eileen's delighted expression with one of my own.

CHAPTER SEVEN

My mother was all smiles the next day, humming as she cooked us bacon and eggs. My dad, still wearing his neck brace, turned the Sunday paper slowly, occasionally looking over the top to regard his wife.

Mum doled out food and put a heap of fried bread in the centre of the table. Dot, Dad and I exchanged a look.

'You're encouraging us to eat saturated fat? Mother, are you feeling OK?'

She grinned, picking up her knife and fork. 'I just thought we deserved a treat today,' she said, taking a bit of bread. 'It's been an upsetting time lately . . . But things are looking up.' She beamed at me.

'She's happy you've made a friend,' said Dot astutely. 'A special friend.'

'He's just a boy and it was just an evening. No big deal.'

Mum and Dot smiled at each other.

'Well, we'd like to check him out, wouldn't we, Jack?' Mum turned to my father. 'Make sure he's good enough.'

'Have we gone back in time to the nineteen-fifties or something?' I forked up a piece of bacon. 'Should he have asked Dad's permission first?'

'That would have been nice,' my father said, and finally put down the paper, giving me a little wink. 'But probably too much to ask in this day and age.'

'Well, maybe some other time . . . ?' Mum sipped her tea. 'We could have him over for lunch?'

'We'll see,' I said, vowing to put that off as long as possible. 'I'm going for a walk after breakfast. Have you seen my parka? It's freezing out there.'

'That thing's too small for you.' Mum shook her head. 'But it's in the spare room. I was going to give it to Dot.'

I ate half my egg, then pushed my plate away. 'OK if I go now? I need some fresh air.'

Mum started to look disapproving but checked herself. 'Fine, but don't be too long. You haven't finished the homework I set you last week yet.'

'I'll be back in an hour or two and then I'll get right down to it.'

* * *

76

It was truly freezing as I stepped outside. Gazing up at the sky I remembered the nearly-full moon the night before and how serene it had looked. Tonight it would be full.

I whistled for Bobby, who was mooching around outside Dad's shed, and slipped the lead around his neck. He rubbed his soft ears against my legs.

'I wish I had your coat,' I told him, stroking his back. 'Where shall we go?'

Bobby looked at me, big-eyed and indecisive.

'Up the hill a bit?' I suggested. 'Up to "no-man's land"?'

Bobby barked, which I took as agreement, and we set off, soon finding ourselves negotiating the thickset trees where no path existed. It was a beautiful, bright day and I felt light and, for once, uncomplicated as we climbed. Thinking of Evan's easy banter as we'd sat eating in Fabio's the night before, making Eileen laugh and keeping Mr Garry, who was at least eighty and usually most unimpressable, impressed with his tales of teaching surfing on the Gold Coast last summer. It was a life of sun and good times that bore no resemblance to my upbringing here in this endless cold, and I couldn't really relate. But I like a good story, and Evan was a good storyteller.

Suddenly Bobby stopped. Stiffening, he backtracked,

ending up caught against a stubborn tree trunk.

'What's the matter, boy?' I bent to cuddle him, looking ahead of us to see what was there. At first there was nothing, but then I made out something behind a couple of trees. A dark shape. Hiding.

I caught my breath, still stroking Bobby.

'Who's there?' I asked, sounding more confident than I felt.

The shape moved and a face appeared around the trunk of one of the trees.

'Luca?' I stood up, relieved, and then looked down at Bobby, who was shaking and snarling at the same time.

Luca moved so that he was completely exposed. I saw him give a pleading, friendly look at the dog, who ignored it, barking ferociously instead.

'Bobby, shush.' I kneeled again, putting both arms around the quivering animal. 'Luca's nice. He won't hurt you.'

But Bobby was trying to break free, thrashing about as I struggled to hold on to him. I'd never seen him like this before.

'Take him home.' Luca's voice was firm. 'He's frightened.'

I noticed then that he had backed right away.

'What's the matter?' I said, still trying to control

the dog. 'Are you OK?'

Bobby continued to attempt to escape from my grip. His body moved powerfully and I struggled to hold him as his jaws snapped angrily, turning his gentle face wild, predatory.

'Bobby!' I felt the strength in my arms fade as his body strained against them.

'I'm sorry,' Luca said breathlessly. 'I didn't think—'

Suddenly Bobby reared up, snapping viciously into the air, and I gasped.

'Run, Jane . . .' Luca backed away, his face grimacing as he did so. Suddenly he lurched forward, gasping as though in pain.

'Luca!' I watched his hands flex and unflex uncontrollably.

'Please.' He shook, and his eyes had grown much bigger, the green turning darker and wild. 'Just leave me!'

'But—'

'Go!' he screamed then, and dropped to the ground.

I looked down at the dog, whose snarl was weaker, curious now, as well as afraid.

I grabbed his lead and yanked him back.

'Come on, boy,' I panted and pulled the terrified animal with me, relieved when Bobby finally cooperated and we began moving. Then I was aware only of the adrenaline pumping through my veins, and of me running faster than I'd ever done in my life. Running down through the dense wood, which tore at my clothes as I moved. Running until we got back down to Dad's shed.

We reached the back of the house and as I bent over, out of breath, I watched Bobby rush in through the open back door before I looked up to where we had been.

'Who are you?' I whispered up at the woods.

Still panting I walked slowly, treading as lightly as I could, away from the house, back towards Luca. But the sound that pierced the air stopped me in my tracks.

A cry, sad and low, coming from high above.

And then, once again, I felt no fear, only a pull to the boy in pain.

Take me back to him, I heard a voice inside my head say. He's in trouble. Take me back.

And then everything went black.

CHAPTER EIGHT

'I'm sorry,' Luca said, rubbing my shoulders fiercely. 'Jane, I'm so sorry.' He sat back as I blinked up at him. Slowly my eyes took in my surroundings. We were sitting under some tall, thick trees, like oaks, soft green grass beneath us. To my left, a wide, clear river babbled soothingly. I was shaking, sitting up and trying to hug myself.

'Where are we?' I asked.

'Nissilum,' said Luca, watching my face. 'My home.'

'I don't remember getting here.'

Luca turned to sit beside me and rubbed his eyes. 'You will remember, gradually. Something I'm not looking forward to.'

'Why, what happened?' I frowned. A memory was edging in. The woods, Bobby was there . . . and Luca. I concentrated but nothing else was coming.

He fidgeted next to me. I noticed the colour in his face for the first time. He looked well. Healthy. I realised that it was warm here and I was beginning to bake in my coat. I shrugged it off.

'Luca,' I said seriously. 'Tell me the truth. The whole truth.'

He pursed his lips, closing his eyes for a second. As he opened them again, he started talking.

'I told you I was immortal,' he began. 'But that I am more or less, to all intents and appearances at least, human.'

'Yes. And?'

'Well, there's something else. Something that I don't like, but I can't help.'

'What?' I said, my breath quickening.

'I am also a member of a breed of wolf. The Hunter Wolves.' He sighed heavily. 'We're werewolves.'

And then, there it was, a picture in my head of Luca, like an animal, writhing and wild in the woods.

I stopped breathing for a second. 'I see,' I said lamely. 'It makes sense.' I turned to him and it was then it dawned on me. 'It was you. The night of the accident. You were the wolf.'

Luca nodded. 'I was on mortal Earth when I realised it was too late, the moon was full and I had to turn.

But the trees were so thick and my wolf form had to break free. I just ran and, before I knew it, I was crossing that mountain road, and then I saw the car . . .' He paused, dropping his head. 'But I was going so fast, I couldn't stop.'

I stayed silent, still trying to take this in. Gentle Luca, a vicious . . . beast?

'Once a month I am unable to stop myself turning. It doesn't matter where I am, as long as it is the day of the full moon.'

I stared, then laughed, frightened, wanting none of it to be true. 'You're serious. This isn't a joke?'

'You didn't think my being immortal was a joke,' he said quietly. 'Why are you so surprised that I'm a werewolf?'

I looked at him, slightly hunched over, still in his black coat. 'You're so serene . . . and elegant. I suppose it's hard to believe you could be something so brutal.'

'Brutality is not encouraged here,' Luca said. 'This is a place where people like me, and the others that live on Nissilum, restrain our most violent impulses.' He paused. 'At least, we're supposed to.'

'Others? Other wolves?'

'Other creatures from the dark worlds.' He gave a short humourless laugh. 'The kinds of creatures you mortals only read about in books.'

'You mean vampires and wizards?' I blinked.

'And angels and witches,' he said, utterly straight-faced.

'Wow,' I said, because it was all I could come out with.

'I didn't think it through,' said Luca apologetically. 'That all this might be really frightening for you.'

'Maybe it hasn't properly sunk in yet,' I said carefully. 'But I don't actually feel that frightened. Not now anyway.'

'Really?' He peered at my face.

'No. I mean. It just feels like one more layer of weirdness.' I laughed. 'And I've met scarier people than you.'

'Oh?' He looked almost disappointed.

'There was somebody at school . . .' I began.

'She hurt you,' he abruptly finished for me.

I stared at him, not blinking. 'How did you know that?'

'I told you. I'm very perceptive.'

'You are.' I held his gaze a moment before looking away. We sat in comfortable silence.

'It's a peaceful place,' he said at last. 'Nissilum.'

I glanced about me at the sharp greens and browns of

the trees, hearing the birdsong and the soft bubble of the river, and a stillness that made me feel safe.

'Yes,' I agreed. 'It is.' I had so many questions I didn't know where to start. But Luca, intuitively, started talking.

'We live pretty much like you do,' he began. 'We work, we provide for our families. We socialise . . .' He hesitated. 'And we have learned to live with our natural enemies.'

'Vampires,' I said, remembering from somewhere that werewolves and vampires were rivals.

'Yes . . . and the witch community.' He laughed. 'They are not violent but they are sly and insidious. They can do harm by just talking to you. The laws here state that any malevolent behaviour is severely punished, and most species abide by it. But there is the occasional renegade.'

'But who's in charge? Who rules this world?'

'The angels.' He smiled. 'The Seraphim. They are a little self-righteous, as you might imagine. But they do a good job. Because they are made with no evil inherent in them, they are the natural governors.'

'Do they have wings and, you know, harps?'

He laughed. 'Wings I have never seen. And harps are something you mortals have made up I think. But they do have spectacular powers if they choose to use them. Shapeshifting, telekinesis. Super-strength. All-seeing, all-knowing. But they are strict with themselves about that. Trust is a huge part of their philosophy. Trusting each other and all of us who live here on Nissilum, to behave. Not to abuse our gifts. They live in the Celestial Palace and its grounds.'

'And what about your family?' I asked him.

'My immediate family is my parents and my younger sister and brother.' He rubbed at his knees. 'They are good people, and they abide by the laws of Nissilum. I wish I could do the same.'

'You are a good person,' I said softly. 'I know that.'

Luca took my hand then and held it in his. His fingers were long, elegant and strong.

'This is my favourite place,' he said, letting go and looking around us. 'It's known as the Water Path. It's where I found the notebook.'

'I read some of it. It made me sad.' I puffed out my cheeks. 'Who'd fall in love? It sounds so painful.'

'When the love is taken away it is,' he said, stretching his long arms. 'Or if you fall in love with the wrong person.'

'I suppose.' I looked around us. 'So how did I get here, to the Water Path?'

'I brought you.' He smiled. 'I didn't know whether it would work, but when I found you lying in the wood, I just picked you up and here you are.' He hesitated before adding, 'I think it was a joint effort, actually. You must have wished it too.'

Beside us the water rippled and spat, and I saw a frog, its chest puffing and receding, watching us from a small rock. A breeze caused the tops of the trees lining the riverbed to sway gently. It was so calming.

'Hmm. Maybe.' I shook my head slowly. 'But I'm beginning to think Eric was right. You really are a superhero.'

'Eric?' Luca looked lost.

'Just a kid who works in the town shop.' I smiled. 'I made him feel like an idiot for even saying it. But he was right.'

'I'm not a hero. Far from it. I caused the accident that put your dad in hospital.'

'The truck was a death-trap. It was an accident waiting to happen.'

'That's very gracious of you,' Luca said, sombre. 'But I am to blame.'

I turned to him and took hold of his hand. 'Without your help my dad would have . . . Well, I couldn't have done that on my own.' I squeezed his fingers.

'You're embarrassing me.' Luca's lips twitched. He took off his coat, and for the first time I saw properly his lean, lithe body in sweatshirt and jeans. I stared until I felt his eyes on me and I turned away quickly to look at the river.

'What's it like?' I asked, not looking at him. 'Turning into a wolf?'

'Painful.' Luca grimaced. 'As though every organ inside of me doubles in size.' He put his hand on his chest. 'And my heart literally feels like it will burst. It only lasts a few minutes, but my body changes shape and my human form has to adapt too quickly – it carries risk of a heart attack.'

'God.' I put my hand where my own heart was beating. 'It must be terrifying.'

'Yes. Which is why it is only supposed to happen once a month.' He paused. 'Werewolves cease to exist if they abuse their power.'

'Why would you want to turn any other time?'

'To protect loved ones. Or if you are angered beyond human limits.' Luca shook his head. 'Or in extreme situations.'

'Poor you,' I said.

'It has its advantages,' he smiled. 'The speed, for example. That is always there, even when I am human. And the strength.' He lifted his arm. 'It doesn't look much, but the power in this could destroy a brick wall in seconds.'

It was such an unremarkable arm. It was long and lean, but it didn't look anything special. Without thinking I reached over and with my fingertip stroked along the underside, where the veins ran down to his palm. I had never touched anyone like this. And a month ago, I would never have believed I would be doing something so intimate. I took my hand away and we sat in silence for a few minutes.

'You can heal, too, can't you?' I said. 'You touched my scratch and it disappeared soon after.'

He nodded. 'There are other things, too . . . You'll learn about them in time. But I brought you here to show you that I am not delusional, that I was telling the truth,' said Luca eventually. 'And so that you would be less afraid.'

'I'm not at all afraid. In fact, apart from my family, I feel safer with you than with anyone.'

Luca looked at me. 'Even your boyfriend?'

I flushed. 'How do you know about that?'

'I saw him,' he said flatly. 'The night we met on the track up to your house.'

'Oh.' I felt a twinge of disloyalty. Whether to Evan or Luca, I wasn't sure.

'It's OK,' said Luca. 'It's inevitable I suppose.'

'Never was for me.' I picked at some long grass, growing between the rocks. 'And he's not even my boyfriend.'

'What's he like?' asked Luca, ignoring that.

'Older. Attentive. He's been living in Australia.'

'So he's tanned and fit?' Luca said wryly. 'Good for him.'

My lips twitched. 'But he can't break a brick wall with his hand.' I looked half smiling at Luca. 'He's not a superhero.'

He shrugged. 'But he's mortal. He's not as complicated.'

'Suppose not,' I said, wondering if that was true. 'I know nothing about him really.'

A silence fell between us.

'Anyway,' said Luca at last. 'It doesn't matter, you and I are friends.'

'I hope so.' I held on to one of his slender hands. 'I'll never forget what you did for me.'

'I'd do it again in a heartbeat,' said Luca, though he didn't look at me.

I swallowed, confused at how I felt. Feeling so close and peaceful and safe with the boy sitting next to me, but wanting Evan to want me too. Was that all it was? That I wanted a boy like Evan to want me?

'You should pursue this Evan,' said Luca, reading my

thoughts. 'Mortal girls are nothing but trouble.' He sighed. 'And then there's the long-distance thing.'

I laughed. 'Now that's not really a problem, though, is it?'

'No.' He grinned. 'But it's what I'm going to tell myself.'

The sound of footsteps startled us, and I quickly turned to see a long-limbed girl of about twelve, hair in two thick, straight, dark plaits, coming towards us. She kept her eyes on me as she came, then spoke to Luca.

'I thought I'd find you here,' she said. 'Ulfred needs you to clear out the barn, Luca . . . Who is this?'

'This is Jane. Jane, this is my sister, Dalya.'

'Is she a Hunter?' said Dalya, looking me up and down. She dropped on to the grass next to us.

'She's . . . a mortal,' said Luca cautiously.

Dalya's eyes widened. 'You've been back to mortal Earth?' She shook her head, disapprovingly. 'You're not supposed to—'

'No, and you won't tell anyone, Dalya,' he said, sternly. 'It's under control.'

I looked from one to the other. 'Under control?'

Dalya smiled impishly. 'He means he won't fall in love with you.' She looked almost triumphant. 'He can't, or he'll—'

91

'That's enough.' Luca grasped her hand tightly. 'Now be nice to Jane. She's my friend.'

'Luca hasn't got any friends,' Dalya told me, flatly. 'He's antisocial.'

I bit my lip to hide a smile; Dalya and Dot were like two peas in a pod. 'Makes two of us. Luca and I have a lot in common.'

'He just reads all these mortal books that he took from Earth one time,' she went on. '*Huckleberry Finn* and *White Fang* and *Franny and—*'

'*Zooey*,' I finished. 'I've read those too.'

'How did you get here?' Luca asked her. 'You ran?'

'No, I came on Sabre.' Dalya gestured behind her. Further in the trees a small black horse was tethered to one of the trunks. 'I brought India with me too, but I left her further back. She won't come through the trees.'

Luca looked at me. 'I wanted to show you the Celestial Palace, but there's no time now.'

Dalya hopped from one foot to the other. 'That's what I came to tell you. Mother is on the committee for the Great Ball. She said we all need to help with the arrangements. She's calling a family meeting.'

Luca rolled his eyes. 'I'd forgotten about that.'

'What's the Great Ball?' I asked.

'The annual Nissilum celebration of peace,' explained

Luca. 'The angels host it at the Celestial Palace to keep good will amongst the species.' He paused. 'It's where angels, vampires, witches and wolves all meet and pretend they don't hate each other. It would be amusing, if one wasn't required to wear a suit and be polite for hours on end.'

'Luca always gets roped in to serve drinks and usher people about,' Dalya told me. 'It's because he never has anyone to take.' She looked at me, her brown eyes bright and mischievous.

Luca frowned. 'Stop it, Dalya. The Great Ball is not for mortal girls.'

'She could pretend. Mother would be overjoyed that you have a mate.'

I raised an eyebrow.

'That's "girlfriend", in mortal terminology,' said Luca firmly, giving Dalya a gentle prod in the arm.

I chewed my lip. 'It sounds kind of . . . interesting,' I said slowly. 'Fun, even.'

'Really?' Luca stared at me. 'Are you saying you'd like to come?'

'I don't know . . .' I threw up my hands. 'I mean, it's no more weird and frightening than anything else right now.'

'True.' Luca looked down at the grass.

'I'd have to wear a dress, right?' I said, warming to the idea. 'Only I'm not a dressy kind of girl.'

'That is the custom.' He looked serious for a minute. 'Jane, I don't think this is a good idea. If anyone found out that you were mortal . . .'

'She could be one of our southern cousins,' said Dalya excitedly. 'There's so many of them, and nobody knows them very well.'

'When is this ball?' I asked.

'A few weeks' time,' said Luca.

There was a moment's silence before I spoke.

'I suppose I could come.' I picked up a tiny stone and threw it into the water. 'If you want me to. After all – in for a penny, in for a pound.'

Brother and sister looked at me blankly.

'That's "What the hell!" in mortal terminology,' I said, tongue in my cheek.

Luca raised an eyebrow then turned to Dalya. 'Well, if this one can keep her mouth shut long enough, then . . . we'll see.' He got to his feet. 'Now it's time for you to go back to the land of pennies and pounds.' He lifted his arms and stretched, his T-shirt rising to reveal a firm, olive-skinned stomach. 'You'll need to close your eyes and tell yourself to go home.'

Like Dorothy, clicking her red shoes together.

'Is that all?' I asked.

'That's all.' He picked up my parka. 'Here, I'll help you with your coat.'

I pushed my arms through while he held it. As I zipped it up I felt the underside rip noisily.

Luca and Dalya regarded me, amused.

'You need a new coat,' said Luca, laughing. 'You've grown out of that one.'

'What are you, my mother?' I grinned.

Dalya rolled her eyes impatiently. 'Come on,' she whined. 'I want to watch her go.'

'Close your eyes,' said Luca softly. 'And give yourself the instruction.'

I did as he said and pushed all thoughts out, except for one.

Take me home.

And the sounds of the water and the trees faded until there was nothing, except for the voice in my head.

CHAPTER NINE

I arrived back exactly where I had left, lying at the base of a tree. I opened my eyes slowly to see a familiar dusting of snow over the winter leaves and sat up, stiffly. I looked up at the sky, wondering if I had fallen straight through the universe from Nissilum. Did it exist in the universe? I shook my head. It wouldn't help to analyse anything too much. None of it would make sense.

I imagined my mother had been pacing the kitchen for hours by now, worried witless about where I'd got to, but when I walked through the back door, she was standing doing the washing-up, humming softly. At the sound of my footsteps, she turned and smiled at me.

'Hello, darling. Nice walk?'

I looked up at the clock. It was eleven-thirty. I'd left for my walk at a quarter to. I blinked. It wasn't possible . . . Maybe time stands still in Nissilum.

'Bobby's in a strange mood.' She peeled off her gloves and hung them over the tap. 'Was he chasing after birds or something? He was all worked up.'

I shrugged. 'He was a little overexcited, that's all.'

'Hmmm.' She looked at me. 'Lunch will be ready in an hour. And Dot's over at Cassidy's house. Why don't you go into the living room and talk to Dad.'

It wasn't a question, it was a sugar-coated order. Mum doesn't like company while she's cooking.

'OK.' I got up, unzipping my parka. 'But I need to change first.'

The living room door was closed as I went past to the stairs, and I heard a low voice and figured Dad was on the phone. In my bedroom, I quickly changed, putting on the first things I found on my chair.

As I pulled my fingers through my tangled hair, my eyes fell on the photograph sitting on top of my chest of drawers. It was of my parents, back when they were first married. Mum was wearing a full-length, blue, satiny dress, her dark hair curled up in a chignon at the back of her neck. She looked stunning. I picked up the photograph and studied her face. I could see myself in her. My colouring and my eyes. I looked down at her dress, wondering if I'd ever look good in something so elegant and feminine. I shook my head. Would I ever make it to the Great Ball? Back on mortal Earth, Nissilum and its tranquil, luscious beauty was fading already.

I replaced the photograph and opened the top drawer. There lay the notebook. Proof that Nissilum and Luca existed. I took it out and put it under my pillow so I could read it later in bed.

I went downstairs and into the living room to find Evan sitting on the sofa with my dad. I blinked as Evan got quickly to his feet.

'Oh hi.' I covered my nerves by doing a quick inspection of my clothing. Not too bad: leggings, clean T-shirt and a short black cardigan. 'Um, what are you doing here?' I asked awkwardly.

After our evening the week before, Evan had told me he was going to be out of town with his dad for a while and that he'd call for me when he got back. I wasn't sure he'd meant it at the time. I hadn't exactly been the most sophisticated company on our date. I'd practically bolted out of the car when he'd driven me home.

'I went for a drive,' Evan said easily. He came over and kissed me softly on the cheek, his lips moving close to my ear as he whispered, 'I wanted to see you.'

I looked across at my dad, who didn't look like he'd heard, before allowing myself a shy smile.

'This is my dad,' I said, stupidly.

'Yes, I know,' said Evan smiling. 'We've met.' He looked unbelievably gorgeous in scruffy, faded jeans and a denim shirt. He ran a hand through his messy blond hair. 'I was just asking your dad about his work. You didn't tell me he was a carpenter.'

'Evan's done some woodwork out in Australia,' said my father, handing Evan a beer. 'I'd hire him in a heartbeat if I wasn't so stretched financially these days.' He rubbed carefully at his neck. 'I could do with the help while I'm getting over this injury.'

'I did some work at a boatyard on weekends, for one of the wooden boatbuilders. I loved working with wood. Learned a lot too.' He took a swig of beer. 'One thing I'm going to miss about back home.' He shook his head. 'I think I'm getting under my dad's feet. I need to find something to keep myself occupied.' As he spoke he gave me a careful sideways look, his eyes smiling as he licked a drop of beer off his lips.

I thought the expression 'jelly legs' was made-up until I saw him do that.

I swallowed. 'You could teach me to drive,' I said without thinking. 'I mean, if you're serious?'

'I am,' he said, his eyes on mine. 'And it would be my pleasure.'

I glanced at Dad, hoping to God he hadn't noticed how

I was acting, but he was busy rubbing Bobby's back, who'd come panting and friendly into the room.

'Oh, but I haven't got a car yet,' I said, already trying to get out of it. 'I'm not getting it till next year.'

'Not a problem. When do you want to start?'

Dad nodded appreciatively at Evan. 'No time like the present,' he said, giving me a wink.

I opened my mouth, trying to think of another reason why I wasn't ready, but I couldn't come up with anything.

'After lunch,' said Dad. He nodded at Evan. 'You'll stay for lunch, young man? Anna always makes enough for five anyway.'

'So I've heard,' said Evan glancing at me. 'Thank you. I'd like that, Mr Jonas.'

'I'll inform the cook,' said Dad jovially, walking through to the kitchen, leaving us alone together.

Evan looked me properly up and down, grinning. 'I hope you don't mind me just dropping by, but it was the only way to get to see you again.'

I shrugged but couldn't keep the smile off my face.

'You look so pretty,' said Evan and, before I could say anything, moved closer to me, his hand brushing my back, sending tiny electrical impulses up my spine. Then, resting his hand on my waist, he drew me gently towards him. I stayed rooted to the spot, wondering what to do with the sparks flying around my insides, but Evan seemed happy to do all the work. 'I couldn't wait to see you again,' he said softly. 'I haven't stopped thinking about you. I really like you, Jane. You're different.'

I turned slowly, not wanting to spoil the moment by saying or doing anything clumsy or stupid. But as I was grappling with this, Evan lifted his hand and stroked my jawline, stopping to raise my chin with one finger. He bent forward, bringing his lips to mine, and I felt the softness of his mouth as he kissed me. Gently at first, then more firmly as I tentatively kissed him back. I moved my arms around his strong, lean chest, my fingers traced the dips between his ribs, aware that the hunger I felt right now was most definitely not for food.

But the sound of the door opening broke the spell and Evan pulled swiftly away. We both looked to see Bobby in the doorway, gazing up at Evan with a kind of adoration.

'Well, the dog likes you,' I managed to say, over the pounding of my heart. 'So, you've got somebody's seal of approval.'

'As long as I have yours,' said Evan, pushing my hair off my face. 'I don't care about anyone else.'

'Dinner's ready!' came my mother's voice from the kitchen.

101

'You haven't met my mum properly yet,' I whispered. 'She's the real gatekeeper in this house.'

Evan bent to give me one more soft kiss on the mouth. 'No worries. The ladies love me,' he said, pulling back with a grin. 'You'll see.'

CHAPTER TEN

'Here you go,' Mum said, handing Evan another beer.

'Uh . . . no thanks, Mrs Jonas.' He shook his head. 'I'm driving.' He glanced at Dad. 'Two's my limit.'

Dad nodded his approval as Mum handed him the beer instead and smiled at Evan.

'So teenagers aren't all drinking and looting any chance they get,' she said, sitting down and taking the lid off the casserole. 'Good to know.'

'Mum. Nobody goes looting.' I rolled my eyes, realising that her looks weren't all I'd inherited from her. We shared the same social skills too, apparently. While Evan had been washing his hands before lunch I'd warned her not to interrogate him about the time he'd gone missing. I just hoped she wasn't going to let her curiosity get the better of her.

I glanced at Evan, hoping she wasn't totally putting

him off, but he was smiling.

'It's OK. I've seen my fair share of wasters . . .' He paused. 'Back in Australia, there were hundreds of them, drinking till they passed out.' He held out his plate and Mum heaped a huge spoonful of pork in white wine on to it. 'I was always too dull to join in.'

'Dull?' I said, catching his eye. 'Why don't I believe that?'

Evan wrinkled his nose. 'It's true. I'm not one of those enigmatic types. I never sat in my bedroom writing poetry and smoking marijuana. Ask my mum. She was practically begging me to rebel. Just so I could be like all the other kids in the neighbourhood.'

I felt Mum's eyes on me but I didn't meet them, and the table fell quiet as she continued dishing out food.

'I must admit,' Mum said, when we'd finally all been served, 'I was secretly hoping you'd lead Jane astray. I'd like to see her go a bit wild. She needs to get out more.'

'What?' I stared hard at her. Great PR job, Mother. I turned to Evan. 'Feel free to run like hell. It's not going to get any better than this.'

Evan shook his head and speared a bean with his fork. 'I have no intention of going anywhere,' he said, confidently. 'Sorry to disappoint you.'

I chewed my food and smiled at the same time, unable

to look at Mum. She generally had a nose like a sniffer dog when it came to bullshit, but she seemed to be buying Saint Evan, because she beamed at him as he devoured his food.

'What a sensible boy. Your mother clearly did a good job bringing you up.'

I glanced warily at Evan, but his face was impassive. 'She's a good person,' he said evenly.

He was definitely ticking all the boxes. Pity my mother couldn't shut up.

'She must miss you,' Mum went on, ignoring my eye signals. 'You're so far away.'

Evan shrugged and forked up pork and potato. 'I guess,' he said, uncomfortably.

'Who is your fath—' Mum began, but I cleared my throat loudly, cutting her off. This was turning into an interrogation.

'Evan's going to teach me to drive,' I announced quickly. 'Isn't that great?'

Mum raised an eyebrow. 'That is great. Just make sure no one sees a sixteen-year-old in possession of a vehicle. Particularly not the local constabulary.' She picked up her wine glass and took a sip. 'They're dying to arrest someone around here.'

'Really.' Evan swallowed a mouthful of food. 'I bet

they've got their eye on me already.' He glanced at me and gave a subtle wink. 'The stranger in town.'

'Well, I'll put them straight,' said Mum. 'It will be my pleasure. A clean-living, responsible boy will really wind them up.'

Dad and I exchanged a smile. Mum's hatred of authority was legendary in our family. Weird, considering she was a model citizen in so many ways.

'Your mother's a dark horse you know,' Dad had told me, more than once. 'She wasn't always so sensible.'

I could never really get my head around My Mother the Anarchist, but today the subject was proving a handy diversion because Evan had relaxed again. So relaxed in fact, that he missed his mouth with his fork and gravy splashed clumsily off his chin.

'Oh God, I'm sorry,' he said, pushing back his chair. 'What a klutz.'

Mum was already on her feet. 'Stay there, I'll get you another napkin,' she said, darting into the kitchen.

I grinned at Evan as he wiped his beautiful chin.

'Thank God for that,' I said. 'I was beginning to think you weren't human.'

Evan flashed me a look of what I took as confusion.

'Who's not human?' Mum had appeared next to him, holding out a fresh napkin.

'No one, Mother. It was a joke.'

'A joke, yes.' Her eyes brightened slightly, but her smile looked a little forced. I swallowed, beginning to feel nervous myself, until Evan cut the atmosphere.

'I'd love some more, if there's any going?' He gestured at the casserole dish. 'It's delicious, Mrs Jonas.'

'Call me Anna,' said Mum, snapping back to normal. 'Mrs Jonas makes me feel so old.'

Evan smiled, tilting his head back to look up at her, and just for a split second I saw her eyes close and then open quickly. She put one hand on the table.

'Mum? Are you OK?'

'I'm fine. I think I moved too fast out of the kitchen.' She rubbed at her forehead. 'It gets so hot in there with the oven on.' She smiled, ignoring Dad's anxious expression and started moving around the table to her seat.

'One spoonful enough?' she asked Evan brightly. 'How about another potato?'

'Great, thank you.' As he held out his plate, I wasn't sure whether I was imagining the faint pulse in his cheek. But his eyes darted across to me at last and the look he gave me was warm, melting again, and I relaxed. But there was a strange awkward silence, interrupted only by the scrape of Evan's cutlery on his plate. I tried to catch my mother's eye, but she seemed intent on looking straight ahead of her as she ate. Dad, noticing my unease, winked at me, putting his knife and fork together.

'That was delicious, Anna,' he said. He looked over at Evan. 'Good to see a healthy appetite around here. Jane and her sister aren't big eaters.'

'Hope that's not a diet you're on.' Evan nudged my elbow. 'You're perfect.'

Flames shot up my neck again. I shrugged. 'We do eat.' I flicked a glance at my father. 'He's exaggerating.'

'I was just the same at her age, Jack,' said my mother, uncharacteristically coming to my defence. 'There was a time, when I was sixteen, that my appetite just vanished.' She looked thoughtfully at me, as I willed the conversation to take a new turn. 'I was in love at the time.'

I raised an eyebrow. 'You were?'

Mum nodded absently, probably on her way down memory lane. Dad took over.

'It wasn't with me,' he told Evan. 'Unfortunately.'

Evan took a drink of water. 'Must have been quite a guy. I don't think anyone or anything could put me off my food.' He knocked my leg under the table. 'Not even the girl I love.'

I held my breath. Was it possible that a boy like him could ever love me?

'Quite right, too,' Mum said vaguely. 'Never lose your head over love.'

Evan's eyes lowered. 'No,' he said quietly, but his hand found mine and he gripped it for a second. I squeezed it back, my legs turning to jelly again.

Mum had come back down from wherever she was. 'Anyway, it was a long time ago. I was young and . . . silly at the time.' She leaned over to Dad and gave him a kiss on the cheek. 'And I have my wonderful Jack.'

I groaned and rolled my eyes at Evan. 'I'm really sorry. She's not normally like this.'

Evan's jaw seemed to tighten a little, and I felt bad. He must have been thinking about his own parents. I stood up.

'I'll clear the plates,' I said quickly. 'That was really good, Mum. Thanks.'

'No problem,' she waved her napkin dismissively. 'A pleasure in fact.' She and my dad smiled at each other.

'You want a hand?' Evan pushed his chair back, but I shook my head.

'You're the guest,' I said, smiling. 'Talk to Mum.'

'You have an interesting scar,' my mother said to Evan, as I collected up the dishes. 'How did you get it?'

Evan looked blankly at her.

'The scar,' Mum said, pouring herself another glass of wine. 'On your neck?'

Evan opened his mouth, hesitating, before he touched the spot on his throat with his finger. 'This? I got it when I was working on the boats in Australia. Some hot metal sparks bounced off my neck ...' He rubbed at it gently. 'Only a metal disc left a little imprint.'

'Oh Lord,' said my mother, though her tone was almost bouncy in contrast to a few minutes before. 'Must have hurt.'

Evan nodded. 'Just a bit.'

'Poor you,' I said, touching his arm. 'Will it be there forever?'

'Forever and ever,' he said, mockingly, but his eyes were soft.

'Go and get the cheesecake, Jane,' Mum said, spoiling the moment. 'It's in the fridge. Second shelf.'

Evan winked quickly at me as I moved to do my bidding.

'Cheesecake's my favourite. You're a great cook, Anna.'

'Rubbish.' I saw her smile, pleased. 'You'd soon get sick of my repertoire.' She tapped my arm as I walked through to the kitchen. 'Ask Jane.'

'I hope I get the chance to get sick of it,' Evan

said, daringly, and I glanced back at her. But her lips were turned up, smiling.

After lunch, Evan insisted on helping Mum with the washing-up, and Dad went to pick up Dot from Cassidy's house. I put stuff away in a kind of daze. In the last three hours I'd visited a world inhabited by werewolves and vampires, and introduced my boyfriend to my parents. Who said I led a dull and uneventful life? Things can change in a heartbeat. I looked out of the window at the tops of the trees and in my head remembered the sound of rushing of water, and sad, green eyes, and that delicate, kind boy who'd showed me that there truly is a whole world out there waiting to be explored. A sudden feeling of melancholy came over me as I struggled to see how that boy could possibly fit into my life.

'I'm going to watch TV,' said Mum, drying her hands on a tea towel. 'You two can amuse yourselves.' She whistled for Bobby, picked up a newspaper from the counter and wandered through to the living room.

Evan rubbed his eyes and then stretched lazily. When he dropped his arms his eyes found mine and he moved closer to me.

'So, how about I teach you to drive?'

Evan's car was a beat-up old Saab he said his dad had loaned him for the duration of his stay. It seemed tinny and . . . well, tiny, compared to my dad's truck. It was also freezing. I wrapped my arms round myself in the front seat.

'Sorry about the lack of heating,' said Evan as he turned the key to start the engine. 'And it's not the most reliable of motors.' He checked in the wing mirror and we began reversing out down the track. 'Consider this a baptism of fire.'

I glanced at him. 'Sorry about my mum's . . . over-sharing today. She's not used to visitors.'

Evan's face was impassive. 'She's nice,' he said. We'd come to the bottom of the track and he turned the car around in the right direction, brushing my leg with his hand as he changed gear. 'And I'm not used to visiting.'

I relaxed and stuck my hands between my legs, thinking. 'I'm trying to picture your dad? I recognise the name, but . . .'

Evan didn't look at me, concentrating on the winding mountain road. 'Bill Forrest,' he said. 'He lives just the other side of Bale with my stepmother. She has a daughter . . . Your age I think. Sarah Emerson?'

I froze. Of course. Sarah's mum had kept her name. I

112

suppose I'd assumed that her dad, Bill, was her real dad. She'd never said otherwise. The one time I'd seen him was two years before with my mum after another bullying session from Sarah. Mum had marched round to his house, ready for war and he'd played the whole thing down. My mouth went dry.

'Bill Forrest,' I turned to Evan but he didn't respond, except to change gear, 'is Sarah's father?'

'Sarah, yeah.' His tone was light and then he glanced quickly at me. 'My stepsister's called Sarah.'

'Stop the car, please,' I whispered. I put my hand out to the dashboard and the glove compartment door fell open. Evan, not hearing me, reached across and firmly shut it.

'Old car,' he said, rolling his eyes and this time smiling at me. But my expression was defensive. My good mood had evaporated.

'Jane,' he said, his eyes narrowing, 'did you say something?'

'Sarah is the bitch who made my life hell at school,' I said, unable to keep the bleating tone out of my voice. 'She's . . . she's horrible.' I stared hard at him as his face took on another look. Realisation.

'Oh God.' He slowed down to a snail's pace. 'I had no idea.'

Out of the corner of my eye I saw Dad in his brand new truck with Dot waving manically in the front seat. Evan lifted a hand limply in greeting. They both grinned at us as they drove past. I could hardly bring myself to smile. I'd known he was too good to be true.

'Let me out.' How to describe how I felt at that moment? Flat, disappointed. And angry all over again.

'Jane . . .' Evan pulled up to the verge and stopped the engine. 'I can't believe Sarah . . . ?' He shook his head. 'She seems a nice kid.'

'Ha.' I stared ahead of me and then closed my eyes. 'A nice kid she is not.' I felt him shift beside me, saw out of the corner of my eye his hand creeping over to mine. I jerked my arm away before he could touch it.

'Hey.' His voice was gentle. 'I am not my sister.'

I swung my eyes to look at him. The curve of his cheekbone, the tiny lines at the corners of his eyes, his soft, full lips, the glow of his perfectly tanned skin against his denim shirt.

No, much much prettier than his sister.

But the thought of him, laughing about me with Sarah. Living in the same house as that poisonous . . . I was shivering again, but not from the cold. All the happiness draining out of me. I felt shrivelled up and small.

'Does she know?' I asked quietly.

'About you?' He breathed out, his finger tapping the steering wheel nervously. 'She knows I've met a girl.'

'But does she know my name?'

'No.' He pressed his lips together then and turned slowly, cautiously in my direction. 'Not yet.'

'I don't want her to know we . . . we were dating.' I swallowed realising that Evan and I were now past tense. At least, I couldn't see a future.

I grasped the door handle and pressed down to open it.

'Please, Jane. Don't go.' Evan turned me towards him, his beautiful face pleading. It almost melted me, but Sarah had spoiled it all. And she wasn't even here.

'I want to go home,' I repeated coldly.

He said nothing and I climbed out of his car, slamming the door. It had started raining, large drops of cold water, and I hugged myself as I walked quickly back to the house.

Mum was feeding the dog when I appeared in the kitchen, wet through. Miserable.

'That was quick,' she said, straightening up. Her eyes took in my face 'Sweetheart? What happened?'

'Nothing.' My voice was flat. 'I'm going upstairs.'

She moved towards me. 'Did he . . . What did he do?' She reached out her hand.

'He didn't do anything . . . I don't want to talk about it.'

'But—'

'Please.' I walked past her and into the hall. As I reached the stairs, Dot skittered out from the living room.

'I missed him,' she wailed, tugging at my hand. 'I missed Evan!' She swung on my arm, before she realised I was not smiling.

'Janey.' She stopped. 'What's the matter with you?'

'Nothing, Dottie,' I stroked her hair.

Everything's wrong, I thought.

And then I moved past her and began climbing the stairs to my room. I knew she was looking up at me, anxious, but I just couldn't comfort her. It was all I could do to comfort myself.

Later, lying on my bed, I heard the phone downstairs ring and my mother called up to me, but I turned out my light and ignored her.

I pressed my face against my pillow and longed for a friend. Someone I could trust. I'd begun to think that friend could be Evan, but the only person I could see in my mind right then was a tall, dark, delicate boy with the kindest eyes I'd ever seen.

CHAPTER ELEVEN

The next day began with a fresh fall of snow. I woke to see ice draped around the panes in my bedroom window and pushed my quilt up to my neck.

Downstairs, Dot's excited voice urged my father to go outside and play snowballs with her.

'You're late!' I heard my mother yelling to my sister above the sound of the radio in the kitchen. 'Get in the truck and Dad will take you to school.'

Dot's protests faded and then the back door shut with a loud bang. At the same time, Mum switched off the radio and the house stood in silence. I waited for her to shout at me to get up, but there was only the sound of footsteps in the hall and the back door opening and shutting again.

As much as my family drove me mad sometimes, I didn't like being alone in the house. Even though Mum had probably just gone outside to get the post from the box at the end of the track, I felt agitated. The house was eerie.

I turned over and slid my hand across the sheet then under the pillow, my fingers touching the hard case of the notebook. I dragged it out, and levered myself up to lean against the headrest, and examined the shabby cover once again. It had to be decades old, and holding it I felt a pleasant thrill. I was holding on to a piece of somebody's life, somebody's feelings. I opened the journal to where I had left off the last time.

There were more drawings, some done in ink-pen: ornate, detailed – a sketch of a face caught my eye and I turned the book to study it at the right angle. It was a slender face, rigid cheekbones, deep-set eyes, framed by curls. I couldn't tell whether it was male or female. By the side of it was a sketch of gates and a large, grand building. I stared at the face again – something about it registered as familiar, but I couldn't think how. Then I turned the page to find another short entry:

December, she wrote. *Another freezing day and I'm beginning to think you aren't real. That I simply dreamed you . . . If it weren't for the pendant you gave me, I would certainly think so. I keep it somewhere safe and when she's asleep I think of you, but you don't come.*

Have you forgotten me already? My mother is getting better. Today she ate a whole bowl of soup, even some bread. It's such a relief, when only a few months ago I thought she would never recover. But she is strong. I read to her at night and sometimes I want to tell her about you. About how much there is between us. And I get angry, because none of this is simple. And she would never understand. I've thought endlessly about us, and every way I look I can't see a way it would work between us. But then how can I ever be without you? Sixteen years old and I feel my life is over. At least, if you are truly gone forever, I will be lonely forever.

The entry stopped abruptly then, but I lingered on that last sentence. Melodramatic as it was, something about it resonated strongly with me.

I shut the book quickly, not wanting to dwell on how it made me feel. Then I slipped the notebook under my pillow and lay back. By now I should have felt happy. At the beginning of something wonderful. But instead I felt muddled and sad. I wrinkled my nose, willing the melancholy away, and thought of Evan. The crinkles around his eyes and their colour, that unearthly bright blue.

I rolled my head on the pillow and my eyelids drooped,

but a scratching sound opened them again. I shifted and propped myself up on my elbows. A familiar face looked down at me.

'Luca?' I grabbed the quilt with one hand and sat up properly. There were two pink spots on his alabaster cheeks, but the green of his eyes was as intense as ever.

'Good morning, Jane.' He perched on the bed, rubbing at his knees. His coat was covered with bits of twig and flakes of snow. 'Sorry to wake you.'

'How did you . . . ?' My eyes darted to the window, which swung open.

'I hope you don't think this is indecent.' He grinned, studying my quilt. 'Visiting an unmarried lady in her chamber.'

I shuffled back down under the covers. 'It is a little indecent,' I said, smiling. 'And quite a risk.'

'Ah. I saw your mother walking to the town,' said Luca. 'I figured it was safe to come in.'

I shook my head.

'God knows what she'd make of you,' I said wryly. 'You look like a Victorian urchin.'

He looked blank. 'I have no idea what that is, but I'll take it as a compliment.' He started undoing the buttons on his coat and shed it. He wore only a white T-shirt and dark-blue carpenter jeans. He looked delicate. Pale. Regal.

'You must be freezing.' As I spoke an icy blast from the open window drifted over to the bed. Luca seemed unaffected.

'I've been on the move,' he explained. 'I'm still warm from travelling here.'

I yawned, looking at the alarm clock.

'It's very early,' I said. 'Has something happened?'

He shifted on the bed. 'Not exactly.' He paused, sniffing and picking at an invisible thread on the bedspread. 'But I have had a request from my mother,' he went on. 'She wants to meet my . . . girlfriend.'

I raised an eyebrow. 'You have a girlfriend?'

The pink in his cheeks spread across his face. It was adorable.

I waited a beat before putting him out of his misery.

'OK,' I sighed. 'So you told your mother about me?'

He hesitated, then, 'Not me. Dalya. The demon.'

'Oh.' I smiled sympathetically. 'So . . . ?'

He looked a little pleading. 'I wouldn't ask . . .'

'But you need me to pretend?' I stuck my arm out of the bed and gestured to my hoodie. 'Pass me that – and close the window would you?'

Luca stood obediently and did as I instructed, bringing my sweatshirt over to the bed. He perched on the edge,

121

watching me as I wrapped myself in the hoodie. I sank back against the pillow, surprised at how unselfconscious I felt in front of him.

'My parents are going to spend time with the greats,' said Luca. 'They will be away for a week or so.'

'The greats?'

'What you call "grandparents".' He wrinkled his nose. 'Which is a very long-winded term if you ask me. You people are weird.'

'I hardly think you're in a position to call mortal traditions weird,' I said, raising an eyebrow.

'Perhaps.' He eyed me, amused. 'The point is . . . I have foolishly agreed . . . to bring you to our midday meal today.'

It was clearly meet-the-parents week. I suppressed an ironic smile.

'If this is too much,' Luca began, 'I will understand.'

For a minute I thought of Evan. But what was the point?

'It's fine,' I said. 'I wasn't doing anything anyway.'

Luca gave me a curious look. 'It's a liberty,' he said, glumly. 'You're spoken for, I know that.'

I tried not to give anything away in my expression. It was humiliating somehow to have to admit that I'd made a mistake with the smooth-talking Australian boy.

'You know what,' I said, brightening, 'I'd like to meet your family.'

'Really?' The serious green eyes lit up. 'Wonderful!' He grabbed my hand with his, and it was as though I had sunk my fingers in warm, soothing water. Momentarily I closed my eyes, enjoying it, before I stopped and pulled away. We looked at each other for a few seconds, neither of us knowing what the other was thinking, before the thud of more snowfall against the bedroom window made us both jump.

'I'm ready when you are,' said Luca then.

I took a deep breath, glancing at the slag heap of clothing on my chair.

'Oh dear,' I said, sighing. 'I haven't got a thing to wear.'

Luca waited with his back turned as I dressed in jeans and a plaid shirt and my trusty, long grey cardigan.

'I'll have to steal something from my mother I suppose,' I said, tugging one plimsoll over my heel. 'For the ball.'

'It's not for a couple of weeks,' Luca said, finally turning round. 'I would offer to pay for something, but . . . our currency would not be accepted on mortal Earth.'

I grinned. 'Oh, I'll think of something,' I said, then looked down at myself. 'Something more suitable than this. Your mum's going to take me for a boy.'

'No chance of that,' Luca muttered, and for a second our eyes met, in an awkward kind of acknowledgment.

'I need to call my dad,' I said. 'Tell him I'll be out for a bit. I think he's picking up some timber this morning, but this snow probably means he'll be back early.' I picked up my address book and flipped through to find Dad's number.

'Don't you have one of those portable telephone things?' said Luca, looking curiously at the book.

'Nope.' I located Dad's mobile number, which I still hadn't memorised. 'No point.'

'Quite right,' said Luca. 'I am amused by the mortal obsession with constant communication. What do you all find to talk about?'

Keeping my finger on the right page, I closed the address book and poked him with it.

'Not everyone shares our antisocial tendencies, Luca,' I said. 'But for the record, it baffles me too.'

'You'd better make your call,' he said gruffly, looking out of the window. 'I do appreciate this, Jane.'

'No problem.' I opened the bedroom door. 'Stay here. I'll be right back.'

Downstairs, I left a message on Dad's phone. Mum was still out somewhere and when I ended the call, I glimpsed a piece of paper on the table with her handwriting on it. *GONE FOR A WALK TO ABIGAIL'S HOUSE*, it began. Abigail was Mum's best friend and she lived the other side of Bale, which meant Mum would be gone hours. *EVAN CALLED. TWICE. LAST NIGHT.*

I held my breath. Should I call him back? Right on cue the phone rang, and I stared at it for a few seconds before picking up.

'Hello?' I said cautiously.

'Jane.' It was Evan, sounding distinctly less self-assured than usual. 'I feel so bad about Sarah. I had no idea. Honestly . . .' He paused. 'Can we at least talk about it?'

I hesitated before answering. 'I don't know . . .'

'You know you can trust me,' he went on. 'You do know that, right?'

'Yes . . .' I said uncertainly. Did I know that?

'I can't stand the thought of you being mad at me over her. She's not worth it.'

I said nothing, waiting.

'And the thought of not seeing you . . . What can I do to make it better?'

'I don't know. And I'm busy today,' I said, winding the phone cord around my free fingers. 'I'll call you.'

'OK.'

Evan sounded so despondent I felt like I should say

more. Give him more. But Luca was waiting for me. I swallowed, torn and guilty, but a movement from upstairs resolved me.

'I'll call you,' I repeated. And I hung up.

When I got back upstairs my bedroom was empty. The window was still open, creaking, and I walked over to shut it, looking down to our yard as I did. Luca was lurking behind Dad's shed, fully wrapped in his coat. He lifted a hand to wave at me. I grinned. I hadn't thought through how I would get him out of the house the conventional way.

I put another layer on – the poncho – and sprinted downstairs to where he stood.

'This won't take long,' said Luca. He slipped around the back of the shed and I followed, glancing behind me to check that nobody had seen us.

'Now, leave most of the talking to me,' he said brightly, walking ahead of me. 'All you need to know is that your father runs a farm and we are distantly related through second cousins of my father's, whom he doesn't remember.' He paused. 'He has an appalling memory, which will work well for us.'

'Right.' I tramped after him, my mind racing. 'Anything else?'

126

'Don't mention pounds and pennies,' Luca went on. 'We trade in krenels.' He turned and smiled wryly. 'I'll explain the denominations of that some other time . . . And stick to simple words and phrases. None of your mortal gobbledegook.'

'Thanks very much.'

Luca stopped. 'Seriously,' he said. 'Everything else is just as it is here. Shops, restaurants, schools, even fashion. Though we tend not to wear those horrible neon colours you all like.'

I shook my head. I should have felt annoyed but I found his chattering delightful somehow.

'Oh.' Luca stopped, biting his lip. 'And we don't have cars or trains or trucks or aeroplanes. We don't need them.'

'Is that it?' I smiled at his back.

Luca hesitated before going on. 'No televisions, or computers, or telephones. You'll think we are primitive; our lives are much simpler than yours.'

We had gone deep across the mountain by now and had been moving so fast I felt out of breath. I stopped and, a few feet in front of me, Luca intuitively came to a halt also.

'How will it work, getting there?' I asked, panting still. 'Only I've never consciously travelled to a parallel world.'

Luca slowed down in front of me. We had reached a small clearing. He stopped altogether.

'I'm not sure, but it has happened once, so it should happen again,' he said. 'I know it has something to do with what you want. You have to will it.'

I remembered the night of Dad's accident. Sitting in that car wanting – willing – someone to help us. It had worked then. And it had worked when I'd been worried for Luca in the woods.

'I think I need to hold on to you,' I said, feeling suddenly awkward.

He held out his arms. 'Come on then.'

I moved closer, holding him, noting how his long body felt different to Evan's. It was slighter, but athletic and strong. I pressed my cheek against his coat, felt his heartbeat and his arms closing around my body.

'OK?' he whispered into my hair.

I nodded and shut my eyes, picturing the Water Path, the grand trees, the sound of the water. I began to drift, and Luca's head rested on mine as he held me.

I had no memory of the journey; my first conscious thought was of a breeze lifting my hair and a familiar rushing sound. I looked into the river, hurrying on its way somewhere, pushing past embedded rocks which stuck

up above the surface. A huge bird soared elegantly, following the river. It looked like an eagle. I blinked as I watched it fly. I'd never seen an eagle. From this distance it looked huge, but not ungainly. Just magnificent.

Luca silently watched with me.

'I read more of the notebook,' I said at last. 'She was my age, that girl.'

'Yes.' Luca leaned back on his elbows. 'And it doesn't have a happy ending I fear.'

'Who was she?' I said, more to myself than to him.

'I believe she was mortal.' Luca pressed his lips together. 'And her . . . lover, I think he was one of us.'

'A werewolf?'

'Could be.' He hesitated before going on. 'There is a rumour about a male, living on Nissilum, generations ago, who ceased to exist. People say it was the love of a mortal girl that killed him.'

I turned slowly to look at him. 'Is that why you are reluctant . . . to fall in love with a mortal?'

Luca nodded. 'Although to me, the notion that one can control one's emotions in that way seems ridiculous.' He sighed, sitting back up and holding on to his knees. 'But according to my mother, it is perfectly possible to control such things. To decide not to love. Just a matter of ruling with your head, not your heart. Not very romantic.' He shook his head. 'But, given what is destined to happen to those of us who fall . . . it is probably better to keep mortal relationships platonic. Better still never to engage with mortals in the first place.'

I felt vaguely rejected. Stupid. I mean, I knew what I felt with Luca was different. Safer, calmer. Perhaps it was less exciting?

'You need to get yourself a proper girlfriend,' I said flatly. 'Not a pretend one.'

'Hmmm.' Luca didn't look at me. 'I haven't met an immortal girl yet who inspires those feelings in me. I don't think I ever will.'

His answer pleased me, though I disliked myself for it. I didn't want him, but I didn't want anyone else to be with him either.

'Anyway, I thought it was a good thing to come here first,' said Luca, changing tack.

'Before you meet my family. It's a calming place. I don't want you to be nervous.'

'I'm meeting a bunch of werewolves,' I said half smiling. 'What's to be nervous about?'

Luca chuckled and as he turned to look at me I saw how his green eyes danced. When he laughed his normally serious face lit up. It jolted something inside me.

I smiled back at him, then looked up at the pale-blue sky.

'Shouldn't we get going?' I said.

'Yep.' Luca got to his feet and held out his hand to help me up. 'Particularly since we are going the slow way.' He noticed my puzzled face and added, 'We're walking.'

Luca and I walked for miles, but he held my hand all the way and I found we were moving briskly, covering the distance quickly. We crossed a vast field of rape and came to a stony path, and then a pretty gate, covered in wisteria. Luca stopped in front of it.

'The south is divided from the north by a vast river. Northerners pay a toll to cross the bridge into the southern region. We also have to apply to cross over first. My father hates filling in forms. And as I said, his memory is not good. Neither he nor my mother will question you too closely on your family.'

'OK.' I nodded. 'Good to know.'

He pushed through the gate and we walked up a wide gravel drive of sorts, flanked by apple trees. Ahead of me, I saw the front of a large old cottage. It was idyllic.

I felt a mixture of nerves and excitement, and behind that a kind of acceptance. I didn't feel like a stranger in a strange world. I felt somehow at home.

We reached the front door and Luca turned.

'Ready?' he said, touching my sleeve.

'Ready.'

'Ulfred! They're here!' a familiar voice shrieked. Dalya, her dark hair falling to her waist, stood in front of us. Her eyes travelled up and down me.

'What is she wearing?' she whispered rudely to Luca.

'"She" is standing right here,' said Luca, cuffing her lightly on the shoulder.

'Luca?' I looked over Dalya's head to see a tall woman with short, dark hair coming towards us. She wore a long, silky-looking shift dress with what looked like a piece of hewn leather around her waist as a belt. On her feet she wore elegant suede moccasins. Her skin was pale, and her eyes were green like Luca's and Dalya's. She craned her head as she came nearer, gently placing her hands on Dalya's shoulders to move her to one side.

Up close, I saw she had silvery-grey streaks at her hairline. And her eyes, a rich hazel-brown, were almond-shaped. She was beautiful.

'Hello,' she said, extending her hand. 'My name is Henora. You must be Jane?' She glanced briefly at Luca, who looked a little tense. 'I'm so pleased to meet you.'

'Likewise,' I said, then blushed. 'I mean . . . I've heard

132

so much about you.' I didn't dare look at Luca.

'I have prepared some food,' said Henora, turning and gesturing for us to follow her.

Dalya scampered past us and down a long corridor, at the end of which I saw a man, an older version of Luca, waiting in what had to be the kitchen.

'My mother's favourite flower is the lily,' Luca whispered behind me. 'And she doesn't eat meat.'

I nodded subtly, wondering exactly how it worked out for a vegetarian werewolf at the full moon.

We walked through into a large but homely room, with rough-painted walls and a large window. A huge stove glowered in the corner and a pale wooden trestle table was set with wooden platters. There was no cutlery, but earthenware mugs next to a jug of water.

Luca's doppelgänger stood placidly at one end of the table. He beamed from ear to ear.

'Welcome Jane,' he said, as Dalya clung on to his arm adoringly. He stepped closer to me, taking me in. 'I am Ulfred. What a fine-looking girl.' He leaned forward slightly. 'Unusual.'

'Jane is still wearing her workwear,' said Luca, not looking at me. 'She came straight from her father's farm.'

I nodded, my mouth frozen in a clueless grin.

'Good girl,' said Henora approvingly. 'Family loyalty

We reached the front door and Luca turned.

'Ready?' he said, touching my sleeve.

'Ready.'

'Ulfred! They're here!' a familiar voice shrieked. Dalya, her dark hair falling to her waist, stood in front of us. Her eyes travelled up and down me.

'What is she wearing?' she whispered rudely to Luca.

' "She" is standing right here,' said Luca, cuffing her lightly on the shoulder.

'Luca?' I looked over Dalya's head to see a tall woman with short, dark hair coming towards us. She wore a long, silky-looking shift dress with what looked like a piece of hewn leather around her waist as a belt. On her feet she wore elegant suede moccasins. Her skin was pale, and her eyes were dark like Luca's and Dalya's. She craned her head as she came nearer, gently placing her hands on Dalya's shoulders to move her to one side.

Up close, I saw she had silvery-grey streaks at her hairline. And her eyes, a rich hazel-brown, were almond-shaped. She was beautiful.

'Hello,' she said, extending her hand. 'My name is Henora. You must be Jane?' She glanced briefly at Luca, who looked a little tense. 'I'm so pleased to meet you.'

'Likewise,' I said, then blushed. 'I mean . . . I've heard

known for their friendliness to cats. Let alone this bunch of alpha canines. I waited for the penny to drop.

But Ulfred's attention was elsewhere now, he tousled Dalya's hair and asked his wife if he could help her with anything.

Luca took the opportunity to flash me an encouraging smile, but I felt nervous, my mind beginning to race with the potential for all of this to go horribly wrong.

The sound of the main door banging made us all turn to see a boy of around fourteen striding noisily down the hall.

'Lowe.' Henora shook her head, a small smile on her lips, defying the firmness in her voice. 'Late . . . as ever.'

The boy walked through into the kitchen. Like Luca, he was slender, with the same delicate features, but his hair was lighter, curling slightly and he had Dalya's deep brown eyes. He started taking his boots off, his eyes on me as he spoke to his mother.

'Cadmium had me hacking down the hedges inside the palace gates,' he said. His voice, not quite broken yet, was husky and a little petulant.

Henora smiled. 'This is Lowe,' she said turning to me. 'He has spent the morning at the Celestial Palace, preparing the grounds for the Great Ball . . .' She glanced quickly at Luca. 'He could have done with some help you know, Luca.'

Luca grunted, watching as his younger brother tapped mud from his boots on to the stone floor.

'I had other plans today,' he said calmly. But for the first time I detected a slight edge to his voice. 'And you know I'm not much good at manual work.'

Lowe gave a short laugh and slapped Luca lightly on the shoulder. 'Not much good, or not much interested?' he said jovially before turning to Henora. 'I like to do it, Mother. Luca is a delicate soul. You know that.'

Though some years younger than Luca, Lowe had the authoritative air of an older brother.

Henora smiled indulgently at him, before moving back to the stove.

Ulfred came forward. 'Introduce your guest, son,' he said lightly.

'Oh . . . yes.' Luca flushed a little. 'Lowe, this is Jane . . . My friend from the south.' He glanced at me. 'Jane, this is my little brother, Lowe.'

Lowe and I nodded in greeting and I felt him appraising me, not very subtly.

'Lucky Luca,' he said slowly, coming closer. 'She is wolf . . . I presume?'

'Of course,' Luca said. 'What else would she be?'

Lowe shrugged. 'I just don't recognise her, that's all.'

'You don't know everybody in the whole world,' piped up Dalya, to my relief. There was something too clever about this boy.

'True.' Lowe's eyes lingered only slightly on me before he turned to survey the table. 'What's for lunch, Henora? I'm hungry.'

'Roasted vegetables and braised owl,' she said, stirring something in a pot on the stove.

I blanched. Braised owl?

Luca nudged me gently. 'It tastes like rabbit,' he whispered. 'If you've ever sampled that.'

I nodded. I had. I hadn't liked it much either.

'The meal is ready,' said Henora. 'Take your seats.'

Luca and I were sat side by side, while Lowe and Dalya briefly squabbled about their own seating.

'I want to sit next to Ulfred,' she whined.

'Very well, brat,' Lowe said sharply. 'Have your own way. Again.'

'Lowe,' said Henora, 'mind your temper.' She frowned at him as he pulled his chair in roughly.

'He's all male,' she told me, not without a hint of pride in her voice. 'With the impatience that goes with it, too.'

'Whereas Luca's more like a girl,' Dalya said idly. 'I mean that in a nice way.'

'Why thank you,' said Luca, dryly, but he looked quite

affectionately at his sister.

A bowl of something pale lurking under blackened vegetables in gravy was placed in front of me.

'This looks delicious,' I lied, prodding at a slimy pepper-like thing on top. There was still no cutlery anywhere on the table.

Henora handed bowls to everyone, putting only a heap of vegetables on her own plate.

'We must go back to the physician soon, Hen,' said Ulfred, gesturing at her food. 'You will grow weak again if we run out of supplement.'

'Oh don't fuss, dear,' said Henora. 'I am perfectly well.'

'Henora takes a pro-supplement,' explained Luca. 'Her red blood count suffers because she does not like meat.'

'I will not eat my brothers and sisters,' said Henora firmly. 'That is why I go to the locked caves at full moon.' She raised an eyebrow at her older son. 'It has been thus since long before you were born, Luca . . .' She turned to me. 'And are you a meat-eater Jane?'

'Uh . . . I am,' I said, deciding not to elaborate. I suspected that the notion of killing and then eating an animal raw was far more alien to me than it was to Henora.

She nodded, accepting this. 'I am a bit of an oddity, I admit.' She sighed. 'But I have very strong principles in that regard. And I won't be shaken.'

The table fell quiet. No prizes for guessing who was the boss in this house, I thought, feeling wistful about my mother. She and Henora would get on like a house on fire.

Ulfred picked up a piece of meat with his fingers and tore at the flesh, his strong white teeth making short work of chewing. I was riveted by the sight. The others, I noticed, ate in a similar way. Of course. They were animals. Dalya bent forward and licked at the gravy on her bowl unselfconsciously. Her long tongue lapped like Bobby's at his water dish.

As my eyes travelled around the table, I realised, blushing, that Lowe was regarding me with some amusement. When our eyes met he too lifted his food in his hand, attacking it hungrily. As a large piece of owl disappeared into his mouth, he wiped his chin showily with the back of his hand. His eyes had never left me.

Henora looked over at me, anxiously. 'You don't like your food, Jane?' She gestured at my untouched food.

'Of course.' Understanding that years of mortal table manners would have to be dispensed with, I picked up a large chunk of meat and put the whole thing into my mouth, swallowing as fast as I could. At least this way I would not actually taste the owl on its way down to my stomach. I took a large drink of water and tried chewing on the next piece of meat, hoping that my inadequate teeth would not let me down.

As it turned out, eating like an animal was liberating. If I could just rid myself of my mother's horrifed face, it was a sensible way to eat. Tearing at meat with your teeth – particularly when it is attached to bones – means that not a single morsel is wasted. My mother would approve of that at least.

'I expect Luca has told you about the impending Great Ball, Jane?' Ulfred changed the subject, pouring himself a glass of water. 'You should come . . . I don't think a southern wolf has attended for some time.'

'Not for years,' put in Henora. 'Not since Tarn offended Celeste in the last quarter.' She looked across at me. 'You'll know Tarn, of course. The Patriarch of the south.' She sighed. 'He has a temper on him worse than Lowe's.'

Lowe widened his eyes in mock outrage.

'And as you know,' added Ulfred. 'Celeste abhors all forms of aggression.'

'Oh yes,' I said, nudging Luca's foot with mine under the table. We were heading for deep water, conversationally speaking, and any minute now my mortal ignorance would be revealed.

But Luca simply gave me a serene look in return.

'Well, Celeste *is* the Queen,' he said, helpfully. 'Sort of. It is her duty to set an example.'

'She didn't do a very good job with her great-son,' said Henora. 'And where is he now?'

'He's locked up, isn't he?' said Lowe. 'Raphael was incarcerated when he went on that rampage . . . About three years ago, I think.' He turned to me. 'He had a tantrum because the food was not served quickly enough. He tore through the palace and destroyed every piece of china and glass he could get his hands on . . .'

Lowe was clearly enjoying relating the story. I saw Luca looking a little impatient.

'And his great-mother ordered him to be institutionalised,' Lowe finished, taking an enormous portion of meat and vegetables. 'Crazy.'

'And we haven't seen his father for decades.' Henora sniffed. 'Celeste's handmaid is very tight-lipped about the matter, but there are only so many excuses one can make for a man who is supposedly the Legal Enforcer for the land.'

Legal Enforcer? Must be like a lawyer, or a judge or something, I thought, chewing on another chunk of grey meat, noting that owl was indeed as disgusting as rabbit.

'I heard he went mad too.' Lowe said. 'Physicians couldn't do anything for him.' He looked around the table and settled on me. 'And eventually he faded away.'

'That's just gossip.' Ulfred looked disapprovingly at Lowe. 'I met Gabe, he was a good man. It's a tragedy if he has truly lost his mind.'

Dalya was observing all of us with a rapt expression.

'He died,' she said in a hoarse whisper. 'I know that can happen if—'

'Of course he didn't die.' Luca rolled his eyes. 'Nobody dies here.'

Henora and Ulfred exchanged a strange look.

'Who did you say your father was?' Lowe asked me, casually.

'Peto,' Luca said before I could open my mouth. 'He runs a farm . . . practically in the wilderness in Hallacre. Unlikely you'll have met him . . . Or his family.'

'Peto?' Lowe narrowed his eyes, thinking. 'No. I don't believe I do know him. Must be as antisocial as you, Luca.' He smiled wickedly at me. 'I'm amazed my brother managed to strike up a conversation with you, Jane. He's not known for his silver tongue.'

Lowe was a little obnoxious, I thought protectively.

'Maybe he doesn't feel there are many people

142

worth talking to?' I eyed the boy boldly over the rim of my mug.

Ulfred glanced from Luca to his brother and then to me, and gave a loud, good-natured laugh. 'Now, children,' he said, then, winking at me, 'behave.'

'Don't mind Lowe,' said Henora. 'He likes to stir up trouble.' She cuffed her younger son gently over the head. 'And he loves his brother really.'

I smiled, but the friction between Luca and his brother had not passed me by.

Dalya was not the only troublemaker in this family.

After lunch Henora ordered us all out into the garden while she made fresh mint tea. 'Excellent for the digestion,' she said, picking a handful of mint from a flowerbed by the back door and going back inside. Ulfred muttered something about visiting an elderly neighbour and disappeared.

The garden was the size of a vast field. Three horses ambled at one end. I recognised one – Sabre – from before. Dalya raced off immediately to see him, while Luca and I settled ourselves under a large cedar tree where a plain wooden table and two benches were placed. Lowe stayed at a distance, throwing a ball up into the air and catching it, occasionally casting a glance in our direction.

Looking at the back of the house I realised it was enormous and ancient. It resembled the old drawings of medieval houses I'd seen in History textbooks. And the garden had an old-fashioned feel to it, the lawn springy and the flowerbeds ornate. It seemed incongruous that it was a place occupied and tended by what were in fact . . . animals. Everything was so proper.

Luca tapped my hand, which lay on the table. As ever with him, I felt a kind of soporific contentment. I lazily turned my head.

'Thank you,' he said. 'I hope this is not too much of an ordeal?'

'It's . . . an experience,' I said carefully. 'But I like your parents. They've been very welcoming . . .' I paused. 'God knows what they think of me?'

'God knows?' Luca looked bemused. 'You mortals and your gods.'

'It's just an expression,' I said. 'Everyone says it.' I sat up. 'Anyway, you must believe in God. You have angels governing you!'

'Ah.' He scratched his head. 'But they symbolise order and morality. Who knows whether there is an almighty being governing them?'

'I'm totally confused,' I said, and saw his lips twitch. 'You mean you personally don't believe in a God?'

'I don't know. I believe in something beyond ourselves, something physically intangible. Yes. But I have not given it a name.'

I thought for a minute. 'I suppose that's pretty much what I think, too,' I said eventually. 'Even more so now.'

We smiled at each other. 'See,' said Luca, 'we're a match made in heaven.'

I rolled my eyes at the pun, but I felt happy and close to him. I felt right somehow.

'Do you think they believe I'm for real?' I said then. 'Your parents?'

Luca scratched at the rough wooden tabletop. 'I think they're prepared to believe good in everyone,' he answered. 'They are big on the benefit of the doubt.'

I frowned. 'But they think I look too odd. My face is too round . . . My eyes are grey!'

He laughed. 'As to that, they are broad-minded, also. Like mortals, werewolves are capable of genetic anomalies. It's true, we have longer faces, and bigger jaws, and our eyes are generally a variant on brown, not blue, but I believe only one thing has struck them as truly unusual.'

My breathing quickened. 'My cluelessness?'

'No,' he knocked my hand almost shyly. 'Something a lot prettier.'

I felt grateful for the shadows cast by the cedar's hanging leaves.

I had never felt beautiful or pretty. Not even close. I wasn't blonde, and curvy, and vivacious. I was straight up and down, unfashionably pale. I shook my head.

The sound of Dalya shouting at Lowe diverted us, and we looked up to the bottom of the garden to see her wrestling with him by her horse, Sabre.

'Leave him, Lowe!' she wailed. 'You overexcite him.'

Lowe slapped the horse hard on its rear and it skittered over to the other side. He jeered triumphantly at his sister. 'You mollycoddle that animal. He's not a pet.'

Dalya stamped her foot and uttered a loud sob. She turned on her heel and marched towards the house, leaving Lowe grinning after her. He stopped when he caught us watching him, and his expression turned darker. Shooting us a sour look, he plucked a rose from the bush in the bed next to him and tore the petals off roughly.

'He's not at his best today,' Luca said, frowning. 'But he's not a bad kid.'

'Hmmm.' I felt unsettled by Lowe's aggression. 'I wouldn't like to be alone with him at the full moon.'

Luca laughed. 'He's just like Henora,' he went on, as Lowe scattered the petals on the grass. 'Opinionated and traditional. What you might call patriotic.'

'Or a boy with too much testosterone,' I said, without thinking. I caught Luca's raised eyebrow. 'I mean . . .'

But Luca was grinning at me as I floundered. 'You're probably right about that.' He said. 'He's "all male".'

Henora appeared, carrying a tray with glass cups and a kind of transparent kettle full of greenish hot water. She placed it on the table and sat down on the bench opposite us.

'Thank you for your hospitality,' I told her, as she poured tea into the cups. 'You have a beautiful house.'

Henora smiled at both of us. 'I am so glad to meet a friend of Luca's,' she said. 'We were beginning to despair—'

'Mother,' Luca said warningly. He took a sip of his tea. 'You know I choose my friends carefully.'

'Yes.' She leaned back. 'And I admire you for it. I am glad to see you happy, that's all.'

Luca continued to sip his tea, looking ahead of him.

'So, are you coming to the ball?' Henora asked me, putting her cup down. 'As Luca's guest?'

'I . . .' I caught Luca's eye. 'I would like to, yes.'

'Excellent.' She beamed at me. 'It is an interesting event. One has to be on one's guard for much of the time . . . There are elements of our society that could cause trouble given half a chance. But in general most

147

people behave themselves.'

I nodded.

'I will take care of Jane,' said Luca seriously. 'It will be fine.'

Lowe strolled over to the table, picking up a cup and emptying it in seconds. He put it roughly back on the table.

'I need to get back to the palace,' he told his mother. 'Cadmium wants me to work inside this afternoon.'

'Of course,' Henora said. 'Off you go.'

'I'll join you later,' Luca said to his brother. 'I will see Jane home and then come and help.'

Lowe shrugged, turning to face me. 'Good to meet you, Jane,' he said. 'I am looking forward to seeing you at the ball.'

'Yes.' I was thrown by his now friendly manner. 'I'll see you at the ball.'

Lowe leaned forward then and made to kiss my cheek. As his mouth came closer my breath caught in my throat as I heard him whisper, 'I'll be watching.' Then in an instant he was pulling back, as if he had never spoken, but his eyes pierced mine. I glanced away, my heart beating so loudly I was sure the others could hear it.

With a nod at his mother, Lowe turned and bounded towards the house.

I had a cold, uneasy feeling about Luca's little brother.

'I had better be going soon myself.' I looked at Luca and Henora. 'My father needs me back to help.'

'Of course,' said Henora. 'We thank you for visiting. Give our regards to your family . . .' She nodded at Luca. 'Luca will see you are safely away.'

Luca and I slipped out of the house, with a hyperactive Dalya following us to the stony path beyond the wisteria gate.

'I won't tell,' she said to Luca. 'I promise I won't.'

'You'd better not,' he said sternly. 'You know what could happen if you do.'

She looked solemn. 'You can trust me, brother.' She turned to me. 'Goodbye, Jane. Good luck.'

We watched her slip back through the gate, before we began trudging to the field of rape and all the way to the Water Path.

'I'm not sure Lowe is as trustworthy,' I said as we walked. 'He suspects me.'

Luca shook his head. 'He's flexing his muscles,' he said. 'He's moody and impetuous, and he can be abrasive. But he is loyal. I think.' He looked down at the ground as he spoke, his face darkening. 'But perhaps it was foolish of me, bringing you here. I didn't think . . . Lowe is sharp, it's true.'

149

'He said something to me.' I linked my arm through Luca's. 'When he said goodbye, he told me he would be watching me.'

'I'm sure there is nothing to be anxious about.' Luca reached for my fingers with his free hand. 'But maybe I should have been more careful.'

We were approaching the Water Path and already the sound of the river could be heard.

'I will see you again soon,' Luca said. 'We need to make arrangements . . . for the ball.'

'Are we being foolish?' I said, surprising myself. His younger brother's behaviour had unsettled me.

'Perhaps.' He sighed. 'But I won't leave your side all evening. You will be safe with me.'

'I know.' I smiled while squinting in the fierce sunlight.

We stood quietly and, though I wanted to go home, I felt reluctant to leave him.

'Go, then,' said Luca. 'Back to your boyfriend.' Though he smiled, there was a sadness in his green eyes and I hesitated, wanting in some way to reassure him.

But I said nothing.

CHAPTER TWELVE

I can't sleep at night, and when I do, I dream of you. In my dreams it is all so simple. You and I are together, everything is going to be all right. Easy. But when I am awake the weight of all that's between us and all that divides us lies heavily on me. Mum is nearly fully recovered, but she is fragile. Her treatment has taken more out of her than the disease. She needs me. And I can't leave her. But the thought of never seeing you again is, well, it's unthinkable. I tried to come to you, but it didn't happen. I willed it with all my might, but you have cut off from me. It is only by writing this down that I can connect with you. I know I am being unfair. I wish I didn't have to choose.

I shut the book, my own heart felt heavy, troubled by something. What became of her, I wondered, the author of this diary? What happened to the boy she loved?

I was sitting in the window seat of Dad's office reading, staring out at the winter that seemed permanently on our doorstep. The house was empty again. My parents had gone to collect Dot from a sleepover the other side of town. Getting up with the book under my arm, I wandered through to the kitchen and opened the fridge.

I was halfway through making myself a sandwich when a knock on the back door startled me. Nobody comes up here without warning. It couldn't be Luca – he was away with his family. I held on to the bread knife and padded cautiously to the door.

'Who is it?' I said slowly.

'It's Evan.' His voice was low, humble-sounding.

I looked down at the bread knife, holding it behind my back, and flipped the latch on the door to open it.

Snow was falling on his scruffy blond hair and on his grey duffel coat.

'Hi,' he said, rubbing his gloved hands together. He took a step forwards. 'I know you don't want to see me. And I understand how you must feel about me living with . . . But I want to explain . . .' He smiled wryly. 'Do you think I could come in – for a while?'

I bit my lip but opened the door wider. Evan looked and sounded adorable. He took a tentative step inside, brushing the snow off his hair.

Realising I was still holding the bread knife, I dropped my hand. Evan's eyes grew wide as he saw it.

'Whoah. I really don't want to the get on the wrong side of you, Jonas,' he said, catching my eye then, grinning. His perfect teeth and his perfect mouth. The tiny lines at the corners of his eyes crinkling.

'I was holding it,' I said dumbly. 'When you knocked . . . I wasn't going to . . .'

'Attack me?' he said, smiling still. 'I know that.'

I raised the hand holding the knife. 'I'll put this away,' I said, turning towards the kitchen. 'Come through.'

Evan followed me to the kitchen. I pushed the breadboard with my half-made sandwich on it to the back of the counter and dropped the knife into the sink.

'I'll make some tea,' I said, my back to him. 'Take a seat.'

As I filled the kettle I could feel his eyes on me. Once I had plugged it in and dropped a couple of teabags into the pot I turned and drew out a chair next to him.

Evan still had his coat on, the grey wool made his eyes seem bluer than ever and his hair was perfectly dishevelled. He put his still-tanned hands on the table and stared at me.

'I talked to Sarah,' he said finally. 'About what she did.'

I felt a familiar thud in my stomach.

'Oh God.' I slumped back in my seat. 'I can just imagine what she said about me.' I stared angrily at him. 'She's poisonous.'

'She's grown up a bit,' he said seriously. 'She said she feels really bad.'

'Hmmm.' I chewed my lip. 'I'll believe that when I see it.'

'Well maybe you should,' he said then.

'Should what?' I sat up slightly, frowning.

'See it?' He rubbed at the table with his finger.

'If I saw her ever again it would be too soon,' I said firmly. 'You just don't understand, Evan.' I threw up my hands. 'How could you? You've always been perfect, I bet.'

He waited a second before replying. 'So, you've known me all my life have you? You know everything about me?'

'No . . .' I began, flustered. 'Of course not. But look at you. You have no Achilles heel. You're untouchable.'

A strange expression crossed his face but he didn't look away.

'No one is untouchable.' His voice was quiet. 'And not

154

me, for sure.' I watched as his eyes wandered around the kitchen, settling on a family photograph Mum had stuck on the windowsill. A much younger me, with short curly hair. My dad, with more hair, and my mother, smiling and looking down at baby Dot. His eyes lingered on it for a while, and I swallowed. Evan's family was broken. Scattered. And here I was trying to detach him from the few relatives he had. I rubbed my hands together, feeling at fault somehow.

Evan turned from the photograph and his face softened. 'But it's not about that. It's not about the past. It's about the future. I've never felt this way about any girl before. I want you in my life, Jane. I can't stand the thought of this just . . . ending.' He looked up at me, holding my gaze. 'And for better or worse, Sarah is kind of in my life too. If she apologised to you – *really* apologised – would you consider being my girlfriend?'

Would I consider being Evan's girlfriend? I nearly laughed out loud. Instead I kept my expression steady.

'I can't imagine being friends with Sarah,' I said. 'After everything she did . . .'

'I know it's asking a lot.' He reached out and twined his fingers through mine. I didn't pull away. How could I?

'I don't know.' I shook my head. 'You don't know her like I do.'

Evan held my hand tighter, his thumb gently massaging mine. 'Worth a try, though,' he said. 'For us?'

I smiled then but rolled my eyes. 'You're good at this, aren't you?' I said. 'Getting what you want?'

He pulled me a little closer to him, putting one hand out to stroke the hair off my face.

'I just can't walk away from this,' he whispered, his lips coming closer to mine. 'From you.'

And I felt my resolve melting away as I gazed back at those eyes, those cheekbones and the small sprinkling of freckles on his tanned nose. As our mouths came together and I felt the softness of his lips on mine, I knew I wanted to make him happy. We kissed each other tenderly and slowly before I forced myself to pull away.

'OK,' I said, quietly. 'But not yet. I'm not ready yet.'

'Cool. Whatever you want.'

'It's all in the past, I guess,' I said, more brightly than I felt. 'I've got to put it behind me.'

He smiled, and reached out to hug me to him. 'You're a brave girl.'

'I'm not brave. I feel like I just . . . let things happen to me.'

'Even better,' he said playfully, pressing his lips to my cheek.

* * *

I thought about Sarah while I was watching TV with my dad and Dot, who lay sprawled across the sofa, snuggled up to him. I tried to rationalise what she'd done. Was it just harmless schoolgirl stuff? Was she older and wiser . . . and nicer now? The prospect of seeing her, talking to her, normally, was unimaginable. But maybe it would lay it all to rest. And give Evan and me a chance.

I gazed at the screen, not seeing what was playing out in front of me. I couldn't believe that she had changed. Not really. And it would take every ounce of my backbone to give her a chance.

Mum wandered in with a pile of ironing. She dumped it on an armchair and plumped down next to me at the end of the sofa.

'You made it up with Evan, then?' she said quietly, tapping my knee.

'Kind of.' I tucked my legs under me.

'What did you fight about? He seems such a nice boy.'

'He is.' I hesitated. 'But his sister isn't.'

Mum frowned. 'Who's his sister?'

'Sarah. Sarah Emerson.'

'You're joking?' Mum said loudly, causing Dot to look over at us, curiously. 'Well, I can see why you'd be angry about that.' She shook her head. 'That silly, spiteful girl is Evan's sister?'

'Stepsister, actually . . . And Evan thinks she's changed. She's really sorry apparently.' I sighed. 'She wants to apologise.'

My mother raised an eyebrow. 'And what do you think? What are you going to do?'

I hesitated. 'I think . . . I think I'm going to let her apologise,' I said then, a slight smile on my face.

Mum rubbed my knee. 'That's very big of you, darling. I'm not sure I'd be quite so forgiving. But then again . . . Evan might be worth it.'

'Yes,' I said, looking back at the television. 'I think he might.'

CHAPTER THIRTEEN

Fabio's was empty but for the familiar figure sitting on a stool by the counter. My heart skipped its usual beat as I approached Evan.

I hadn't seen him since he'd come to talk to me a week before. I hadn't felt ready. There was so much to think about. Not just about Sarah, but about him. Everything seemed so intense all of a sudden. And then there was Luca . . . That was intense, too. In a different way. I'd spent a lot of time out walking the dog, poring over the mysterious girl's notebook. Entry after entry of heartache. Whoever she loved had just disappeared and the loss was nearly killing her. It frightened me. To get so attached to someone, and to have them just disappear . . . I'd shut the book away in my drawer, unable to read any more. It hadn't helped me much, it had just made me feel more apprehensive. What was I getting myself into?

I should really lighten up, I suppose.

Evan turned intuitively as I came up behind him.

'Hello stranger.' He slipped one arm around my waist and his lips brushed my cheek. 'What can I get you?'

'A Coke, please.' I climbed up on to the stool next to him, running my eyes over his black jeans. He took off his denim jacket and draped it on the back of the stool, and it was hard not to notice his muscular, tanned arms as he waved at Eileen.

'A Coke for the lady,' he said, as Eileen came over to us. 'And another iced tea, please.'

'Coming up.' Eileen beamed at him and started getting our drinks. 'What are you two up to today?'

Evan looked at me. 'Want to come for a ride?'

I nodded. 'But somewhere safe. I told you how uncoordinated I am.'

'Rubbish. I'll bet you're a natural,' he said, smiling.

Eileen placed our drinks on the counter and I took a swig of Coke straight from the bottle.

'I missed you. I thought, after I saw you . . .'

'I know.' I looked down at my Coke. 'I just needed some time to think.'

'I understand.' But I heard a slight edge to his voice, a little defensive. For some reason I felt the need to explain myself, but what I could say?

'Sometimes I just need to be by myself.' I looked at Evan now. 'You must know that feeling.'

'Sure.' He picked up his tea and drank some more, but he seemed a little tense still.

'Evan?' I said quietly. 'It's just the way I am.'

'And it's exactly what I like about you.' He smiled properly at me then, and I felt myself relax.

'So,' I said, 'where shall we go?'

Evan was patient with me as I attempted to drive his car along a deserted training field. We were miles from home in a place he had researched beforehand. After ten minutes I gave up as the car was bumping and stalling under my control.

'Rain check?' I asked him, unbuckling my seatbelt.

Evan shook his head, but we swapped seats and I relaxed now that I was safely in the passenger seat. Evan drove round in a circle and then stopped the car.

'The army used to use this place,' he said. To the left of us a row of Nissen huts stood abandoned and eerie. I glimpsed machinery of some kind, rusting away inside.

'It's a bit creepy,' I said. 'How did you find it?'

'Dad told me about it.' Evan wound down the window and the freezing air nipped at my cheeks. 'He was in the services . . . way back. It was the reason he moved here in fact.'

'Did you live here, then?' I asked. 'I mean in Bale . . . Did you come with your dad?'

Evan shook his head. 'No . . . they'd broken up by then. My parents. He came here alone. Said they trained in this place. Like a kind of crude barracks or something.'

From out of the silence came a piercing bark – more of a howl, really. I pressed my face against my window and for a second or two I thought Luca would come bounding out to me. I swallowed. The sound stopped abruptly.

'Was that a wolf?' I turned to Evan.

His face darkened. 'A what?'

'A wolf.' I gestured outside. 'Didn't you hear it?'

Evan shrugged. 'Didn't hear a thing.' A slow smile crept on to his face. 'Are you scared, Jane?'

I stared at him. He was still smiling, but there was a sharpness to his eyes. It was difficult to see in the low light though. Maybe I was imagining it?

'Of course not.' I fronted up. 'I'm not that easily scared.'

'Good. I wouldn't want that.'

I nodded, but I wasn't looking at him, I was looking at his reflection in my passenger window. Of him, staring at the back of my neck. I felt a prickle of discomfort.

I flipped back to see his face, friendly, with the little creases around his blue eyes.

I relaxed again.

Evan rubbed my leg and it sent tingles through me. This time I enjoyed them. Looking down at his strong brown hand, I didn't want him to take it away. I shifted and met his eyes.

'You OK?' he said softly. Then he leaned across and put one hand on my thigh, pulling me in towards him. I looked at his soft, partly-opened mouth and I put my hands on either side of his face. We kissed and I felt my whole body responding to him. As his hands moved up to my waist, I felt his fingers touching the skin there, and I realised I would let him do whatever he wanted.

If I wasn't careful.

I pulled away, breathing hard. 'Not yet,' I said. 'Not in this place.'

Evan looked hungrily at me and gave me one final hard kiss before sitting back and putting his hand on the ignition key.

'Bad girl,' he said, but I saw his smile.

'Is the lesson over for today?' I asked coyly, wrapping my arms around my body. 'Because I'd like to get out of here . . . If that's OK.'

Evan started the engine and we drove smoothly out of the field. As we came up to the exit, a line of crows sitting astride the fence cawed anxiously at the car. As Evan pulled out on to the road one of them suddenly took flight, shrieking menacingly close to his window.

Evan didn't flinch, though the bird was quite terrifying. Up close, its beady eyes trained themselves on him.

'Shut the window,' I said, alarmed, 'it's going to peck your eyes out!'

'It won't hurt me.' Evan's tone was assured, and though I should have found that comforting, I felt almost suffocated by the noise.

'Evan, please!' I reached across him and pressed the button to close the window.

When I sat back in my seat, he glanced at me, amused.

'You need to toughen up,' he said laughing. 'There are more dangerous things than crows out there in the big bad world.'

Though he squeezed my hand reassuringly, I felt a shiver travel up my spine.

'I've been thinking,' said Evan, as we drove back on the road to Bale. 'I might stay around a little longer.'

'Really? You mean, for the summer?'

'Maybe.' He flicked on the indicator to turn right. 'Would that suit her ladyship?'

I fake-shrugged. 'Doesn't matter to me.'

'You're harsh.' He laughed. 'I know you don't mean that.'

'I suppose it would be fun.' I rubbed at the steamed-up window. 'We've only just got to know each other. It would be a shame if you left.'

'I'll take that as your boundless enthusiasm. I kind of like how understated you are.'

'You mean rude?' I said, dryly.

'No. Not rude. It's kind of sexy in fact. Back home, the girls are just so "up" all the time. Fake. You know what I mean?'

I nodded. 'No danger of that with me.'

Evan smiled, then screwed up his eyes a little, as though he was thinking about something, then started to slow down.

'Can I run something by you?' he asked then, turning to look at me. 'And if you hate the idea, then that's fine.'

'What?'

'Will you consider meeting Sarah?' he said.

I dropped my eyes away from his. 'I told you I would—'

'I mean today? She wants to.'

165

'Right.' I looked down at my hands, feeling cornered. 'Does it have to be today?'

'No.' He pulled up outside Fabio's again. 'But she's waiting for you, in there.' He gestured at the café.

'Oh my God.' I swallowed. 'I'm not ready.'

'It'll be fine,' said Evan. He took a hand off the wheel and grasped one of mine. 'And you can leave any time you like.'

I breathed out deeply. 'OK. But it's not going to work.'

'Just give her a chance.' Evan leaned across and kissed me on the cheek.

For a moment I stood by the door, my eyes wandering round the room until they settled on the back of her blonde head. Thick, straight, glossy hair, perfect as usual. I felt fear creeping inside me. All at once I was there again. Sitting with my back to her in the classroom, hearing her whispering loudly to Mariella, with the odd word emphasised. *Ugly cow. What the hell is she wearing?* Sarah was coarse, I remembered that.

I took a deep breath, catching Eileen's eye. She smiled but her glance flickered over to where Sarah was sitting on a banquette by the window and she frowned. Eileen was one of the few people who knew what had happened. Thanks to Dot's big mouth of course. But I was grateful for her protective gaze as I walked slowly over to Sarah. As I reached her elbow, she turned carefully and her eyes swept over me. I held on to my nerve.

'Hi,' I said, awkwardly.

'Jane.' Her husky voice was softer than I remembered. Less arrogant. 'I'm glad you came.'

I said nothing, but moved to sit on the banquette opposite her. I shrugged off my coat, keeping my eyes down a little.

Sarah was drinking a latte in a tall glass, she pulled it towards her and took a sip.

'How's home school?' she asked, but without her regular sarcasm. 'Beats Mrs Parkinson's Maths period I bet.'

I gave a small smile. 'It's different, yeah.' I fiddled with the fake flower placed in a small spot in the centre of the table.

'Jane, I'm really sorry,' Sarah said hesitantly. 'About everything I did.' She flopped back in her seat a bit. 'I was a monster.'

I frowned slightly. I never thought I'd hear Sarah apply that term to herself. It seemed so odd coming out of her perfect little rosebud mouth. She had come out with far worse, of course.

'Yeah. Well . . .' I didn't know how to respond. But

maybe a part of me didn't want to make it too easy for her. After how she'd made me feel for so long.

'I thought about it a lot,' she went on. 'After you left, well, I began to notice how everyone at school saw me. They kept away from me. Like I was contaminated.' She turned her face up in a perfect expression of remorse. 'Everyone hated me.'

Those big, baby-blue eyes looked so hurt. I felt something like bile coming up from my stomach.

No, they hated me. You made them hate me.

Freak.

But Sarah was oblivious to my internal narrative.

'I told myself that I'd make it up to you. But I knew you'd never want to see me. When Evan told me he was seeing you . . .' She shook her head. 'I felt like it was a sign.'

'A sign?'

'Yeah. That it was time to talk.'

I chewed at the inside of my mouth. Time for her to talk.

'Let's just forget it,' I said, lightly. 'I accept your apology.'

'Seriously?' Sarah's eyes widened, innocent and grateful. 'Just like that?'

I shrugged, anxious to leave. I wasn't going to hear

anything I believed. No point in sticking around. 'Sure. It's all in the past.'

'Jane, you're . . .' Sarah slid one bangled wrist noisily over the table, reaching for my hand, but I didn't move. 'You're so nice. I would hold a grudge forever if you'd done to me what I did.' She sighed, drawing back her hand.

'Don't worry about it.' I started putting my coat back on. 'Life's too short.'

Her expression grew misty and confused for a second before the familiar toothy smile kicked in.

'You're so right,' she breathed, picking up her bag and glancing out of the window. 'Is Evan outside? Can you guys give me a lift back home?'

''Course.' As she turned to pick up her sweater I rolled my eyes, making sure I wore no expression when she turned back again.

Eileen winked at me as we walked out, Sarah in front. I gave a wry smile in return.

'Hi!' Sarah waved excitably at Evan who was still outside in the car. She rushed to the front passenger seat.

'You know what, I'm going to walk,' I said, bending down to talk to Evan through the window. 'I could do with some exercise.'

Settling herself into the front seat, Sarah craned up out

of the window, a catlike smile on her face. 'So great to talk. I hope we can be friends.'

I nodded in the absence of a civilised response. Sarah and I may no longer be enemies, but we would never be friends.

'I'll catch up with you tomorrow,' Evan said in a honeyed voice. 'Thanks, Jane.' He gestured subtly at the side of his stepsister's head. She was already bent, riffling through something in her bag.

'Of course.'

I stepped away from the corner and stood for a bit watching as they drove away. I saw Sarah lean in to Evan closely as he drove, as though whispering in his ear, and his head moved towards hers, forming one dark shape. My stomach clenched at their closeness.

A girl he hardly knows.

Of course, Evan's like that, I told myself, turning away. He's friendly and warm. It's just his way.

But I was cold as I walked home. A kind of chilly confusion had caught hold of me.

I'd done the right thing. So why did it still feel wrong?

CHAPTER FOURTEEN

'You're not concentrating.' My mother's eyebrows knitted together as we both sat in front of the computer screen. She shut down the window illustrating the lineage of the Tudors and studied me. 'Perhaps a boyfriend isn't such a good idea after all.'

'I'm just tired,' I said, grumpily. I hadn't slept properly for days. I hadn't dreamed of anything either.

'Well, you're not sleepwalking at least.' She sighed and put the lid back on her pen. 'That phase is over, thank goodness.'

I grunted, thinking how I missed it, in a way. I missed Luca.

'What is it?' Mum leaned closer, her hand creeping over to mine. 'I thought it went well with Sarah.'

'Yeah it went OK.' I wrinkled my nose. 'It was kind of nothing in the end . . . After all that.'

'And now you feel flat?' She held on to my hand. 'Now that weight has come off.'

'Maybe. I suppose it was a bit of an anticlimax.'

'What did you want? A cat fight?'

'No . . .' I looked restlessly around the kitchen. 'But it was too easy.'

'Well, that's good.' Mum let go of my hand and started gathering up pens and books. 'Drama is not good. Believe me.'

She set her lips and I wondered what drama she had let go of.

'Mum, have you still got that blue dress?'

'Blue dress?' She stopped what she was doing. 'I don't think I . . .'

'The one you're wearing in the picture. On my chest of drawers . . . It's satin or something like that.'

Mum thought for a second then her face softened. 'Oh. That dress.' She relaxed in her seat. 'I haven't thought about that for years. Your grandmother made me that dress.'

'Grandma Ellen?' I sat up.

'She made it when she was recovering . . .' Mum said wistfully. 'You remember she had breast cancer when she was in her fifties.'

I nodded. Grandma Ellen had made a full recovery

before I was born. Still alive and very much kicking, albeit hundreds of miles away.

'I wish she'd make a dress like that for me,' I said, staring into space.

'And so the day has come!' Mum clapped her hands together. 'My little boy finally wants to be a girl.'

'Mum!' A flush was creeping up my cheeks. 'It's just a beautiful dress, that's all.'

'It's yours,' she said, happily. 'If I can find it . . . and if it fits you.'

'Really?'

'Let's go and look for it now.' Mum got up, shooing away the dog, who looked curiously at the two of us. 'It's somewhere up there. It must be.'

An hour later, I stood in my parents' bedroom holding the blue satin dress. We'd found it in the attic in a huge suitcase, along with the rest of Mum's discarded clothing from decades ago.

'Can I have this, too?' I'd said, clutching a striped sailor top, perfectly faded with a wide boat neck.

'Of course,' she said, smiling. 'I never took that off when I was a teenager. Your grandma used to beg me to wear a dress . . .' She stopped and we stared at each other and started to laugh.

'I know,' Mum said, shaking her head sheepishly. 'I was just like you once.'

'Here,' she said now as I stood half naked in her bedroom. She took the dress from me, holding it so that I could step into it. 'Pull it up gently.'

I did as I was told, slipping my arms through the delicate sleeves. Mum moved behind me to zip it up. I was holding in my stomach, certain that something so exquisite and tiny would be too small, but as Mum stepped away from me I realised it fitted perfectly. I looked down to see the blue satin shimmering like two-tone, hugging my waist and hips comfortably. Now that I had actual breasts the top filled out, leaving just enough room to make it sophisticated. The neckline ran straight from one shoulder to the other, dipping a little lower in the centre.

Mum fiddled with something at the back, then put her hands on my shoulders, pushing me towards the mirror.

'Look,' she ordered, and I raised my head to examine my reflection, opening my mouth slightly at what I saw.

'God,' I said breathily, 'I don't look like me.'

With nothing covering up my neck and shoulders my hair draped in big dark curls on to my bare flesh, which was pale, but I had to admit, flawless. And for the first time I acknowledged my shape properly. It was a woman's shape, not straight up and down, not skinny, but not fat either.

'You're perfectly in proportion,' she said, adjusting the neckline a little. 'My beautiful girl.'

'I wouldn't go that far,' I said awkwardly, though it was hard not to gaze admiringly at the vision in the mirror. 'But I could scrub up well, I suppose.'

I saw my mother roll her eyes behind me. 'You'll have to get that boyfriend of yours to take you somewhere where you can show it off.'

I looked back at my reflection and smiled. 'I'm sure something will come up.'

'I'll have it cleaned,' said Mum, brushing at the fabric. 'I just hope you don't grow any more before you get the chance to wear it.'

Suddenly I felt a jerk of excitement at arriving at the Great Ball in this wonderful dress. It transformed me, even I could see that.

I pulled the notebook out again in the afternoon, finding the right page, and turned to lie on my stomach on my bed. The middle of the book was covered with more drawings. She'd sketched the interior of a house. A large room with ornate lights hanging down and a man and a woman wearing what looked like bathrobes. The floor of the room was chequered black and white. On a table were glasses and a large jug or vase. A girl lay curled up on a couch; she had long hair. Her clothes were nondescript, but she wore trousers and a shirt.

I flipped forward a few pages and found a very short entry.

Bitterly cold. Always so cold here. My mother says we are going to move. Now that she's getting better, she wants to live somewhere warmer. I don't care. I don't care about anything any more. You are gone. And my choice seems clearer than ever.

I frowned. Luca had said there was no happy ending to this. There was nothing to stop me reading through to the end of the book, but I didn't want to. In a strange kind of way I needed to hang on to each entry. It made me feel closer to Luca. I had a feeling that once I had read everything and finished the book then he might fade away.

I got off the bed and put the book away in my drawer, burying it beneath my underwear, where it couldn't be found, and then paused to look out of the window.

The trees were looking a little greener now. Spring was on its way.

I turned to see the Breton striped top on my chair.

I slipped it on over my T-shirt and gave myself a quick inspection in the mirror. It was cute and it smelled of my mother.

Feeling in a good mood, I decided to take Bobby for a walk into town.

Downstairs, I flipped through my address book to find Evan's number, and after dialling the number I waited, excited at the thought of a spontaneous meeting.

'Hey.' The familiar girl's voice on the end of the phone startled me. So much so that I was speechless for a second or two.

'Hello?' Sarah's tone was back to its insolent drawl. 'Anybody there?'

I cleared my throat. 'Um . . . It's Jane.'

'Oh hi.' Just like that, the petulance turned to something much more syrupy sweet. 'How are you, Jane?'

'Fine.' I hesitated. I had nothing to say to her. 'Is Evan there?'

'Hold on a minute, babe, I'll go and find him.'

Babe?

Heavy footsteps got louder and I heard his breathing. I adjusted my own, which was all out of sync.

'Hey, Jane, I was just about to call you,' said Evan. 'You ran off yesterday before I had a chance to make plans with you.'

'Oh,' I said, coyly, pleased. 'I didn't exactly run off.'

He laughed, a slow affectionate laugh, making my insides somersault. 'Good. Want to do something now?'

'I was thinking of taking the dog for a walk. I thought, you know, we could hook up?'

'Want me to come up the hill?'

'It's a mountain. But no . . . I thought I'd take him down to town. He likes the chance to mingle with other dogs from time to time.'

'Does he indeed?' Evan teased. 'Do you think he'd mind a pitstop at my favourite café?'

'He loves Eileen.' I smiled. 'She spoils him with leftover burgers. Shall we meet there in, say, half an hour?'

'I can't wait,' said Evan.

It was finally warm enough to wear my jacket loose, with just my new-old striped top on underneath it, as Bobby and I made our way down the track and over on to the rugged path leading to Bale. I breathed in deeply, remembering how spring can make you feel so exhilarated when it appears out of nowhere. A few degrees higher in temperature and everything changes. I lifted my face up to the sun and felt my heart lifting too. I was glad I was meeting Evan. He was right, I had rushed off. I'd got things out of proportion. Whatever her reasons, wasn't it good that Sarah Emerson was trying to make amends?

Bobby scampered ahead and I picked up my pace to catch him before he ran into the road.

'Bobs!' I jangled the lead to entice him back. Unsurprisingly he wasn't tempted but stood obediently, waiting for me to catch him up. I slipped the lead on him, pausing to give him a rub.

'I'm happy, Bobby,' I whispered into his silky head.

Bobby cocked his head to one side, bemused, and I ran a finger over his soft ear.

'Right then,' I told him. 'You want one of Eileen's special horizontal milkshakes?'

Bobby gave an enthusiastic bark and I stood and tugged his lead.

'Let's run,' I said, lengthening my strides. 'All the way there.'

By the time we reached Bale's main street I was out of breath and way too hot, so I slowed. I had to compose myself before I saw Evan. I stopped and put my hands on my knees, gradually recovering my breath, before straightening up and taking off my jacket, running my hands through my hair to calm it down.

'OK.' I puffed my cheeks. 'I think I'm ready.' I pulled the dog along the pavement and when we reached

Fabio's, I stood slightly on tiptoe, peering over Eileen's net curtain.

He was in there, perched on a counter stool as usual. And next to him, swinging from side to side on her seat, tossing her silly blonde mane around, was Sarah.

I dropped back on to my feet, my breath coming quickly now.

He brought her? Why?

Bobby whined, confused as I remained standing on the spot. I looked down at him as though he would provide some remedy to the situation.

'Shut *up*!' I heard her say; loud, confident.

'Seriously.' Evan's voice, more gregarious than usual. 'They're vicious animals. They're not cute.'

In spite of myself I raised my head again to look at them. Evan had his hand on her shoulder, rubbing it as he talked. His face was animated and his free hand thumped the counter.

'They are! Koala bears are cute!' she protested.

Was she even wearing a skirt? All I could glimpse was acres of black leg.

'They bite,' he said, lunging at her as though to nip her cheek with his teeth.

I was suddenly freezing cold. I shivered, touching the

top of Bobby's head with my palm.

And I felt nauseous.

'Behave yourself, you,' I heard him say. 'Jane will be here any minute.'

I couldn't hear what Sarah said in response. I tipped my head against the glass, but all I heard was a rushing sound in my ears.

I stayed there though. Tired all of a sudden. And humiliated.

Sarah had spoiled everything. Or was it Evan?

Then I looked down at Bobby, who was cold too I could tell. He looked back up at me. 'Come on, boy,' I said quietly. 'Let's go home.'

Keeping my head down I put my jacket back on, hugging it to me, as the dog shuffled alongside me in apparent sympathy.

The walk back was slow, and the clouds had gathered. The sun had gone in.

Oh boy, had the sun gone in.

When we finally got back to the track, I released Bobby and watched him fly up to the house. Watched as Dot appeared out of the back door, home from her sleepover and come forward to cuddle him. Spotting me, she waved, smiling, and I lifted a hand limply in return.

I couldn't face anyone right now. I knew where I wanted to be.

Dad's bench was covered with bits of branch and leaves. I brushed some aside and sank back, lifting up my legs and crossing them underneath me. I closed my eyes and felt a kind of damp, flat feeling in my heart. A familiar feeling I hadn't had for weeks. Ever since . . . since I had met Luca, I realised.

'I wish I could see you,' I said aloud, keeping my eyes shut. Where was he? Why had he just . . . left me?

A crunch, the sound of boots on leaves, made my eyes snap open.

'And here I am,' he said. Softly, sorrowfully.

I turned my head slowly to look at him. There was no mistaking the sinking of my heart.

'I ran all the way,' said Evan, clearing a space on the bench to sit next to me. 'What happened? One minute I saw you outside Fabio's. The next you'd disappeared.'

I didn't speak at first. I didn't trust myself not to unleash a rant. But Evan was waiting, oblivious to my pointed silence.

'Jane?' He rubbed my shoulder but I shrugged him off rudely.

'Leave me alone,' I said, before he was settled. 'You've ruined everything. You and your sister.'

'Will you let me explain?' he said cautiously.

I stared at him, shaking my head.

'Why?' I frowned. 'Why did you invite her along? I said I forgave her. It doesn't mean I want anything to do with her.'

'She invited herself along . . .' he said calmly. 'She's pretty forceful when she puts her mind to it.'

I remembered how he'd looked with her. Relaxed, playful. And his words: '*Jane will be here soon.*'

'You like her,' I said, turning my face away from him. 'And that's OK. She's much more your kind of person. Insensitive. Shallow.'

'Jane.' His voice rose a notch. 'You don't mean that. You know we're special, you and I. You really think I'm shallow?'

I fiddled with the lace on my trainer. 'I have no idea who you are. You change . . .' I hesitated. 'Sometimes I see you and I don't like it . . .'

He reached out and took my hand. 'I just know how to handle people like Sarah. Remember all those fake bimbos I told you about back home? I grew up with girls like Sarah. I learned how to humour them.'

I sniffed, my eyes still down on my trainers. 'Well,

you learned good, is all I can say. You sounded pretty convincing to me.'

Silence.

'I want her to accept us,' he said eventually, much more humbly. 'She's one of those spoiled, demanding types. You of all people know that. My dad adores her. She wants to go out, I have to take her. She wants to act all girly and flirty, I have to humour her.' He sighed. 'I know it makes me sound like I've sold out. Like I'm not brave enough to be real with her. But I'm still the black sheep in our house. I need to prove to my dad that I'm grown up . . . You are so important to me . . . I'm just trying to juggle everything. Keep everybody happy . . . you know?'

I felt ever so slightly bad. Maybe, just maybe, I had overreacted a little. Maybe he *was* trying to do the right thing. Play the long game.

But he wasn't completely off the hook. Not yet.

'The thing that gets to me,' I said, 'is that she's got her own way. Muscling in between us. It just seems like from now on it's going to be the three of us. I know her. I know exactly how she operates.'

He shook his head. 'I won't let that happen. In fact I had a plan . . . I was going to tell you about it . . .'

I kept my head down, waiting, as he cleared his throat.

'Let's go away somewhere, just the two of us . . . Camping or something.' He waited for me to respond, as I remained fascinated by my footwear. Eventually I lifted my head.

'Better bring a three-man tent,' I told him dryly. 'Just in case . . .'

'Is that a roundabout way of accepting my offer?' A faint smile played on his lips.

I shrugged. 'I don't know . . . You always manage to make me feel . . . ridiculous. Like I'm paranoid or something.'

'You're very far from ridiculous,' Evan said seriously. 'Though you might be a teensy bit paranoid maybe . . .' I could tell he was holding his breath, and I gave him what he wanted. A smile.

'Maybe next weekend.' I sighed. 'There's a spot on the other side of the mountain. My dad used to take us there when we were little. It'll be nice this time of year.'

'Great.' Evan shuffled closer to me and put an arm tentatively around my shoulders. 'I'm sorry I upset you.'

''S OK.' I could feel my legs getting cramps and I uncrossed them, kicking at the ground. 'Just keep her away from me.'

'It will be done,' he said, drawing me into him. 'From now, it's just you and me.'

CHAPTER FIFTEEN

The days rolled by and I began to lighten up. Not see the doom and darkness in everything. Lose the paranoia. I had allowed myself to be convinced by Evan that my distrust was all in my head. I supposed it made sense. For as long as I could remember I had been wary of most people . . . And when I met Sarah that wariness turned into something much darker. She was out to get me. I was different and I had to be punished. That was my lot. Everyone was my enemy, except for my family.

And Luca.

I had never felt a moment's real fear with him, which thinking rationally, was plain . . . irrational. I mean, he was a werewolf! A dangerous predator. But Luca had shown me all his dark corners, not hidden them.

Maybe fear is in not knowing? Trust is about knowing?

I wasn't stupid, I knew that the attraction I had to Evan was partly down to the enigma of him. And the fact that he was so golden he glowed. The shallow part of me wanted that golden boy, wanted to believe in him. His beauty seemed to reflect any that I had. So that was why I spent my days fantasising about spending the night under the stars, the other side of the mountain, with my boyfriend, refusing to think about his sister, trying not to let Luca in.

Not that Luca was around.

I took the dress and held it against me in front of the mirror. The two-tone satin shimmered and my face glowed along with it. I saw myself stepping through the great palace to its grand ballroom. Elegant, womanly with Luca holding my arm proudly. But would I ever get there? Wasn't it just a ridiculous fantasy?

I shivered as I realised how much it would bother me if that were true.

Because I wanted to be the princess at the ball. I wanted to dance with a handsome boy and have everyone gazing at me. I guess there's no girl in the world that doesn't deep down want that.

I shook my head, embarrassed at my train of thought. I never usually had any truck with that kind of romantic stuff. Never wanted to dress up. But putting on that dress . . . seeing myself as a boy might see me . . . it changed things.

And that dress didn't belong here on mortal Earth. It belonged to another world. Where I was another Jane.

And it belonged to me and Luca.

A knock on the door brought me out of my thoughts.

'Jane.' Dad's voice. 'I need some help getting a table in the van . . . Your mother and sister have gone into town. Can you give me a hand?'

'Just coming.' I lay the dress on my bed and grabbed a sweatshirt.

Dad had finally finished Mrs Benjamin's table and it was enormous. I gaped as he opened the shed door.

'I'll do the brunt of this,' he said. 'I just need you to guide it through the doors.'

'Dad. You shouldn't be lifting anything yet,' I said, giving him a stern look. 'Let's wait and Mum and I can do it.'

'It needs someone stronger than your mum . . . at one end at least.' He sighed, gently rubbing his shoulder. 'But perhaps you're right.'

'I could call Evan. If you can hang on twenty minutes?'

Dad shook his head. 'I'll give Mrs B a call. Maybe she can wait another day and your mother can help.'

'OK.' I moved to lean against the van, where Dad joined me.

We stood in easy silence, looking at the table, through the shed door.

'You like him, then?' Dad said after a while. 'Evan.'

I looked sideways at him.

'I guess,' I said, a little shyly.

Dad nodded. 'Seems a good kid. Seems like a bit of a loner, too.' He caught my eye. 'I don't want you to be hurt.'

My skin prickled. 'He's staying around for the summer, he told me.'

'Good. Just be careful that's all.'

I shrugged. 'He wouldn't hurt me. Not on purpose, anyway.'

'Jane.' Dad pursed his lips for a second. 'You're very young. I can see how a kid like him – worldly, travelled . . . that kind of thing – would appeal. But he's independent. I can see that. I'm just not sure you should set your heart on him.'

'I'm not,' I said, annoyed. 'What is this? You don't like me having a boyfriend.'

'Not at all.' Dad smiled. 'I suppose every father says

189

this about his child, but you're special, Janey. A special girl. And you're sensitive.'

'I can look after myself. I'm not a child any more.'

Dad continued smiling at me, moving closer and putting an arm round my shoulders.

'You remember when he came to lunch. And your mother talked about being in love.'

'I remember. She couldn't eat.'

'That's right.' Dad chuckled. 'Well . . . when I first met your mother, she was pretty cut up. She didn't tell me everything . . . but I got the distinct impression that this guy – her "first love" – had really broken her heart. She told me he had been a free spirit . . . always a little unavailable . . . that she'd known they would never end up together deep down because of that, but that he felt like her soulmate, and she fell for him. She was devastated when it ended.'

'What happened?' I asked, curious. 'How did it end?'

'He just disappeared.' Dad shrugged. 'She tried to contact him, but she never saw or heard from him again.'

'Poor Mum,' I breathed. I turned to look at Dad. 'But then she fell in love with you.'

'It took a while. But she knew I wasn't going anywhere and I adored her. And eventually, she came to love me.'

I squeezed his arm. 'Mum loves you, loads. It's obvious.'

'I know. I wasn't her first choice.' He tightened his hold on my shoulder, leaning in to kiss the top of my head. 'But she told me when we got engaged that she knew I was the right choice.'

'Of course you were.' I snuggled into him. 'The other guy would never have made her happy in the end.'

'So, I'm just saying . . . that all that glitters may not be gold. Don't give away your heart until you're sure. Fool around a bit. Have fun. But keep something back.'

I nodded. I was pretty sure that Evan was the right choice. And he wasn't unavailable, was he? He was gorgeous. Kind. He always seemed to find the right words . . . when I had doubts, anxieties. Evan always said the right thing. He wanted me. And I wanted him.

But he wasn't my soulmate. I couldn't completely trust him. Not yet.

CHAPTER SIXTEEN

Evan stood back and surveyed his handiwork. The old army tent he had borrowed from his dad swayed a little in the breeze. But it was upright at least and sturdy. 'It'll be a bit chilly tonight,' he said, taking my hand. 'But I'll keep you warm.' He wrapped an arm around my waist.

It occurred to me that maybe he wasn't planning separate sleeping bags.

I bit my lip. 'Evan . . .' I began. 'I don't think I'm ready for . . . I mean, I've never done it . . .'

Evan studied me, a smile playing on his lips. 'Done what?'

Heat flooded my cheeks. 'Evan! You know what I mean!'

'Oh,' he said, his eyes widening. 'You mean . . . *that*?'

'Yeah.' I willed the colour out of my face. 'Just in case you were expecting—'

He cut me off, grinning. 'There's no hurry to do anything. I'm just happy to be spending a whole night in your company.'

'OK . . . Good.' My embarrassment subsided and I looked around us. Evan had driven us five miles or so around the mountain to the spot I'd talked about. It was stunning. The trees were less dense, and the view down into the valley was pure green. No houses, no people. Just the birds in the trees and the odd fox at night.

'I'll light a fire,' Evan said, starting to pick up slim branches of wood for kindling. 'It should keep us going till we go to sleep – we can cook over it too.'

'Great.' I joined him searching around for more firewood and we spent twenty minutes in easy silence. When we'd gathered enough, Evan got to work lighting the fire, while I unpacked the food we'd bought. A couple of steaks, some baking potatoes and some tomatoes to roast. I was starving. I groped in the bottom of the bag to find some cutlery, but there was nothing.

'Damn, we'll have to eat with our fingers,' I said, pointlessly turning the canvas shopping bag upside down.

Evan looked up. 'I have some in my shoulder bag,' he said, squinting in the sudden sharp sunlight. 'In the boot of the car. I'll get it out in a sec.' But the crackle of wood catching alight diverted him and he turned back to the fire to stoke it and add more kindling.

'I'll get it,' I said, dashing round to the car, while Evan, not hearing, had his back to me, concentrating.

I opened the boot, immediately locating his shoulder bag. As I lifted it out, my eye caught something on the floor of the boot, what looked like rolled-up papers. Letters or something, tied together. Tucking Evan's bag under my arm, I reached back in to pick them up. Glancing over the top of the car at Evan's bent form, I tried pushing the ribbon up to release the papers while clamping the bag under my arm. But the weight of it was too much and it dropped with a thump on to the ground.

Sighing, I dropped the papers, still tied together, and was about to pick them up, when I felt his hand on my shoulder. Startled, I jerked, nearly hitting my head on the door.

'Careful,' he said, almost curtly. 'I said I'd get it. You go and look after the fire.'

I turned to look up at him, taken aback by his tone. But his expression was friendly.

'OK . . .' I glanced subtly back down at the papers.

He put his hand on the boot door, pushing on it slowly to shut it. 'Mind your hands.'

I backed away as he shut the boot firmly. And though

he smiled at me then, I was aware of something prickly, something tense about him.

'Come on,' he said briskly. 'Let's get the dinner on.' He picked up his shoulder bag and put one arm around me.

As dusk fell, Evan and I lay back, full from barbecued meat and potatoes, waiting for the stars to come out. It was always my favourite thing, to lie there with my father, while he pointed them out and I watched as they grew brighter in the sky.

I lay with my head on Evan's chest, listening to the thump of his heart, while he stroked my hair with one hand. I felt as close to relaxed as I had ever been with him, the heat of the fire crackling in front of us, and the half-bottle of beer Evan had persuaded me to drink had made me sleepy.

'Your parents seem like good people,' he said, quietly, breaking into the silence. 'Contented.'

'They are.' I remembered my conversation with Dad. 'My dad's a laid-back kind of person, whereas Mum's quite highly-strung . . . emotional, I guess. They complement each other.'

Evan shifted and I lifted my head to support it with my elbow. 'I'm sorry about your parents splitting up. It must have been hard on you.'

He put his hands behind his head. 'It was a long time ago. I'm over it now.' He sniffed. 'You're lucky, to have both of them though.'

This struck me as an odd thing to say for some reason, though obviously it was true.

'When did they meet? Your mum and dad?'

I shut my eyes to think. 'I think Mum was in her early twenties. Dad was a bit older.' I hesitated. 'She was getting over some other guy . . . she told us, that time at lunch? I can't imagine my mum in love . . . you know, getting excited about going on dates . . . acting all girly and giggly.' I smiled into the woods. 'I wish I'd seen it.'

Evan's face was serious, almost hard. 'Broken hearts . . .' he said darkly. 'Now there's a lesson for us all.'

My dad's words came back to me. 'You don't think it's worth the risk – falling in love?'

He pulled a face. 'I didn't say that . . . Just . . . maybe if we choose who we love more carefully we limit the possibility of getting hurt.'

So Evan was a cynic. I guessed it was understandable, but he was wrong. I sat up, feeling a little woozy from the alcohol. 'That's the point, isn't it? You can never know for sure that someone will be there forever . . . You just have to trust that they will. If nobody trusted, then it would be terrible.' I shut my mouth, realising I was telling this to myself as much as to Evan.

'People get hurt . . .' his voice sounded distant now. I watched for a smile, a sign that he was being light-hearted, but his face was impassive.

'Oh.' The penny dropped. 'Somebody broke your heart? A girl?'

'I didn't say that. It's just good sense to be on your guard.' He closed his jaws and in an instant his face changed as he regarded me softly. 'Though there are exceptions. To every rule.' He pulled me towards him.

I put my arms around him, but I felt confused. Evan seemed to be on a downer tonight. Yet he was so intense with me at the same time. I couldn't work him out. Just when I started to relax with him he'd do or say something that made me unsure again. It was like he was two different people.

I felt him kiss the top of my head, his hands moving down, slipping under the waistband of my jeans, and my uncomfortable thoughts were replaced by desire. I wasn't ready to sleep with Evan. Or anyone. Not for a long time. But I wanted his hands on me, I felt myself moving so that his hand could stroke the skin at the bottom of my spine, expertly circling a spot with his thumb, making me wriggle at his touch. I lifted my head to look at him, and his hands took my face and then suddenly we were kissing, more urgently than ever. I tipped my head back and let his lips find my neck, arching my back slightly, feeling my whole body react.

'I could make a big exception for you, Jane,' Evan said breathlessly. He pushed up my T-shirt, and I realised I didn't want to stop this now. I was tingling, expectant, and he nuzzled my head with his, gripping my waist with his strong hands.

'Evan.' I forced myself to pull away. 'If we don't stop now, then I don't think—'

He put a finger to my lips, silencing me, then traced the outline of my mouth.

'It feels right, though, doesn't it?' he whispered. 'You and me.'

I nodded, it had felt more than right a few minutes before. It had felt perfect.

'We can wait,' I said. 'It doesn't have to be now, does it?'

He brushed a lock of my hair to the side of my face, his eyes, intense, studying me for a long time. Then finally he dropped his hand and his gaze.

'It doesn't have to be now, no. But I think we both want it to be.' He spoke to the ground.

'But we'll want it again. There'll be other times,' I said softly.

'Fine.' His voice crackled, coldly. 'There's no hurry.'

Ignoring my hurt expression, he got to his feet, kicking at the dwindling fire.

'Let's go to sleep now. I'm tired.'

I was anything but tired. I was a little stunned and confused. Definitely not tired.

'You go,' I told him, staring at a weak flame. 'I'll just sit here a while. I'm not that sleepy.'

He nodded, tousling my hair, then I watched as he moved towards the tent, zipping it up behind him.

Alone, with only the sound of an owl nearby for company. I felt melancholy descend. Loneliness. Like before. And then tears coming. How could someone so lovely, so attentive, change in an instant to cold and distant?

Cruel.

I swallowed. I wanted to go home. It was all ruined.

Luca? Where are you?

Slowly I got to my feet, stretching. It was very dark, and I turned to look behind me, seeing Evan's car, lurking like a metal beast. Quietly I walked towards it, looking back at the tent for a second, but it was still, no light on. Evan must be asleep already. I trod around to the back of the car and carefully pressed at the boot's handle to open it. With a slight creak, it opened, and I eased it up as far as I dared, bending to get what I'd come for.

I slid the ribbon off and into my hands tumbled documents, a passport, a driving licence and a few newspaper clippings.

I opened the passport. Evan's face – different, younger I suppose, stared up at me. And his driving licence. I squinted in the dark. Him again, unsmiling, blonder. I looked closely at the photo. It was difficult to tell, and his hair was longer, but his scar wasn't there in this one. Must have been taken before his accident.

The newspaper clippings were cut from some local Australian paper. Reports on Evan going missing. A feature on his mother's concern. Her pleas for witnesses. An interview with his dad. A photocopy of a hire car agreement from a year before.

The rest were what I assumed were keepsakes. A swimming certificate, a surfing badge.

Suddenly I felt like I was just prying. I assembled the papers together quickly when one clipping fluttered to the ground. I snatched it up and was just about to roll it in with the others when the headline on it caught my eye: *GIRL CLAIMS SHE SAW MISSING BOY ATTACKED*. A photo of an attractive, busty girl sat above a claim she had seen Evan Forrest being attacked the night he went missing, but had run out of fright.

I stopped reading. Too much information to take in. Evan certainly had some baggage. A story to tell.

I felt the leaves rustling behind me and all at once I was flustered. Grabbing everything, I hastily tied the ribbon. There was no further noise and I relaxed slightly, though my heart had resumed beating quicker than normal.

I threw the bundle back into the boot and gently closed the door on it, my hands resting on the cold metal as I waited for my breathing to regulate. I lay my head against the car then. Feeling almost numb with the events of the past half-hour or so. I felt my eyelids drooping as tiredness took hold of me, and I felt conciousness fading away.

The hand suddenly on my back frightened the life out of me. I shrieked and whirled round to face him.

'What are you doing, honey?' said Evan.

I turned, hoping that my trembling wasn't visible.

'I . . . my face was hot,' I said weakly. 'From the fire.'

Had he seen me looking? How had I not heard him come up behind me?

He nodded, looking at me without expression for a few seconds. But then, to my relief, he smiled.

'You *are* tired,' he said gently. 'You were asleep standing up.'

'Was I?' I swallowed. That would explain why I hadn't heard him. 'How long have you been here?'

'I heard a noise. And when I looked out of the tent you were nowhere to be seen. When I came out I saw your feet and the top of your head. You were slumped against the car, out of it.' He rubbed my arms. 'You need to get into the warm. Come on.'

He took my hand and led me back to the tent. I wasn't sure I wanted to lie down next to him but I had no choice.

Inside the tent, Evan gently helped me take off my hoodie, socks and trainers. 'You may as well leave your jeans and T-shirt on,' he said, bashing at a cushion and placing it at one end of my sleeping bag, which he then unzipped.

'I'm really sorry . . . about earlier,' he whispered when I was safely wrapped up. 'I guess I got a little carried away. You're just so lovely . . . and sexy. I was frustrated . . . An idiot. Do you forgive me?'

I managed a smile at that. 'It's cool,' I said, and closed my eyes.

'Evan,' I said after a few minutes, opening my eyes.

'What?' He cocked his head, his expression soft.

'Did something happen to you . . . back in Australia?'

He frowned. 'No . . . What made you ask that?'

'Nothing . . .' I shook my head dismissively. 'I just wondered . . . I mean, it seems as though there's

202

something you're not telling me?'

And there it was again, the narrowing of his eyes for a second, before he remembered to smile. 'Go to sleep, Jane,' he said, softly. 'You're exhausted.'

It was true. I could hardly keep my eyes open. I shrugged sleepily. ''Night, then,' I murmured, feeling myself drifting off.

'Sweet dreams. See you in the morning.' I felt him pulling my sleeping bag up to cover me properly.

Within a minute I was waking up again, my mind whirring, but I kept my eyes shut and nestled my head into the pillow. Evan held my hand across his sleeping bag as he lay down too, and it helped, because the last thing I remember in the darkness as I peeked out through a slit in my eyelids was his expression.

Smiling and serene, watching me as I slept.

In the morning I opened my eyes to see him still watching me and smiling, as though he had been rooted in position all night. Even with his hair all messy and the slight shadows under his eyes, he was still the finest-looking specimen of a human being I had ever seen.

'Morning,' he said quietly. 'You sleep OK?'

I rubbed my eyes. I dreaded to think of my bed-hair and I needed to clean my teeth.

Evan, supporting his head with his hand, resumed smiling at me. 'You snore . . .' he said, teasingly. 'In a totally adorable way.'

'Oh God.' I closed my eyes. 'Did I keep you awake?'

He pursed his lips. 'Me and the entire population the other side of the mountain, probably,' he said. 'But it's OK.'

I groaned and sat up, looking down at my rumpled T-shirt, my head clearing, remembering . . .

'I'm going to get dressed,' I said, gesturing at the tent opening. 'So, would you mind . . . ?'

'Right . . . Of course.' Evan wriggled out of his sleeping bag, and I was relieved to see that he too had slept in his jeans. 'I'll get another fire going, make some breakfast.'

He disappeared out of the tent and I quickly got dressed in a pair of scruffy tracksuit bottoms and a faded black T-shirt, pushing my trusty trainers on to my feet. Hardly making an effort, but this morning I didn't care.

Outside, there was brilliant sunshine; my heart couldn't help lifting at the feel of heat on my face. I avoided looking at the car, sitting with Evan's life tied up in a bundle inside it. That last newspaper clipping playing on my mind. I chewed on the inside of my mouth, wondering what to do. Maybe I should forget about it? It was none of my business. He must have his reasons for not telling me . . .

But why was it in the back of his car? Why had he brought it all the way over from Australia?

We were going home today. Maybe I could ask him about it, sensitively, when we were safely out of the wood. For some reason I was uneasy about what reaction I'd get . . . And I didn't like the idea of being so remote when it happened.

I watched Evan as he busied himself with the lit fire, breaking a couple of eggs into a pan, prodding at them with a spoon as they spat and sizzled. He turned then and seeing me watching, grinned contentedly.

'Want some coffee?' he said. 'Or tea?'

I smiled, allowing myself to flash forward in time to Evan and me in our own kitchen, fixing breakfast. I stopped myself. How ridiculous. We'd only just met.

He did look cute, though, as he cooked the eggs, and filled the billy kettle with water from the huge bottle we'd brought with us. Practical. Taking care of me.

I settled myself down next to him, leaning my head against his arm.

'Thank you,' I said, 'for doing this.'

'I want to do it,' he said, calmly, placing the kettle on a makeshift griddle. 'I like looking after you.'

I felt negative thoughts drifting away. I was being a drama queen. I really needed to calm down and relax.

'This is fun,' I said, nudging him, feeling guilty somehow. I yawned then. 'Wake me up when the eggs are ready.'

I drifted off for a doze, the sounds of Evan clinking about with the egg pan, lulling me to sleep.

'Mum!' I shouted, dumping my bag in the hall. 'Dad! I'm back.'

The house was silent, though the clock in the kitchen ticked noisily. Sighing, I walked through and turned on the cold tap for a glass of water. Taking a long drink, I stared out at the yard. Dad's shed was locked up. I wondered idly if Mum and he had got the table into the truck.

I sat down at the table, feeling flat. I'd been looking forward to seeing them all. Evan and I had had a good morning. The strange events of the night before had seemed harmless. I hadn't brought up the papers in the boot of the car. It was nothing to do with me. And though it was intriguing, in a sad, morbid kind of way, it was for Evan to tell me, if he wanted to. If it had been the other way around, I would have been furious if he'd pried into my business and asked nosy questions.

And he had not stopped apologising about his macho behaviour.

'I guess I'm just a guy,' he'd told me. 'Turned on by a beautiful girl. But I'm more than happy to wait. For as long as you want.'

The clock chimed two p.m. I relaxed back in my chair, wondering about what to eat. I'd had a huge breakfast, but I was still hungry. Must be all the excitement . . . nervous energy. But if I carried on eating like a horse, I'd never be able to fit into that blue dress.

Thinking of the dress inevitably led me on to thoughts of Luca. It had been nearly two weeks since I'd seen him. It was odd. I didn't like it.

Perhaps he had lost interest in me now. Perhaps Lowe had been working his particular brand of meddling malice.

I didn't want to think about the other possibility. That this whole thing could just be in my head. Made up. Like some kind of psychosis.

I crossed to the fridge and took out a slice of quiche and a pint of milk. Pouring myself a generous glass, I sat down at the table and thought of nothing but satisfying my hunger. It was so unlike me, this appetite; it was as though I was trying to fill another void. Not one in my stomach. One closer to my heart.

When I'd finished I wondered whether I should take the dog out. Maybe see Evan again? I had nothing else to do and for once I didn't want to be alone.

But I didn't want any old company.

I sighed and leaned back, wondering whether to raid the biscuit tin, when a soft thudding sound made me sit up straight and and look out of the window.

'Dad?' I said, seeing nothing there. I got up and dumped my plate and glass in the sink, peering out into the front yard. A flicker of a shape moving behind the shed caught my eye and made my heart do a quick flip.

I waited silently, watching as the shape moved carefully into view and I allowed a smile to creep over my face.

There he was. A little flushed, his dark hair flopping sweetly over his face. He smiled back.

Keeping my eyes on him, I opened the window wide.

'Hey you,' I said, happily. 'I was beginning to think you were never coming back.'

Luca's face coloured a little, pleased.

'I'm sorry,' he said, his green eyes doleful, apologetic. 'I got caught up in all the work at the palace. Celeste was personally supervising the preparations and she has the eyes of a hawk. She knows exactly who's shirking their hours and sneaking off.'

'So the palace is all done?' I said lightly. 'Ready for the ball?'

'It is,' he grinned. 'Ready for the grand entrance of Miss Jane Jonas.'

I knew he wouldn't let me down.

'I got a dress. Kind of vintage. My grandmother made it for my mother when she was a teenager.'

'Excellent.' He hesitated. 'I will look forward to seeing you in it. It is bad luck for me to see it before that. An old tradition of the ball.'

'Like a wedding,' I said, raising an eyebrow. 'The groom never sees the bride's dress before she walks up the aisle in it. An old tradition of mortal Earth.'

He laughed, rubbing his arms. 'A fine tradition. Can I come inside, do you think? There is a bit of a chill out here.'

'Sure, but I don't know when my family are getting back, so be prepared to leave at short notice.'

'Of course.' Luca disappeared to wait by the back door.

'I saw your man . . .' he said casually as I let him in. 'Evan. Driving down the hill.'

'He didn't see you?' I asked quickly.

'I'm very discreet.' Luca shut the door behind him and followed me into the kitchen. 'Have you been somewhere?'

'Yes,' I said, with my back to him, so he couldn't see me

frowning guiltily as I filled up the kettle. 'We went camping for a night.'

Luca didn't reply, but when I turned back I could see he was trying to look unbothered.

I plugged in the kettle and sat next to him at the table.

'I missed you,' I said, looking intently at him. 'More than I thought I would.'

Luca sniffed, smiling slightly. 'Sounds like you've had plenty to distract you,' he said, looking away.

'It was just one night, camping,' I said, wondering why I wanted to explain. 'And nothing happened.'

'You don't have to justify yourself.' Luca shrugged.

'OK, then.' I got up and poured hot water into a couple of mugs. As I got out the teabags, I glanced out of the window. All was quiet. We were safe for now. 'You drink normal tea?' I asked, putting the mugs down on the table.

Luca grabbed his and sniffed it intently. 'It won't poison me, I suppose,' he said, his eyes dancing at me over the rim of the mug. He took a tentative sip. 'It's good.' He put his mug back down and watched me as I slurped mine. 'And there I was trying to be polite,' he laughed. 'In front of the refined mortal girl and her careful manners.'

He watched me, every inch of his face smiling. As

though I was nothing but a delight to him. I liked that. I liked it a lot.

'We have an expression, "eat like pigs",' I told him. 'Because us mortals don't all have pretty manners.'

'Thank goodness for that. I like a girl who doesn't stand on ceremony.' He put his hands behind his head.

'A girl,' I said, coyly. 'Just any girl, I suppose?'

He hesitated briefly. 'You know full well not just any girl.' Though he was smiling, his eyes said something less innocent.

And I kind of liked that too.

I reminded myself that Luca and I were friends, nothing more. I fiddled with my mug, determined not to look in any way as though I wanted to flirt back. That would be humiliating.

And the two of us sat listening to the sound of the clock for a while.

'So . . .' Luca began awkwardly after a bit. 'Everything is going well with Evan?'

I covered the disappointment I felt with what I'm sure was a prissy expression.

'Of course it is.' I frowned. 'Why?'

'Nothing.' He clasped his hands together looking even more awkward. 'I just . . .' He seemed to be searching for words.

'You just what?' I knew I sounded cool, but I was annoyed. Annoyed and disappointed that the atmosphere had changed. I didn't want to talk about Evan either.

'I just had this feeling last night that maybe something wasn't right.' He looked straight at me.

He couldn't possibly have known how I'd felt . . . How Evan had made me feel when I'd pulled away from him. I kept my expression steady.

'I sometimes get pictures in my head,' he went on. 'And often they mean nothing . . . But . . . well, I suppose it's what you call a "sixth sense".'

'My grandma had those,' I said dryly. 'Usually after she'd eaten cheese late at night.'

I saw his mouth tilt into a smile.

'You're right. I don't always get it correct. I'm sorry I brought it up.'

'It's OK. Everything's fine. I'm happy,' I said, not knowing whether I was or I wasn't. 'But you'll be the first to know if that changes.'

I sounded way cooler than I felt.

'Good.' His voice was light, but his eyes stayed on mine for a fraction too long. It was like he had seen into my head and picked out insecurity and discomfort. But my pride wouldn't let me admit that. Not even to Luca.

The clock ticking again.

'So.' I leaned forward, refusing to think about that bundle of documents and clippings. 'When is the ball?'

Finally Luca's eyes lit up. 'You still want to come?'

'Of course I want to. I've been looking forward to it for weeks.'

'Good.' He looked relieved. 'It starts early evening tomorrow.'

I bit my lip. 'I'll tell my mother I'm with Evan,' I said, more to myself than Luca. 'I just hope he doesn't call, or come up here looking for me.'

'You'll be back before you know it,' Luca said, studying my anxious face. 'Literally.'

Maybe I won't want to come back, I thought.

'Right. I'd forgotten about the time laws of Nissilum.'

Luca drank the rest of his tea. 'I'm so glad you're coming. It will be a happy night for me.'

'Me too.' I brushed dog hair from his coat and we smiled at each other.

'I had better be going,' he said, getting up. 'I'll see you tomorrow.' He paused. 'If you change your mind I'll understand.'

'I'll be there,' I said, as he stepped out into the yard. 'I promise.'

CHAPTER SEVENTEEN

'Do I really look good enough?' I asked Luca nervously as we stood at the gates of the palace. I had taken ages getting ready for the evening and had been pretty pleased with the result. Putting on the blue dress had turned me from ordinary and shapeless to . . . a girl with curves, with milky-white skin and long glossy curls. The colour of the dress and a little mascara had picked out the grey in my eyes. Everything about me was just so . . . feminine. Like a picture in a magazine. And it made me feel like I was floating just above myself.

Luca's eyes swept over me. If he hadn't been the chivalrous boy he was, I got the feeling he would have given the low whistle my dad sometimes gave my mother when she bothered to dress up. Even in the half-light I could see the glow in his cheeks.

'You really need to ask that?' he said with an impish smile.

I subtly ran my eyes over him. Out of his scruffy clothes I realised he had the perfect slender physique for formal wear. A taut, lean body and cheekbones all the more prominent after a haircut. If I didn't think of him as my weird-looking friend, I would have said he looked . . . handsome. Like a male model. I dragged my eyes away, trying to appear like I hadn't noticed. But the truth was, we made a good couple. We went together. Our pale skin, our hair colour, our personalities . . . I forced myself not to think like that. Opposites attract, I told myself. Opposites like me and Evan.

Luca's hand skimmed mine and he turned shyly back to the queue in front of us.

Henora was unhappy about something, judging from the tone of her voice.

'Let's linger behind a little,' she huffed to Ulfred, picking up the hems of her long, charcoal velvet frock. 'I want to wait until that motley crew go inside.' She gestured at a cluster of small, elfin-faced women, who were hissing at each other on the gravel driveway up to the palace.

'Hen . . .' Ulfred shook his head. 'We have this every year . . . Just ignore them. They have long forgotten how to bewitch. Cadmium has made sure that all sorcery books and implements have been destroyed. For many decades.' He sighed. 'They are keeping up a pretence. It's all they have left.'

Henora's eyes narrowed. 'Perhaps.' But she glanced at Luca and I, standing stiffly a few feet away. 'Luca, Jane,' she growled, 'stay with us. Don't provoke them.'

Luca nudged my elbow. 'Henora is paranoid about the witches,' he whispered. 'Of all the creatures on Nissilum, she fears them the most.'

I looked over at the huddle. One of the women broke free from the others and cast a shrewish glance at the four of us. I saw her eyes roam from Henora, to Ulfred, to Luca and then to me. She rested her gaze on my dress, screwing up her sharp little face. 'A stranger,' she said to her companions, her voice, piercingly high-pitched. 'A pretty one.'

The others followed her gaze, scrutinising me rudely.

'Indeed,' said one. 'A wolf-girl, too. Most unusual.'

'Outrageous,' muttered Henora, pulling me closer to her. 'Dreadful creatures. Ignore them, dear.'

I smiled nervously, but before I had the chance to speak, the witch was beside us.

Luca instinctively stepped forward to guard me. 'Tilly,' he said warningly, 'she does you no harm.'

'Hmph.' Tilly sniffed, a deep inhalation, as though

216

gathering every scent of me. 'I shall be the judge of that, Hunter boy. She has been vetted I hope?'

'There is no need for her to be vetted,' Henora said coldly. 'She is a wolf. Like myself, my husband and my son. Not that it is remotely your business.'

'Oh, come off your high stool, lady,' Tilly sneered. 'I have a right to know who walks in my path.'

'Indeed.' Ulfred bowed diplomatically. 'And I hope we have eased your fears, Miss Tilly. We wish you a good night.'

Tilly pursed her lips, thwarted. 'Very well.' She took a step back, rejoining her group in what seemed a millisecond.

'Silly little fool.' Henora lifted her chin and shut her eyes as though to regain good humour. When she opened them again, a broad smile lit up her face. Her long, straight nose quivered a little. 'Time to make our entrance, I think.'

She swept regally past the witches, with Ulfred, Luca and I in her wake. I hung back, tugging Luca's arm to halt him.

'Are you sure they won't detect I am mortal?' I whispered anxiously.

'I told you. Mint and bay leaf is an excellent foil against the smell of mortal blood. It is written in mythology here. Trust me.' I rubbed at my arms, hoping that ten minutes of rubbing leaves into my skin was enough.

I was beginning to relax when Luca gave me a serious look. 'One thing though, Jane. Don't accept too much wine . . . Or it will be your own mouth that betrays you.'

The entrance to the palace shone with dazzling crystal-white tea lights, attached to a delicate gilt rope. The front of the palace was strikingly like the Palace of Versailles, white and glistening, but solid, like a wedding cake set in stone. Somehow the effect was not sugary or twee, but grand and charming at the same time.

Two sentries stood guard at the gates to the palace, letting guests through. Ahead of us I saw a tall, dark-haired couple. The woman, whose profile was in view, had skin the colour of fresh snow, her thick, black hair hung in a loose chignon at her neck. Around her shoulders she held a fur cape. Her partner, who looked strangely like a young, svelte Elvis, his hair combed into a quiff, wore a stylish take on a dinner suit: his white collar upturned, his jacket draped Teddy-boy style down his long body.

Luca saw me staring at the two of them.

'Vampires,' he said in a low voice. 'They are ridiculously glamorous, but be very careful. They look cool and civilised, but they are master manipulators.'

I shivered, hoping that what Luca had said earlier was true and his blood antidote would work tonight. I suddenly felt vulnerable and Luca intuitively took hold of my hand. 'It will be all right. Just stick with me.'

Eventually we walked into the reception hall. Beneath my feet, marble tiles were polished to perfection, above me a network of snowdrop chandeliers cast light like fairy rain on the tops of our heads.

To the right stood an Amazonian woman dressed in a silver tulle gown. Her white hair was piled elegantly on her head. She smiled warmly at each guest as they passed her. She had startling sapphire-blue eyes and a small upturned nose. Apart from a few small lines around her eyes, she could have been anything from thirty-five to fifty. Her skin looked as though she had spent her whole life underneath a lace parasol, protected from the elements. She clasped her hands together, showing off a large jewelled ring that glinted powerfully.

'Celeste.' Luca's tone was reverent and, as we came closer, her eyes widened fondly at the sight of him.

'How handsome you look,' she said quietly, straightening his jacket in a maternal gesture. 'Dear Luca.' Her eyes turned to regard me, standing awed beside him. 'And who is this?' She raised an eyebrow at Luca.

'This is Jane, Mother Celeste.' Luca pulled me forward gently. I bobbed in an awkward little curtsey, feeling faintly ridiculous.

Celeste laughed. 'How charming,' she said as another group of guests nudged up behind us. 'Excuse me . . .' She turned graciously to greet them and Luca and I continued on towards some grand double doors, through which servants bearing trays of drinks attended to the crowd inside.

I breathed out loudly, bracing myself for what was to come.

'Brother.' A familiar voice halted us. Lowe, standing with a couple of angelic-looking boys his age, waved insouciantly. Whispering something to his companions, he left them and crossed the hall to us.

Luca frowned. 'Shouldn't you be making yourself useful, Lowe? Not just hanging around.'

'I've done my fair share.' Lowe's eyes slid over my dress. 'Gracious, don't you look a sweet sight, Jane?'

The faint derision in his tone made it difficult not to glare at him, but I managed a tight smile.

'Thank you.'

'To think we barely knew of your existence until now,' Lowe went on. 'It seems impossible.' His gaze rested a little too long on me, though I stared unblinking back at him, willing Luca to send him away. Or do something.

'Run along, Lowe,' said Luca, taking my arm. 'I'm sure the kitchen staff are short of a pair of hands.'

'Oh didn't I tell you,' Lowe said lightly, 'Celeste has given me special dispensation tonight . . . to mingle . . .' He paused. 'As a guest.'

'She has?' Luca looked surprised but smiled, pleased for his brother. 'You'd better not let her down, then, I suppose.'

Lowe glanced back at his friends. 'Don't worry about us. We won't embarrass you . . . or your lovely companion.' With an infuriating smile, he drifted away.

Luca shook his head. 'I suppose I do worry about him. He is too . . . what do you call it? Cocky?'

'Cocky is exactly the right word,' I said, dryly.

Inside the great room – the ballroom – the noise was almost deafening. It was more than a hubbub of voices, it was a hissing, whispering nest of creatures. I was amazed at how distinct the assembled groups were.

There was Tilly and her coven, chattering. Tilly's nervous energy gave her the appearance of an agitated little bird, sharp-nosed, her head darting this way and that.

In the corner, the vampires I had seen earlier stood coolly, observing others. The woman with the fur cape held a small, painted, wooden fan in one hand, and I saw her whisper to Elvis as she waved it in front of her, pausing to seize a flute of what looked like champagne from one of the staff. Taking a long drink, she put her head back and hiccuped. I smiled. It made her seem more human at least.

And in the orchestra, seated on a curved stage by a huge stained-glass window looking over the grounds, was little Dalya, bent intently over her violin.

I suddenly wished that Dot was here to see all of this, and felt a pang. She would never know about any of this. She couldn't.

Dalya lifted her head and found us. Two small pink spots appeared in her cheeks and she lifted her bow in greeting.

'Dalya spends most of the evening bored as a snail,' said Luca, waving back at his sister. 'She cannot wait to make her entrance as a proper guest.'

I secretly envied her, observing safely from her place in the orchestra. If it weren't for Luca by my side, I would hardly say I felt at ease. The night opened out before me, unknown and forbidden. I looked almost longingly at the tray of glasses carried quickly past us by a waiter.

Luca followed my gaze. 'One sparkling grape juice won't do any harm,' he said, stopping the waiter to take

222

two glasses from him. 'Though in large doses it's said to have an hallucinogenic quality, so maybe go easy on it.' He handed me a glass.

I drank, to find the taste was like lemonade. Effervescent, but harmless – I hoped.

'I hesitate to break it to you,' Luca murmured over the top of his glass, 'but you are a source of interest already.'

'Really?' I looked subtly about me, my stomach clenching. As my eyes travelled around the room, they met a few curious stares. The vampires in particular gawped brazenly at my dress.

'Come on,' said Luca. 'Let's get this done with.' He took my arm and led me through parting guests to the imposing couple in the corner.

'Hello there,' purred the woman in the fur cape. She lowered her fan, smiling spectacularly at Luca as he approached. 'Rather rude of you to leave it so long to introduce us to your companion.' She extended one long arm towards me. 'How delicious you are,' she said, her smoky eyes taking me all in. 'Where on earth have you come from?'

I opened my mouth, but Luca intervened by kissing her hand.

'Vanya, this is Jane. A distant southern cousin of mine.'

He smiled in a relaxed fashion. 'Jane, this is Vanya. And her husband Milton.' He gestured at Milton who was half turned away in pursuit of more grape juice. 'They rule the vampire nests on Nissilum.'

'Not that we live in such a hovel,' said Vanya. 'We have worked hard to enjoy a more luxurious existence. And it gives our lowers something to aspire to.' She blinked at me and I felt myself becoming almost swept up by her. I looked down at my glass, remembering Luca's warning. 'Heavenly dress,' she said, a tiny laugh escaping her lips. My own mouth was frozen in a smile. 'Very nice for one of your breed,' she told Luca over my head, as though I wasn't present.

Having secured his drink, Milton stepped forward, towering over the rest of us; he held a flute of clear sparkling liquid in one gloved hand, extending the other towards me.

'Enchanted to meet this beautiful creature,' he said. I was fixated by his mouth, wide and red, though his skin puzzled me. Contrary to what I had expected, he had a healthy pallor and his eyes were a regular brown, not the black I had imagined.

Luca nodded warily at him, then, glancing at Vanya, he cleared his throat, attempting more conversation. 'Vanya and Milton are Borgia vampires. A great dynasty.'

Vanya preened in a self-entitled kind of way, flicking her fan back and forth.

'We took the name from some mortal acquaintances of ours, hundreds of years back.' She looked dolefully at Milton. 'We had so much in common with them. Didn't we dear?'

'Exquisite country, too,' Milton added, nostalgically. 'Italy.' He directed a look at me. 'Have you heard of it?'

Borgia? Nefarious Italian family . . . I blinked and drew my hand out of Milton's extended grip, unsure whether this was a trick.

'I haven't, no. Is it beautiful?'

'Very. And the food! Pity we couldn't eat then.'

Luca gave me a slight nudge, reminding me, if I didn't already know, that ignorance was the best policy.

Vanya opened her purse and took out a small compact mirror and a lipstick. Oblivious to her audience, she retouched her lips, pouting at her reflection. Milton was gazing adoringly at her, I noticed.

'Isn't she something?' he murmured, then subtly looked me up and down. 'Though I suspect she has a little competition tonight . . .'

I looked up at Luca to see umistakeable pride on his face and we exchanged a smile. Though I hardly felt comfortable trapped with these imposing vampires, I allowed myself a small rush of pleasure.

Oblivious to any compliments except those directed at her, Vanya snapped her compact shut and replaced it in her purse. She linked her arm through mine and her fur cape rubbed pleasingly against my bare skin.

'Would you like to see the ancestral gallery?' she said quietly into my ear. 'All those fantastically puritanical Seraphim. Gruesome.'

'Why not?' I said, my head reeling a little. Was it the drink? Or was it Vanya?

'I'll take her, Vanya.' Luca smiled amiably but his tone was firm. He moved to break us apart, and slid his own arm through mine.

Vanya's face darkened for a second, but she recovered and smiled broadly. Her teeth were the whitest I'd ever seen.

'As you wish,' she said, in a clipped kind of way, and raised her glass at Milton. 'I need more refreshment darling,' she told him as he obediently took her glass.

Vanya turned to me and I felt Luca's grip tighten a little. 'We must catch up later,' she said, touching my cheek with her finger. Then, with a nod at Milton, she clutched her fur closer around her shoulders and swept off with her beau.

'She's incredible,' I breathed. 'And I feel woozy.'

'Vanya has that effect.' Luca's expression was dry. 'She's a terrible flirt. But she certainly has an eye for beauty.' His eyes flickered shyly over my dress and inside I felt myself glowing.

'I can hardly believe this is happening. It's all so very glamorous.'

'I can't say I enjoy it usually.' Luca pulled me gently in the direction of the great hall, and as we walked a clutch of witches stared imperiously at the two of us. 'I'm normally stuck serving drinks to this lot,' he added in a half-whisper.

At the doorway to the great hall a white-haired man, dressed in a pale-blue and white tailcoat affair, bowed solemnly at us. I nodded in return.

'That's Ned,' Luca said as we passed into the hall. 'He and I tend to spend a lot of time together at the ball. 'He has a good sense of humour. For an angel.'

I laughed. 'They are rather serious, aren't they?'

'Goody two shoes,' Luca said slowly. 'Now, that's one mortal term I approve of heartily.'

'But the angels are supposed to be decent people?' I said. 'Trustworthy.'

Luca stopped and put his glass down on a marble-topped table with what looked like solid gold legs.

'I envy your regard for trust,' he said, and I thought

how soft and kind his eyes looked. 'As you can imagine, it is not prized amongst the population of Nissilum . . . Well, apart from the angels. And as for the werewolves . . . Well, animals don't trust . . . they survive.' Luca's face was serious. Sad.

He hates it, I thought. He hates not knowing how to trust.

'But you trust your family?' I said, wanting to smooth out the anxious creases in his forehead.

'Loyalty is slightly different perhaps.'

And what about me? I wanted to ask, but didn't.

A flurry of waitresses appeared through a door in the hall. Dressed in shades of pale pink, blue and yellow Regency-style dresses they were what could only be described as cherubic. Pale blonde curls, arranged Jane Austen-style and the creamiest skin. I stared, enraptured.

'Very pretty,' said Luca, as they carried their trays through to the ballroom. 'In a sugary kind of way. Not really my thing.'

I grinned. 'They're like something out of a fairy tale. Little Bo Peeps.'

We watched as the last one disappeared through the door.

'So,' I said lightly. 'Have you had any more . . . pictures in your head?'

Luca looked confused.

'You know, about Evan?' I held my breath, hoping the answer was no.

Luca looked as though he was about to say something, but he hesitated.

'Do you mind if we don't talk about Evan tonight? It's just . . . I'm quite enjoying having you to myself.'

He sounded so formal, yet so sweet, I pushed any more questions out of my head.

'Of course,' I said, relieved. 'And me too. I mean—'

'I know what you mean,' he said smiling. 'Come on . . . I'll show you the gallery.'

He led me across the slippery marble floor, so polished and clear I could see the vibrant blue of my dress reflected as clearly as if it were a mirror. At the end of the hall was an ornate staircase, wide at the base, the gold-plated banisters curling prettily outwards. The steps were covered by an ivory-coloured velvet carpet. As the stairs wound round I saw a vast painting, gilt-framed, overlooking the hall.

'That's Cadmium,' Luca said, nodding at the painting. 'Captured in his prime.'

As we climbed up to it I saw an astonishingly good-looking man. Dressed in a white robe, like a handsome blond Roman emperor, a delicate silver and gold crown lay amongst the curls on his head. His blue eyes were piercing, even from a few feet away.

'Fine-looking, isn't he?' said Luca, craning his head to get the full picture. 'I must have seen this painting a thousand times, and every time I look at it, it makes my breath catch in my throat.'

'Where is he?' I whispered, for reasons I couldn't fathom, except that I felt as though I were in a sacred church of some kind.

'Now?' Luca glanced back at the hall, which was empty but echoing the sounds from inside the ballroom. A shriek of laughter cut through the hubbub. 'I haven't seen him all evening. There must be something going on that needs his attention.'

We continued up the ivory carpet, passing a glowing picture of Celeste, smiling benevolently; the ultimate matriarch with sapphire-blue eyes, and a fine, heart-shaped face, she wore a necklace with a semi-circular silver pendant.

'Matilda,' said Luca, nodding at a pretty, buxom woman wearing a white cape. Though like the others she was blonde, her eyelashes were dark, and two rosy spots on her cheeks gave her a more human quality. 'Eldest daughter of Cadmium and Celeste. She's away somewhere,' Luca said vaguely. 'Doing some good work or other. She is married to Reuben.'

Next we passed Dorcas, Matilda's younger sister, Luca said. Unlike the others she had a melancholic look about her, and her hair was a darker shade of blonde, and her skin a little less youthful. I wondered where she was tonight . . .

'What's this?' I said as we climbed further, approaching a gilt frame with no picture, just a plaque beneath it with the name *Raphael* written on it.

'Raphael. He's what you'd call "in the dog house".' Luca turned to me, continuing in a low voice, 'Remember we talked of him when you met my family for the first time?'

'He's . . . mad?'

'That's what they say.' Luca looked about us, checking we were very much alone. 'But nobody really knows for sure. He has always been a bit . . . volatile.'

'So they've removed his portrait to teach him a lesson?'

'It's a gesture,' Luca said. 'Celeste needs to set an example, but she adores Raphael.'

Further up the staircase the next portrait was also missing. Not even a name. I looked questioningly at Luca.

'Raphael's father, Dorcas's husband: Gabriel,' he said. 'Nobody knows exactly what has happened to him.' Luca's face paled slightly.

'Sad,' I said, taking in Luca's sorrowful expression. He nodded, but moved to continue up the stairs.

At the top of the staircase was a large landing and another double-fronted door. Two white chairs sat either side. I glanced at Luca.

'Celeste and Cadmium's reception room,' he whispered, taking my hand and pulling me towards it. He knocked firmly, but there was no answer. We looked at each other. 'Let me show you . . . just for a moment. The view is spectacular.'

He gently opened the door and the light that flooded through the room was dazzling. The whole of the opposite wall was window, overlooking a midnight-blue sky, a nearly-full moon and the tops of cedar trees in the grounds.

A long wooden sideboard with rows of drawers underneath sat against one wall, while in the middle of the room was a large circular table covered in photographs. I moved towards it, my eyes sweeping over the images.

Family photographs. There was Celeste with her daughters, one of her holding a baby, and a large one of Cadmium and a boy of around thirteen or fourteen. To say he looked angelic was a huge understatement. The boy had long, curly hair and was dressed in a pale-blue robe of some kind. His hair looked damp and curled around his neck and shoulders, as though he had been swimming; little drops of water sat on his forehead. He looked serious, with his father's arms loosely around his neck. I moved closer. Something about the boy held my attention.

'That's Raphael,' said Luca quietly. 'He looks sweet doesn't he? But he was just starting to behave oddly . . .'

I said nothing, continuing to stare at the image of father and son. I couldn't explain why I couldn't take my eyes off it – but Raphael was captivating somehow. Shifting my gaze to Cadmium, I saw that his eyes were the same colour and shape as his son's.

'Where was his father?' I asked. 'Gabriel?'

'Gabriel had just disappeared by then.' Luca shook his head. 'Raphael took it very hard.'

'Poor boy.' I frowned.

The sound of footsteps on the stairs startled us and I jerked, knocking the table. Something fell from behind the photograph of Cadmium and Raphael.

'Quickly,' said Luca. 'We must leave.' He turned to the door. I glanced back at the thing on the floor. Another photograph, loose, which must have been tucked behind one of the frames.

'Don't worry about that,' Luca said vaguely over his shoulder. 'We shouldn't really be in here.'

Even so, I snatched up the picture, meaning to put it back on the table, but as Luca opened the door I changed my mind, tucking it as fast as I could into the top of my sleeve, where it rasped against my skin.

I darted after Luca and we stepped out on to the landing, a little breathless.

The footsteps were closer and a figure turned at the bottom of the final flight of stairs. A familiar silver tulle gown and a benign smile stood below us.

'Luca,' said a soft voice. It was Celeste, who held keys in one hand and a glass of water in the other. Again she looked fondly at Luca.

'I was showing Jane the gallery,' he said nervously. 'We came a little too far.' He took my hand again, reassuringly. And we went down to meet her where she stood.

Celeste didn't appear in the least bit suspicious. Instead she gave me what I realised was her trademark smile, full of warmth.

'Your mother must be very happy,' she said, looking from me to Luca. 'I hope you are enjoying yourselves? What a handsome pair you make.'

'Yes.' Luca blushed. I took his arm, unsure whether it was protocol to curtsey to Celeste every time we met.

Celeste began her descent, Luca and I behind her,

but when she reached the empty portraits of her son and grandson, she paused. She reached out to Raphael's and with a hesitant movement traced his name engraved on its plaque.

'I have failed, Luca,' she said quietly. She turned to us both. 'You remember Raffy? The two of you were close once . . . As children.'

I shot a look at Luca, who was silent.

Celeste's face darkened. 'Little Raffy,' she murmured, 'too spirited and sensitive.'

I subtly touched my sleeve, feeling the photograph still in place.

She shook her head, adjusting her décolletage with one hand, then lifting her skirts.

We all moved down to the hall.

When we reached the bottom of the steps and the rowdier sounds from the ballroom, she gave an audible sigh in front of us and retrieved her fan.

'Time for dancing . . . and then the speech,' she said, wryly. 'I do hope the guests are behaving themselves.'

With that she swept elegantly through to the ballroom, leaving us lingering behind her.

'Can you dance?' Luca said, his voice close behind me. I waited for him to put his hand on my waist, but instead he moved to take my arm again.

'I don't know. But I will if you will.'

'Agreed,' he said, and as he pulled me closer to him, I felt a fluttering of happiness.

We walked through to the sound of lively violins playing some classical concerto. The orchestra was in full swing and people were dancing. I saw Vanya, her head thrown back, with Milton's arm circling her waist and a cluster of female witches nearby, holding hands and turning in a circle, their tiny feline faces unsmiling but their movements expert.

'Everyone pretty much does their own thing,' Luca told me with a grin. He took my arm and put one hand gently around my waist, pulling me closer to him. In his black tuxedo and white shirt he looked like an old-time movie star. Classically handsome. His green eyes locked on to mine and he swung me round with surprising skill.

'Everyone is looking at you,' he said. 'The belle of the ball.'

'Really?' I felt myself blushing. It was as if this was some incredible magic dream. Every girl's dream. Holding Luca's gaze as we danced, my insides skipped with excitement. Pure, innocent pleasure. It was all right to feel like that, I told myself. Just for one night. It didn't mean anything. I still had a boyfriend.

Finally I dragged my eyes away, concentrating on

my footwork. Thankfully Luca seemed to know exactly what he was doing. He moved in an assured, unselfconscious way.

'You really can dance,' I said, knowing I really couldn't, but enjoying myself all the same.

'Had to learn,' Luca replied, a little out of breath as he took my arm and I twirled, laughing and swung back to him. 'You don't?'

'It's all part of the ritual humiliation of mortal life for a young person – not having a clue how to dance or talk to boys,' I told him.

'I wouldn't say that,' he said quickly, his eyes darting away as he spoke. I hid a smile, sidestepping an overeager man in a long dark-blue dinner jacket with a matching blue streak in his hair. The man, in his twenties, flashed me a toothy smile.

'Valdar,' whispered Luca. 'Vanya's son.'

'But she doesn't look a day over thirty,' I said, slowing down. I stole another look at Valdar, whose dance partner studied me with narrowed eyes. 'They look like brother and sister.'

'Vanya stopped ageing in her late-twenties, as most of them do. Vampires are so vain.' He pulled a face. 'No pun intended.'

The music stopped and people drifted away from the

dance floor to gather at the sides of the room, by the refreshment tables. A group of young, black-haired boys, guzzled a tomato-red concoction. Blood? I shuddered then, remembering that the people in this room could literally drain the life out of me, if they chose to.

'Do you think anyone suspects I'm mortal?' I said quietly to Luca as we began wandering over to a vacant ottoman-style sofa by the door.

'Mortal?' came a shrill voice next to me, and I froze. Tilly appeared, her wild curly hair in even more disarray. Her slinky velvet dress clung to her sylphlike body. She swooned slightly, and my heart beat slowed down. If she was drunk . . .

'What are you talking about, Tilly?' Luca's voice was light, but one of his hands found mine and held on to it.

'She said something about a mortal.' Tilly's eyes gleamed. 'Is there one here? In the palace?'

'Don't be ridiculous.' Luca's expression was puzzled. 'You've had too much grape juice, Tilly. You're imagining things.'

Tilly lifted her head and trained her almond-shaped eyes on me. 'She said it.' She came closer to me and her nose twitched, as though she was sniffing me. 'You have appeared from nowhere, Miss . . . Who are you?'

'I . . .' I began, glancing over to Luca. 'I'm Jane, a

southern werewolf.' I kept my voice as steady as I could.

'Hmmm.' She lingered closely for a second longer and my breath seemed to freeze in my throat. I remembered what Luca had said: witches can do you harm just by looking at you. My eyes slid away from her.

'I have excellent hearing,' she told Luca haughtily. 'As you well know.'

'Of course,' he said, smiling very convincingly at her. 'But the grapes can tamper with the senses, can't they?'

Tilly looked down at her glass, which was empty, and sniffed. 'Possibly,' she said, her voice crackling. She shook her head in an eccentric motion. 'When are they serving cake?' she said truculently. 'Or do we have to endure one of those dreary speeches before they bring it out?'

Luca's lips twitched in a genuine smile then and my body relaxed.

The sound of metal clinking against glass drew everyone's attention to the front of the room, where Celeste stood patiently waiting for quiet.

'Having a nice time?' Vanya licked her lips uncomfortably close to me and I fought the instinct to jerk away from her. That would certainly give me away.

'Very nice, thank you,' I said politely, noticing for the first time a small diamond stud embedded in her dainty nose.

She smiled, lifting a finger as though to wipe an invisible tear from her eye. 'I find these little get-togethers so touching.'

Milton appeared behind her, wrapping his arms around her willowy frame. 'Such a softie, aren't you, sweetest?' he said silkily. 'Personally, these occasions simply make me hungry.' As I turned I found him staring directly at me, and I coloured slightly. 'No decent food, you see,' he went on. 'Just a lot of drab offerings on trays.'

I smiled, terrified all of a sudden. Milton and Vanya had arranged themselves so that they were hemming me in. My eyes darted around to locate Luca, but he stood the other side of Tilly, who was muttering something into his ear.

The noise in the room disappeared then, as Celeste finally called everyone to hush.

I stepped slowly backwards, but met a solid arm. I kept my eyes on Luca, but he stared straight ahead as Celeste spoke in a gentle but powerful voice to us all. Realising there was no escape for now, I stayed put, only half listening to the speech, much more aware of my pounding heart. Hours seemed to pass until Celeste finished talking, raising her glass to the guests. The orchestra began tuning up and I edged forward.

'Best stay put, darling,' Vanya bent to whisper to me. 'Luca is escorting that wretched Tilly to the powder room.' She smiled at me as I lifted my head to look at her. 'Milton and I will be your company until he returns.'

With a growing sense of panic I watched Luca half pulling, half carrying the reluctant Tilly through the double doors, conscious of Vanya's hand on my elbow.

Come on, Luca, I willed, training my eyes on the door. Instead of Luca, Lowe appeared, following one of the serving girls as she collected empty plates and glasses.

'Lowe!' I called loudly, surprising myself.

He frowned, turning this way and that. To my relief his eyes found me. For one awful moment I thought he was going to turn away and leave me in Vanya's clutches, but he strode across the room, a facetious grin on his face.

'Oh dear. Has he abandoned you already?' he said, nodding curtly at the Borgias. 'Let me get you some more to drink.' With a quick, forceful motion he took my hand and pulled me with him to the other side of the room.

'Thank you,' I said, recovering my breath after holding it for so long. 'I thought I would never escape them.'

'It's nothing,' Lowe glanced about him casually but his gaze came back to me. 'But surely you know your own strength could have overwhelmed theirs . . . if the need had arisen?'

'Yes, but . . . I was off guard,' I improvised, flustered. 'And they are quite overwhelming.'

'Interesting.' He whipped a glass of what looked like water from a small serving girl on her way to another group of guests. 'You are either very naïve, or you have good reason to fear the Borgias . . .' He paused, his stare intensifying. 'Which is it?'

I shook my head as though I hadn't understood him. Inside I realised that Lowe's scrutiny was more alarming than the Borgias'.

I turned as subtly as I could to look at the vampires, but they had vanished. I relaxed again.

'You don't have to stay with me,' I told him. 'I'm sure you have more interesting guests to talk to.'

'Not at all,' he said quietly. 'None half as interesting as you.'

To my relief, Luca appeared in the ballroom, looking around him, worried. Spotting Lowe and me, he hurried over to us.

'I'm so sorry to leave you. But I see you have been rescued.' He patted his brother on the arm. 'Thank you, brother.'

'You should really keep an eye on Jane,' Lowe told him. 'She is like a lamb to the slaughter in here.'

Luca paled a little at that, but he kept his composure.

'Fresh air, I think,' he said turning to me. 'It is getting stifling in here.' He took off his jacket and hooked it over his arm.

Lowe grinned, his sharp, white teeth fully exposed. 'A room full of beasts,' he mocked. 'What do you expect?'

Luca rolled his eyes at his brother and tugged at my hand. 'There is a beautiful garden at the back of the palace. A good place to sit away from the noise.' Brushing past a bemused-looking Lowe we walked towards a large door near the stained-glass window, past the orchestra, where Dalya sat yawning.

The music faded a little as the door shut behind us. The hall we were in was a mass of gilt-framed paintings and spectacular marble tiles, polished to perfection. I could never resist a polished floor, and I found myself twirling, gliding around, picking up the hem of my dress like I hadn't done since I was a little kid. I almost forgot Luca was with me until I stopped, feeling slightly dizzy, and saw him watching me with a grin.

'Sorry,' I said hiccuping. 'I don't usually act like this . . . I guess it's having to be so proper all night. It makes me want to misbehave a little.'

'I approve,' he said, still smiling at me. 'I hope I get the chance to see you misbehave more often.'

'Do you now?' I said, swirling my skirts from side to side. 'Don't let the precious angels hear you say that or they'll throw us out.'

'I wouldn't mind that either,' he said. 'We could go and misbehave in private somewhere.'

'Luca!' I said in mock disapproval. 'And you've been such a gentleman all night!'

'I didn't mean . . .' he said, flushing. 'I meant . . .'

I grinned at his discomfort. 'So, are we going to see this secret garden or not?'

The door was unwieldy at first, but eventually Luca pulled it open and we slipped through and down a small carpeted corridor. All was quiet, but as we walked further down the corridor, we heard the sound of hushed voices coming from a large room at the end. It was dark inside. I glanced anxiously at Luca, who slowed his pace, putting his arm gently out to stop me.

'Who's there?' called a familiar, purring voice.

'Vanya,' muttered Luca. 'It is Luca,' he called loudly.

Vanya appeared in the doorway, her eyes narrowing. 'Well, speak of the devil,' she said. 'Valdar and I were just deliberating over something . . .' She paused, her gaze sweeping over me like a searchlight. 'When is a wolf . . . not a wolf?'

Luca's benign expression was frozen on his face. 'I don't understand.'

'Really?' She stepped closer, much closer, to us and extended a finger to lift my chin with one glossy black nail. I stayed rooted where I was.

'Vanya.' Luca sighed, frowning at the gesture. 'What are you up to?'

'Oh, darling,' she said theatrically. 'We have a little . . . dilemma . . . on our hands.'

My eyes slid uneasily to Luca, whose expression was impassive. Only the slight tick in his cheek gave him away.

'You see the problem is,' Vanya went on, 'that this lovely creature just doesn't smell right.'

I swallowed. It hadn't worked. The mint and bay leaf had not worked.

'You're drunk,' Luca told her firmly. 'And you're imagining things.'

'Don't think so, old boy . . .' Valdar stepped out from behind Vanya, like a giant shadow in the dark. 'I'm not in the least bit drunk and I agree with Mother.' He smiled at me, and there they were, sharp and filed, his teeth glinting in the dim light.

Luca stepped calmly in front of me.

'I suggest you go back to the party and forget all

about this,' he said, looking from Vanya to Valdar. 'You know the consequences of biting and feeding on Nissilum. Is it really worth it?'

'Oh sweet hell, yes,' said Vanya, tilting back her head and laughing. 'For that one momentary break in a lifetime of tedious good behaviour. For that one, sweet drop of mortal blood on my tongue.' She shuddered, dropping her head.

And just as I edged away from her, her hand shot out to grab my arm, twisting it, pulling me close.

'Jane!' Luca shot forward, pushing me back behind him quickly. As I tried to take in what was happening, I was aware of the heat coming from his body and the pulse in his cheek. He seemed to grow bigger and, as I watched, the cotton-silk of his shirt strained over his arm.

'Careful wolf-boy,' Vanya mocked, still clutching me to her. 'I am swifter than you . . .' But with a snap of his jaw, Luca's mouth opened, all his teeth revealed, and he threw back his head and roared, fiercely and shockingly into her face.

'Luca!' I screamed, glimpsing Valdar's alarmed face behind Vanya's.

Vanya meanwhile had shrunk back into her son, pushing them both as far from Luca as possible.

I stepped back too as Luca growled, his shirt torn, and

his arms covered in fine black hair. I didn't dare examine his hands. I looked away and shut my eyes.

'Well, go then,' he growled at Vanya and Valdar. 'Now!'

With one briefly ruffled look at us both, Valdar dragged Vanya firmly back along the corridor, as she snarled and muttered under her breath.

I stayed rooted in position, staring at Luca's back, his shirt shredded, the muscles around his waist throbbing slightly. He didn't turn. Instead he put his head in his hands, rolling his scalp around, making small groaning noises.

'Luca.' I cautiously put a hand out to touch his shoulder blade. 'Are you OK?'

There was a pause and then, still with his back to me, he began slowly shaking his head.

'Damn it,' he muttered. 'I'm not OK.'

I took my hand away, waiting, wondering whether I should go. Leave this place, and Nissilum, right away. But I still didn't move. I couldn't leave him. Not like this.

Eventually, Luca lifted his head, and I saw his body had returned to normal. He turned slowly to face me, and though his eyes were darker green and a little bloodshot, he was Luca again.

'I have done a foolish thing,' he said darkly. 'Bringing

you here, to this place. It was selfish and naïve of me.' He shook his head. 'We must try and get you home. As quickly as possible.'

'And where would that be?' A cool voice spoke out of sight.

Luca and I turned quickly to see Lowe, leaning casually up against the wall behind us, an insolent smile on his face. 'Where is home?'

Luca darted a look at me that said *Keep quiet and let me do the talking*. So I remained silent, making sure however to cast Lowe as resentful a look as possible.

He didn't appear to notice. This time he only had eyes for his brother.

'I knew she wasn't a wolf,' he said coldly. 'I knew it the moment I saw her. Felt her aura.'

'And?' said Luca boldly. 'She is doing no harm.'

'Not now she isn't . . .' Lowe began aggressively, but seeing Luca's pained expression altered his tone to a more wheedling one. 'I'm just concerned for you, brother. You know how this ends. We all know what really happened to Gabriel—'

'I don't care,' said Luca, forcefully. 'You know nothing of this girl. You know nothing of me.'

Lowe was silent for a minute and finally his eyes turned to me.

'So. You have seduced him. You weave your mortal magic and trap him into wanting you. But look at him! He has turned tonight . . . For you.' He stepped right up to me, then, and with a voice dripping in derision, stuck his face into mine. 'I'm telling you this. You will leave here tonight and you will never come back. I will not allow you to ruin him.'

'There is nothing like that between us,' Luca told him. 'If you must know, I was sick and tired of Henora and Ulfred asking if I had a girlfriend. Jane is my friend and she agreed to . . . play the part for tonight.'

I hugged myself. It was true, all of it. So why did I feel so . . . disappointed? Why did I feel kind of foolish? Let down.

'Whatever you say,' Lowe said airily. 'She still doesn't belong here.'

'It was never my intention to hurt Luca.' My own voice cracked. 'But I can see that I am trouble here.'

'No, no, Jane,' Luca said softly, placing his hand on my arm. I gripped his fingers, as though this was the last time I would touch him, not wanting to let him go.

'Yes.' I turned to face him fully, blocking Lowe's view of him. 'I didn't mean to be, but it won't work. Soon enough, everyone will know I am not a wolf. If Vanya doesn't tell them, then he will.' I gestured with my head behind me.

I studied every inch of Luca's face. His tender, green eyes, his finely-honed cheekbones and the dark fringe that fell forward now into his eyes. I wanted to remember this face forever.

'Lowe, leave us, please,' said Luca, firmly.

'I'm not—'

'I would like to say goodbye to Jane,' persisted Luca. 'Allow us that, at least.'

There was a hesitation before Lowe spoke again.

'Very well. You have four minutes to get rid of her.' With that he turned and walked down the corridor. We watched until he shut the door at the end behind him.

Luca turned to me. 'I will come and see you,' he said, quietly but feverishly. 'It will be difficult, because Lowe will report this to Henora and Ulfred . . . I will be watched from now on. But I will do it.' He held my face in one hand and drew me to him, resting his forehead against mine. I felt tears coming, and loneliness.

Though I should have told him that this was the end, that it was better for all of us if he and I never laid eyes on each other again, I did not.

My selfish heart wouldn't let me.

I got to see the peaceful garden at the back of the palace. Luca took me out there and we ran its length, his hand holding mine. When we reached the far side of it, a row of dark, leafy bushes parted in the middle to reveal a well-trodden but unplanned pathway. We crept quietly up to a high wrought-iron gate, which Luca opened, and we slipped through, out of the grounds.

I looked back down the narrow path, across the acres of grass, at the back of the palace, which twinkled prettily – shadows moving behind the stained-glass window of the great hall.

I moved to take hold of Luca, but he shook his head.

'I can't take you, or come back with you,' he said sadly. 'You can do this on your own.'

I felt five years old again, standing at the school gate with my father. Desolate, and frightened that I would never see him again. Safety, familiarity were leaving me.

'I'll come when I can.' Luca clasped my hands and kissed me gently on the side of my head, resting against me. 'Close your eyes.'

I did as I was told, but reluctantly. Sadly. Wishing myself back home.

'Goodbye, Jane . . .' He hesitated. 'Take care of yourself.'

Closing my eyes, I felt a little bit of my world cave in.

CHAPTER EIGHTEEN

It was nearly spring. All at once the cold air had turned dustier, flowers appeared in the woodland. The windows of the house stayed open. My mother started singing again.

Dot and I lay across Dad's bench, the remnants of a picnic at our feet, dozing in the sun.

I had half an hour before Evan was coming to talk to Dad about doing some work for him. Dad's work had picked up again and he could afford the help.

Remembering I still had work to do for my approaching GCSEs, I sighed loudly. I had avoided schoolwork as much as possible the last couple of weeks. I hadn't been able to concentrate on anything much but the flatness in my stomach. I felt deflated, as though someone had let the air out of me. Evan had been conscientiously taking me out driving, while my mother tested me on my theory.

It was a distraction, but since it would be another year before I actually got to drive on my own, I had to force myself a little bit.

'What's the matter?' Mum had asked me one evening as I stared into space at the kitchen table. 'You're very quiet lately.'

'I feel a bit flat, that's all.' I'd stared at the back of the book she held up. 'I don't know why.'

But I did know. I knew the night I came home from the ball, arriving only an hour after I'd left, and running upstairs, tugging off my dress and stuffing it unceremoniously in the wardrobe, and climbing into bed at eight o'clock. I felt as though something had been taken from me. Something integral to my life, to me. And I was angry. With myself, with Lowe, with Luca even. Something I wanted had been held in front of me and then taken away. Just like that. Mum assumed it was something to do with Evan and I didn't tell her otherwise. What on earth could I have said? I just stared out of the window for hours, telling myself that maybe it was for the best. That the dream had shattered. I needed to focus on real life now. I had my future to look forward to.

And I had Evan.

Evan was a little unpredictable and moody, but at least he only lived a couple of miles away. At least I didn't have to sneak around to see him. I should have been grateful to be dating someone like him, who made me feel hot and flustered and shy and confident all at once. I liked his hands on me, I liked his coolness. But . . .

'But what?'

'Jane?' Dot opened her eyes and sat up. She cocked her head to the side, observing me with a frown. 'You're talking to yourself.'

'What?' I grimaced. 'God . . . sorry.' I stretched out my legs, realising my jeans were too short for me.

'You're all funny these days.' Dot snapped a leaf from the bush next to her and started shredding it with her fingers. 'Like, moody and stuff.' She looked sideways at me. 'If that's what being in love is, it's really annoying for other people.'

I laughed. 'Who says I'm in love?'

'You're grouchy all the time, you don't eat anything, and you can't concentrate.' Dot chucked the last of the leaf on the ground. 'That's what happened to Cassidy's sister, Clare, just before she got engaged to Harry. She said being in love was awful and it gives you spots.' Dot peered at my complexion.

'Stop it.' I shoved her lightly. 'Maybe I am in love. I don't know.'

'You must know.' Dot pursed her lips in concentration.

'Do you think of Evan and get that squirmy feeling in your stomach?'

This was true.

'So.' Dot rolled over on to her stomach. 'Why are you sad?'

'I'm not sad. I'm just . . . distracted I guess.' I paused, wondering for an insane moment whether to tell Dot about Luca, about Nissilum. But telling her that vampires are not just the stuff of fiction, but real and living somewhere in another world, was plain foolish. She'd have nightmares for weeks.

Luckily the sound of a car pulling up the track caught Dot's attention as well as mine.

I peeked through the trees, glimpsed the familiar dark blue of Evan's Saab.

'Evan.' I smiled at Dot. 'Let's go and say hello.'

Evan was deep in conversation with my father at the kitchen table when Dot and I walked in, but he lifted his head to smile disarmingly at me. It was extraordinary how I forgot what effect he had on me when I hadn't seen him for a few days.

'Hey, Dot.' He reached out his hand to give her a gentle high-five. 'How's my favourite little sister?'

'Fine.' Dot was uncharacteristically shy, and Dad raised an eyebrow at the two of us.

'Give us half an hour, girls. Then he's all yours.'

Evan gave me one of his looks. Slow, sexy . . . his mouth unsmiling and his blue eyes intense.

'Come on.' I nudged Dot's arm. 'Come and help me tidy my room.'

Upstairs, Dot lounged on my bed, while I attempted to pick up the trail of clothes that had lain untouched for a few days on the floor. The wardrobe was part open, and I glimpsed the blue satin dress. Melancholy stole through me. I didn't want to look at it. I walked across and pulled it out, clumsily reaching out for a hanger.

'Ooh.' Dot looked with interest at what I was doing. 'That's pretty.' She sat up, blinking. 'When did you wear that?'

'This?' I shrugged casually. 'I just tried it on . . . It was Mum's.' I smoothed out the skirts, somehow reluctant to put it away now, and the movement caused something to flutter to the floor.

The photograph.

I had completely forgotten about the photograph. Not looking at Dot, I picked it up and put it on the top of the chest of drawers to look at later. But Dot's eagle eyes were on it. She rolled off the bed and padded over to take a look.

'It's nothing, Dot. Leave it,' I said a little sharply.

She ignored me and held it up to study it.

'A picture of a boy,' she said, looking quite disappointed. 'Why have you got this? Who is it?'

Feeling unprepared, I snatched it from her.

It was Raphael. He looked about fifteen in this one. The same white-blond curly hair, the perfect nose. He wasn't smiling – in fact he looked angry, scowling into the camera, his eyes narrowed.

I studied the picture for a few seconds longer before putting it back on top of the chest.

'It must be something Mum had and has forgotten about,' I said vaguely. 'I'll ask her about it . . .'

Dot had lost interest thankfully. She was busy taking apart the Russian doll by my mirror. I finally got the dress on to its hanger and hung it on the outside of the wardrobe.

'That's enough tidying up for today,' I said, looking at my unmade bed. 'But thanks so much for your help.' I swatted Dot over the head, just as there was a knock on the door.

'OK if I come in?' said Evan's voice. 'Your dad and I are done, I think.'

Before I could speak, Dot had rushed to the bedroom door.

257

Evan's eyes widened melodramatically.

'I finally get to see the Jonas bedroom . . .' he said, in exaggerated awe. He stepped inside, sweeping the room: my unmade bed, the clothes piled hastily on my chair, along with the books, and trainers on the floor.

'I see you haven't had a chance to tidy up yet,' he said, grinning at me.

'We got distracted.' I coloured slightly, willing Dot to take a hint and leave the room.

Predictably, she didn't move.

'Dot,' I said, through slightly clenched teeth, 'don't you have homework . . . or something?'

'Great room,' said Evan, walking over to the window. 'Amazing view.' He turned back to me. 'I'll bet you spend a lot of time in here, right?'

'She hardly ever used to come out,' said Dot. 'But things are a bit different now.' She eyed Evan.

'Good.' He patted her head. 'Mind if I spend a bit of time alone with your sister?'

As if by magic, Dot transformed into a model of compliance.

'Of course.' She skipped to the door. 'Be good,' she trilled as it shut behind her.

I rolled my eyes, but I was laughing now and so was Evan.

'She's so sweet,' he said.

'Yeah . . .' I agreed. 'Though she drives me crazy sometimes.'

'Little sisters,' he sighed. I glanced at him, resisting the urge to say something damning about Sarah.

Evan walked over to where I stood with my back to the window, in front of the chest of drawers. He wore all black today and he'd had a hair cut. His skin still lightly tanned even from the scant sun we'd had the past week. He smiled with his beautiful mouth, putting his arms around my waist, pulling me closer to him, his hands stroking my arms. I felt myself melting, pushing my hips out to his. I nestled my head into the nape of his neck.

'Are you OK, honey?' he said softly. 'You seem a little quiet.'

I pulled away. 'I'm just a bit preoccupied,' I found myself saying. 'With schoolwork . . . I have big exams coming up . . .'

'You need me to help you?' he asked, ruffling my hair. 'I could test you.' He grinned. 'Tutor you.'

I bashed his arm lightly. 'I bet you would. I'm not sure I'd be able to focus . . . with you as my teacher.'

'Maybe you need a break.' He stroked my hair. 'Spend some time with your boyfriend.'

I batted away the inexplicable discomfort I felt

then. 'You're probably right,' I sighed, and watched his eyes wander to settle on something behind me. He frowned.

'What?' I said.

'Nothing.' Evan smiled. 'I just saw a bird . . . out of your window.'

I turned to find nothing but the swaying treetops. 'I don't see it.'

'It's gone,' he said brightly, but he let go of me and moved over to the chest, where he briefly examined his reflection in the mirror above it.

'Let's go out,' he said, in a different kind of voice. Higher, nervy.

'Evan?' I stared at his back, catching his eye in the glass. 'What just happened?'

I saw his expression change, trying to relax. He rubbed at his temples and turned back to face me.

'Nothing happened,' he said dismissively. 'You're so sensitive.'

I stared at him, hurt and confused. 'I was only asking—'.

'Let's go out,' he repeated, refusing to catch my eye. 'You'll need a cardigan or something . . . it's going to be chilly later.'

'Fine.' I riffled through the clothes on my chair,

feeling flustered and flat at the same time. I found a crumpled black cardigan and stuffed my arms through the sleeves, aware of Evan watching me though I had my back to him.

'OK. I'm ready now.' I had no enthusiasm for going out, and was wondering whether to confront him, but Evan always seemed to empty my head of all the questions I wanted to ask.

I felt his hands on my shoulder, heard his breathing as he slid them down and round my waist from behind.

'I'm sorry, I'm a bit moody I guess,' he said into my hair. 'I can't explain it, I just get a sad feeling sometimes.'

He sounded so remorseful that I wriggled gently out of his grasp to face him.

'And I'm sensitive,' I said, scanning his face. 'We make a fine pair.'

He grinned then. 'Never a dull moment at least,' he said.

I smiled back, but I felt unsafe. A part of me wanted to push Evan on to my bed and give way to the strong attraction I felt for him. Another part of me wanted something more steady, more reliable, something I could trust. But I leaned in and kissed him quickly on the cheek. 'Walk? We can take the dog.'

* * *

Evan and I ended up on the other side of Bale, much to Bobby's delight, but to my slight trepidation. We were a little too near to Evan's house for my liking. I wondered if he was going to engineer one of his 'goodwill' missions and take me home to bond with Sarah again. But he showed no sign of it, though he seemed lost in thought as he walked. I was putting on a good show of relaxed contentment, but thoughts, questions were gathering in my head. I started thinking about the cuttings I'd found in Evan's car that night. Wondering if his mood shifts had something to do with that . . . But I didn't know how to broach the subject. I was wary of him. But until I knew, I couldn't feel easy holding his hand, chatting to him. It seemed like a secret he had, and I was beginning to discover that I didn't like secrets. Not one bit.

Eventually, the cluster of cottages that lined one side of the road out of Bale stopped us in our tracks.

'End of the road,' I said. 'I'd better be getting back.'

'Wait,' he said abruptly. 'Not yet.'

I frowned slightly. 'What's up?'

He hesitated for a moment. 'I'm thinking . . . I'm wondering . . . how you feel about me. I mean . . . If you really like me, or are you just bored and I'm like a distraction?'

'Of course not.'

He shifted his feet awkwardly. 'I don't get attached to people. To girls.' He looked hard at me. 'It's not something I take lightly.'

'I know.' Where was he going with this? 'And I really like you. But we've just started going out . . . It's a little early . . .'

'Sure,' he said. 'It's just I'm sticking around for the summer because of you . . . I can't work out whether you see this as casual, like a short-term thing, or whether you want me to stay . . . longer.'

I opened my mouth, taken aback. Only a few weeks ago I'd seen his cynicism towards relationships. All that stuff about choosing to love. What he was saying now didn't make sense.

'What do you want me to say?' I wrapped my arms around my body. 'I hardly know you . . . There are so many things I don't know about you . . .' I took a step closer to him.

'Like what?' A couple of lines appeared on Evan's forehead. 'I've told you everything about me.'

'You haven't told me about why you ran away? You kind of just skimmed over it.'

He drew in his breath and the silence was prickly. 'You really want to know?'

'Of course I want to know.'

I wasn't going to bring up what I'd seen in the back of his car. He'd think I had pried. Gone behind his back.

'You must have felt quite strongly . . . to just disappear,' I said. 'I mean your mum—'

'She didn't care,' he snapped. 'She put on a good show, I'll give her that. But she was lost in her own world. Her boyfriends. The alcohol she got through every night. She didn't even notice I was there most of the time.'

'So you ran away . . . to get her attention?' I said, tentatively.

He shook his head and gave a strange humourless laugh.

'Not exactly. It was her I was running away from. Her fits of anger. The fact that she didn't get out of bed till midday and that our house was dirty and squalid and no matter how many times I cleared up, by the next day it was all filthy again.'

'I'm sorry,' I said, thinking how I took my own mother for granted. 'What was wrong with her?'

'Depressed,' he muttered. 'But wouldn't do anything about it . . . Not until she suddenly realised I was gone. And then she got frightened and started acting like the concerned parent. I guess *she* wanted the attention. She even got to be on TV in Australia.' He shook his head. 'Everyone thought she was a saint.' He looked at me.

'You'd think that, if you met her. She can be so "normal" when it suits her.'

I took hold of his hand, which felt freezing for some reason. 'Evan. I can see how you'd be weird about relationships. I mean . . . I've never been involved with a boy before a few months ago. I have no idea what I'm doing. But I do know I am incredibly attracted to you. And I admire you . . .' I paused. 'I think you're kind of moody sometimes, but you have your reasons for that I guess. Your family . . .'

Evan gripped my hand tightly. 'I've got you now, though. You're like my family . . .'

I smiled as brightly as I could back at him, but his intensity and the responsibility that came with his last statement felt heavy and oppressive. I knew I'd never fall for a regular laid-back type, but was Evan more than I could cope with?

I left Evan in town and walked back with Bobby. I should have been skipping home, ecstatic that someone like him felt that way about me. The freak. But instead I felt anxious. And in a corner of my heart I felt a sort of homesickness.

For Luca. Who made me feel neither of those things. I had no idea how love was supposed to feel, and I guessed that it isn't about feeling at home with somebody or even being understood. That's what friends are for. Being in love is about excitement and challenge and your heart wanting to burst out of your chest.

Wasn't it?

The house was quiet when I got back. Dad was working outside as I came to the end of the track and he waved at me, whistling to Bobby. Mum was doing something in the kitchen and Dot was engrossed in something on TV. I slipped upstairs to my bedroom and stood staring at myself in the mirror. I felt about a hundred years older than I had before I'd met Evan . . . and Luca.

I glanced down, to find the photograph – my souvenir from Nissilum. But it was not where I'd left it. I frowned. I needed that picture.

I went out on to the landing and stuck my head down the stairwell.

'Dot!' I yelled.

'What?'

'Can you come up here for a sec?'

I heard Dot's feeble groan in protest, but she appeared out of the living room, a semi-quizzical, semi-annoyed look on her face.

'I thought you'd gone out with Evan?' she said, craning her head to check out my expression. 'What's the matter with you?'

'Nothing.' I waved dismissively, then dropped my voice to a loud whisper. 'Did you take the photo?'

'What photo?' She screwed up her nose. 'You mean that weird photo of the boy? No.' She rolled her eyes. 'What would I want with a photo of a boy?'

'Fine. It doesn't matter. Get back to whatever crap you're watching on TV.'

Dot rolled her eyes again and turned back into the living room.

I stayed where I was, listening to the TV, to the sounds of my mother in the kitchen. Then I went back into my room and got down on the floor, looking under the chest, under my bed. Nothing.

I growled in frustration. That photograph was my connection with Luca, with a world that otherwise I could easily believe I had only imagined. I sat back on my knees, shutting my eyes. My reality seemed so blurred in that moment. Trying to feel connected to a human boy, someone who was willing to let down his barriers for me. But instead missing a boy whose very existence I couldn't prove to myself, let alone anyone else.

My head felt thick, clouding up, like the worst headache was about to come. I put my hands over my ears, as if that would help. Through the fug in my brain, I could hear words circling, indistinct. I closed my eyes trying to focus on them.

You're not safe.

Clear as a bell, the voice spoke in my head. I opened my eyes, looking around me.

There was no one there.

He is not safe.

The same voice again. My heartbeat was accelerating and I put one hand to my chest.

'Who is it?' I said weakly into the silence of my room.

I can't find you.

'Luca,' I whispered. 'Is it you? Are you here?'

I could almost feel his hands, gently holding my shoulders as I sat, still crouched on the floor. And I put one hand up to take the one I was sure would be there.

But there was nothing.

CHAPTER NINETEEN

Evan was now working part-time with my dad. Helping him out with a few jobs. I should have been pleased. Evan being around more should mean we could start to relax around each other. Mum was even feeding him. But he was a little awkward around her, a bit stiff. He didn't want to talk about his family much and, being my mum, she did.

The truth is when he took a break and we spent time alone together, he was more interested in the physical side of our relationship. Every conversation I started he'd stop by kissing me, or telling me how pretty and sexy I was. He was attentive and gorgeous and he took my breath away, especially when he was outside working with Dad, wearing a faded, floppy T-shirt that accentuated his muscular arms. Yes, I still wanted him. His touch still made my skin tingle. But lately he seemed almost needy.

I wanted us to talk. I wanted him to tell me more about himself, but all we did was lie about, making out with each other.

As hot as he was, that was starting to lose its appeal.

'He's a quiet boy, isn't he?' Mum said after he'd gone home one evening and we were sitting in the kitchen. 'I get the feeling he had a rough childhood.'

'He did,' I said, flipping through my GCSE Maths revision notes. I'd be lucky if I scraped a pass.

'Oh?' She was curious. 'What happened?'

'His mum was a depressive. That's why he ran away.'

'Really?' Mum looked shocked. 'Poor kid. Poor woman.'

'Hmmm.' I put down my notes. 'But it's so hard, Mum. He's so coiled up in that way. He's happiest when he's chopping up bits of wood, or driving around, or playing with the dog . . . doing physical stuff. It's like everything else is out of bounds.'

'Not everyone is lucky enough to have two parents together and relatively sane,' she said, getting up and taking some pastry out of the fridge. 'You should have a little more compassion. I know you had a horrible time at school. But you had us. He's had to mature very quickly. His life has been more complicated.'

Not as complicated as Luca's, I thought.

'But things are different now. He's free of all that stuff . . . yet he still acts like the mixed-up kid.' I sighed. 'It's not like he's *talking* about it . . . I wish he would. But it's hanging over him all the same. I'm not sure I can just ignore it. But . . . I'm not sure I'm ready for it either.'

Or I didn't want to be. It was funny how I had entangled myself willingly with Luca, yet I wasn't prepared to do the same with Evan.

'He's dealing with trauma,' said Mum. 'He's not going to get over it just like that.' She frowned. 'You need to grow up a little. People aren't perfect.'

'I know.' I was being immature. Maybe I had got a little spoiled. Got used to having Luca and Evan meeting all my needs between them. Mum was right. And Luca wasn't here. If he and I really had that strong a bond between us, why hadn't I seen him since the ball? I remembered his words to Lowe that night. He couldn't have been more clear. His feelings for me were just platonic, whereas Evan wanted me as his girlfriend.

I picked up the notes again and scraped back my chair.

'I'm going upstairs to do some more revision,' I said grumpily.

Mum stopped rolling out the pastry to look up at me, concerned.

271

'It'll work itself out, you know,' she said, with a half-smile. 'It always does.'

CHAPTER TWENTY

I pulled myself together after Mum and I had our chat. You can't have everything. And what I had was pretty good. I had a lot to look forward to. Everything was just fine.

So when I looked up to see Luca finally in front of me, I couldn't account for the happiness I felt, along with the shock.

His face had a little more colour to it, his green eyes vivid against his skin. I couldn't help the broad smile stretching over my face. How could I have ever thought he looked weird?

'You came!' I said stupidly. 'How did you—?'

'Sssh.' Luca put his finger to my lips. 'I can't stay long . . .' His eyes ran over my face. 'I'm sorry I haven't been here . . . I was . . . I saw things. I didn't know what to . . .' He hesitated, looking anxious. 'But I couldn't stay away any longer. I had to see you.'

I wasn't really listening to what he was saying. All I could think was that I knew he wouldn't abandon me. Deep down I knew he'd come back. Everything was going to be all right.

I grinned stupidly at him, ignoring his serious expression.

'I'm so glad to see you,' I said. 'I've missed you more than I ever thought—'

He put his hand on my arm and it felt ominous. 'I came to warn you.'

'Luca, what is it? Has something happened . . . ?'

'Listen, Jane,' he said firmly. 'I have been seeing things. Bad things. Things I can't make sense of, but I had to warn you.'

I was starting to feel scared. 'Warn me about what?'

Luca's eyes darted about nervously; he sat awkwardly on Dad's bench, where I'd come to get away from my confused feelings. Or sort them out. Or something.

'Evan,' he said. 'Evan is not good for you.'

I frowned. 'You've been getting more of those pictures in your head?'

Luca nodded. 'He's just not what he seems, Jane. There's something not right about what he's saying to you . . . I don't know why, but I have this feeling he is going to hurt you.'

I stared at him for a few seconds before the smile returned to my face.

'Come on . . . This is a joke, right?'

'I tried to speak to you yesterday . . . I thought you could hear me . . .' Luca held my gaze. 'I know you could hear me.'

'I heard you . . .' I recalled Luca's words the day before. 'You're serious, aren't you?'

He looked right into my eyes. 'I hope not. But I hardly ever get premonitions—'

'Wait a minute,' I interrupted him. 'Premonitions?'

I realised I was glaring at him. As happy as I had been to see him when he arrived, my mood had changed. Why did everything have to be so intense? Wasn't it enough that I was straddling two different worlds; that I had a boyfriend like a Greek god who was inexplicably devoted to me? Now here was Luca, who had come into my life and turned it upside down with his 'premonitions'.

Luca didn't blink, though he did look distressed. Another thing that was bugging me. Why couldn't everyone just lighten up?

'Yes,' he said finally. 'I first had them when I was about eight years old. When my parents turned in the Green Forest – near the Water Path. My father was nearly killed by a renegade vampire. I was turning myself then, though my age meant I returned to human form quickly. I went back to our home and was thrown against the bedroom wall by a scream that ripped through my skull.' He paused for breath, his eyes darkening at the memory. 'Ulfred escaped, though he was badly wounded. He and Henora found me crouched under the bed, shaking.'

'How awful,' I said, inadequately. It was hard to know what to say.

'It's not a gift. It's more of a curse, except – except when it can make a difference. I didn't tell you before, I hoped I'd got it wrong.'

'You *have* got it wrong,' I told him. 'Evan's a little moody at times, but he would never hurt me.'

'Are you sure about that?' Luca watched me.

'Yes!' I threw up my hands, exasperated and angry. 'This is starting to annoy me. I don't see you for weeks at a time, and then you turn up and decide to stir things up for me. Just so that I can't move on. You don't want me, but no one else can have me either.' I shut my eyes and softened the tone of my voice. 'I mean . . . it's probably subconscious or something. You don't know you're doing it. But maybe that's what's happening here.'

'Is that what you think?' he said. 'That I don't want—'

'Stop!' I put my palms over my face, covering my eyes.

'Just leave me alone. I can't deal with this any more.' Somewhere inside I felt bad about what I was saying, but I was tired of feeling confused about me and Luca.

'This is a disaster,' I heard him say.

'Luca.' I sighed, dropping my hands to look up at him. 'I think it's time we both accepted that you and I can never have a normal relationship. It's all too weird, and dangerous, and . . . and I hate keeping secrets. I think we should just get on with our separate lives.'

I held my breath.

'If that's what you want,' he said softly. 'Of course.'

I nodded, turning away from him, too tired to know how I felt.

All I could hear was the beating of my heart as I waited for him to leave.

When I turned back two minutes later a squirrel had positioned itself in the middle of the path, chewing on something. And Luca had gone.

You know that feeling you get after you've said or done something that you can't take back? You feel scared but you feel a little bit euphoric. At first. But when the drama has died down, you just feel flat and regretful and you can't remember why you felt so strongly. And you wish you could take back your words and go back in time.

That's exactly what I felt the day Luca disappeared. Or rather, the day I told him to go. I spent the rest of the afternoon in my bedroom, hating myself, feeling flat and empty. I fought against the guilt for a while, but then I began to panic. Was Luca right? Maybe Evan was bad for me? The more I turned it over in my mind, the more I doubted I'd done the right thing.

I tried willing myself to Nissilum; shutting my eyes and saying it over and over. But nothing happened. I just had to wait until Luca came back to me.

If he ever came back.

In the days that followed I was subdued. Inside I felt wretched. I'd look around the table at my mother and father and Dot, oblivious to the thoughts swirling in my head. My mother would reprimand Dot for leaving her vegetables, my dad would sheepishly thumb through a brochure called *Timber World*, forking food into his mouth. Nobody noticed my glazed expression.

I took to taking the dog for long walks, up through the trees, hoping, I suppose, to bump into Luca. I climbed right to the top once, and stood looking up rather than down, studying the moon as it sat, distant and bashful in the daylight, waiting to turn from a faded white sliver to a glowing presence in the night sky.

Everything was back to normal it seemed. No more pale werewolf-boy.

Eventually I made up my mind. I needed to focus on Evan. I needed to forget all about the stuff with Luca. It wasn't real, none of it. It never really had been. It was just . . . a phase.

I still dreamed of it at night, though. Nissilum. One night I was back there and this time it was Lowe, not Luca, who was waiting for me by the Water Path. He stood, hostile, with eyes narrowed and when I saw him he got to his feet and walked towards me.

'He never wants to see you again,' he told me, his eyes travelling across my face, not with any malice, but with a warning look. 'You cannot come here again.'

And then, as I moved to step past him, his hand reached out to stop me.

'You should have listened to him,' he said then, though I didn't understand what he meant. 'You will see.'

And then he was gone and the trees were filled with eyes and faces. And beyond the trees, whispering bodies moving, watching.

I stepped back and felt one foot stepping into thin air, and I remembered the water behind me. Panicking, I put one arm out to a smiling figure in front of me who reached to take it. But as the arm pulled me closer, I saw the white skin and tumbling dark hair and the ruby-red mouth.

'I'm so glad you're back,' purred Vanya, digging a long, black nail into my flesh. 'I hope we can be friends.'

I opened my mouth but my scream was silent and as I wrenched my arm away, Vanya's smile grew even more lascivious.

'Come again, dear,' she whispered. 'Luca needs you.'

I came back. I found the way back, all by myself and I am writing this next to a curve in the river, waiting for you. I need to say goodbye and see you one more time. And I hope you will know where I am. I will wait for you. Remember, whatever happens, that I wish with all my heart I didn't have to choose. But I nearly lost my mother, and now that she is well again, I cannot leave her. It is part duty, part love. But as for that other kind of love . . . I will never have anything as strong, as thrilling, as I have known with you.

If you don't come, I'll understand. But know that my heart is broken. I am leaving this book here because this is the last time I will come. I hope you will find it and read all that I have been thinking these past few weeks. My time with you has been the most beautiful dream –

that is how I will think of it, at least. Forever preserved in my memory as something precious.

CHAPTER TWENTY-ONE

'I'm never going back,' said Evan, as he lay with one arm around me on my bed.

I rested my head on my elbow. 'Really?'

'There is nothing there . . . except for my mum,' he said quickly, almost as though she was an insignificant afterthought. 'I'd rather be with you.'

'What exactly do you see in me?' I asked him. 'I mean . . . there must be a queue of girls lining up to be with you.'

He gave me a lopsided smile. 'I don't see them . . . I can't get my head around why you can't see how great you are, Jane. You're beautiful but you're not vain. You're clever but you're modest.' He paused. 'You have substance.'

'You're right.' I sighed. 'I can't see it.'

He nodded. 'It's not surprising. After what

happened . . . But you have to try and forget about the past. What Sarah did . . . It was nothing to do with you. It was her stuff. She's got her own "issues" . . . from her real dad. He wasn't a nice person from what I gather. Used to beat up her mum. She had a hard time of it. Felt pretty powerless.'

I attempted a sympathetic look, but I don't think I pulled it off.

'I didn't know that,' I said instead. 'I guess that explains things.'

'You mean like her craving for power,' Evan said.

I laughed then. 'Now you mention it, yes.'

'I'm not saying you should excuse her,' he went on. 'Just try and see how the root of all the bad stuff about Sarah is not about you. You were just in the wrong place at the wrong time.'

'Hmmm.' I picked at the quilt. 'I was happy just hating her and blaming her for everything that's gone wrong in my life. But I guess nobody is born evil.'

'I don't know about that.' Evan shrugged, his voice quieter now. 'But most people are born good.'

'You're so wise.' I prodded him playfully. 'How did you get to be so mature for your age?'

'Crap happening. It can make you examine human nature a little more closely, I suppose.'

'I'm sorry about your mum,' I said, hoping he was going to open up. 'I can't imagine what—'

'It's OK,' Evan interrupted. 'I don't want – need – to talk about it. I've dealt with it . . . I'm dealing with it.' He shook his head. 'Man, this conversation has suddenly got very—'

'Deep? I like deep. Better than shallow, I guess.'

Evan stroked my cheekbone with his finger. 'Seriously, shallow is something you will never be.'

'Oh, I have my moments,' I murmured. 'Definitely.'

Evan leaned in closer to me and, having felt overwhelmed by him only days earlier, I felt glad now to be adored by him. Evan was able to love me. And he lived in my world. It was so much more straightforward.

His mouth softly met mine, his eyes open as he kissed me, and my hips moved involuntarily towards his. Gently he put one hand on my stomach, stroking it through my T-shirt, and I wriggled in response, reaching out to pull his shirt out, touching his strong stomach, feeling it contract. And then his gentleness became something else, something hungry. He slid his palm up higher and then round to my back, where his fingers found the fastener to my bra and skilfully undid it.

'Evan,' I breathed, pulling away slightly in token resistance, when not one part of me wanted him to stop.

He held my gaze as he carried on doing what he was doing, pulling my face towards his with one firm movement and kissing me again, harder. My body was way ahead of my mind, it was giving my feeble brain instructions it had no choice but to obey and I kissed him back, just as forcefully. Before I knew it, my T-shirt was over my head and he was kissing my stomach. I lay back, knowing I should find the strength to stop it, when he looked up.

'Is this OK?' he asked softly. 'Tell me if you want me to stop.'

I nodded, reassured by his words. This wasn't like when we'd gone camping.

'Jane!' My mother's voice rang out from the landing, totally ruining the moment. 'Enough time in the bedroom. Evan should be on his way home.'

I sighed and rolled my eyes at him, and he made a disappointed puppy-dog face in return. He brushed his hair back with his hand, then levered himself on to his knees and began fastening the buttons on his shirt.

I looked down at my practically naked top half, relieved to see that my bra was still covering me – just about – and automatically wrapped my arms around my chest for good measure.

'I'm sorry,' I said, meaning it. 'My mother has obviously had us on a timer today . . .'

'It's fine.' Evan got off the bed and gestured for me to do the same. I put my T-shirt back on and joined him and he put his arms around me, nuzzling my neck with his face.

'I love you, Jane,' his voice said, muffled, and as I wondered awkwardly how to respond, he lifted his head and put a finger to my lips. 'You don't have to say anything back,' he told me, smiling. 'I just wanted to let you know.'

All of a sudden I felt ridiculous for being so hung up on Luca. Evan was just perfect in every way.

'Thanks, Evan,' I said softly. 'That's good to know.' I reached over to do up another button on his shirt.

But I couldn't say it back. I guess my heart wasn't completely there.

CHAPTER TWENTY-TWO

May Day found me standing with my parents on Bale's minuscule village green watching Dot, hand in hand with Cassidy, skipping around a maypole.

'This place is stuck in a time warp,' I said wryly, restraining the dog, who was anxious to join in. 'I swear I just spotted Tess of the D'Urbervilles over by the cake tent.'

My mother dug me in the arm with her elbow. 'Stop it. It's charming.'

'I suppose so.' I waved limply at Dot, who was loving the attention. 'In a nauseating kind of way.'

Ten little girls, dressed in frilly white frocks and their best shoes, giggled and shrieked, tossing ribbons around their heads as the accordion player upped the tempo. It was too much for Bobby, who began barking jealously.

'Go and take the dog somewhere else,' Mum said out of

the corner of her mouth, managing to smile at her youngest daughter at the same time.

'Oh,' I said, mock-disappointed. 'But I'm having so much fun.'

She turned, rolling her eyes. 'Oh go away, spoilsport. Go and find something miserable to do.'

I sighed, tugging Bobby away. 'See you back home, then. After Dot has thrown up from all the excitement.'

I rubbed the dog's ears and wandered over to a stall selling homemade cider. My dad's friend, Ted, lifted his hat in greeting and held out a tray bearing miniature shot glasses.

'Sample some cider?' he said, winking before lowering his voice. 'I won't tell your dad.'

'Thanks, Ted.' I smiled, shaking my head. 'It's seriously tempting but I'd better not.'

'Whatever happened to teenage rebellion!' He emptied the contents of a glass into his mouth. 'Lightweights, the lot of you. Have a little fun once in a while, why don't you?'

I grinned, moving on. He was right, I should have a little fun, and as I rounded the green, passing by the jam tent and then some women assembling the raffle prizes, I wondered if Evan was here. He said he'd come along, though a quaint village fête was hardly his thing.

I stopped and watched a bunch of boys kicking a football around, shouting at each other, and then checked my watch. Half past three. The rest of the afternoon stretched in front of me.

'Want some heather?' said a light, familiar voice. 'It will bring you luck.'

I turned, my skin prickling, to see long, dark hair, plaited loosely, and large dark eyes, staring up at me.

'Dalya,' I breathed, taking in her girlish ensemble of a floral dress with small white collar and a neat knitted shawl. 'What on earth are you doing here?'

'Quiet,' she whispered as Bobby began growling. She placed one palm on his head and the motion quietened him. She obviously had a way with her distant relatives that had evaded Luca. 'I am a stranger, Miss.' Her eyes danced with mischief as she held out the foil-wrapped heather. 'One of your mortal pounds,' she said, smiling. 'And no pennies at all.'

My lips twitched and I just stopped myself from touching her. Her resemblance to her brother was comforting. I dug out a pound from my back pocket and handed it over.

'Thank you, Miss,' she said meekly, staring curiously at the coin before looking up at me. 'I can show you where the heather grows, if you like.' She stared around us, smiling sweetly at a middle-aged couple who were walking by. 'You can pick your own luck.' As her head swivelled back, I wondered at her meaning. But before I could work it out, she gently touched my arm. 'It's not far.'

I looked down at the dog, who had settled himself in a heap on the ground, uncharacteristically passive. 'What have you done to the dog?' I said cautiously. 'He looks like he'd been drugged.'

'Just a little sorcery,' she said, looking pleased with herself. 'He'll be a bit floppy for a while before it wears off.' She turned her face up to the sky. 'In about an hour of your mortal time.' She dropped her head, noticing my anxious expression. 'Don't worry. It's really quite harmless.' She nodded quickly and turned to make her way off the green while I followed her.

Dalya seemed to know exactly where she was going and before long we were away from the crowds, heading for the deserted streets. She moved stealthily, elegantly, finally coming to the base of the mountain, where she stopped.

'Why have you come?' I asked, breathless from keeping up with her.

She studied me seriously, then said, 'Luca is in confinement. Lowe has told our parents everything . . . Luca is unhappy.'

'I'm sorry. This is my fault. I should never—'

'Luca has a mind of his own,' she interrupted me firmly. 'He is also sensitive.'

'I know that.' I smiled sadly.

She sighed deeply. 'I don't want Luca to be hurt. He will follow his heart . . . if he is able to . . . And it's dangerous. But . . .' She paused. 'He is concerned for you.'

'I know . . . But there is no need.' I looked around us. 'I am safe. This is not Nissilum. I have the freedom to make my own choices . . . Be with who I want. Extricate myself if I want. There is nothing to worry about.'

'You don't understand.' She held my gaze. 'He has a sixth sense.'

'Yes,' I said, starting to feel irritated again. 'He told me about his premonitions.'

Dalya's eyes narrowed. 'You don't take them seriously, though,' she said. 'You don't take him seriously.'

'Of course I do. But . . . Luca was not specific. Whether he knows it or not, I think he has his own agenda as far as Evan is concerned.'

She put her hands on her hips. 'That may be . . . But he is not a liar. He is a good, honest person. He wants to protect you.'

'So, what should I be doing?' I raised an eyebrow at her.

'Keep away from him.' Her tone was final, her face expressionless. 'Stop seeing him.'

Irritation flared up again. 'Listen, Evan is here, he doesn't live in a remote, parallel world. He wants to be with me, and he can be. There is no unhappy ending here.'

It sounded good. It sounded convincing enough.

She shook her head. 'You haven't noticed anything . . . odd about Evan?'

'No!' I glared at her. 'And if you think there is something "odd", then tell me. Tell me what I should be frightened of.'

'I can't tell you that. Luca has a feeling . . . a strong feeling.'

'Sorry.' I rolled my eyes. 'Not good enough.'

Dalya paused. 'Very well then. Do what you want. I risked punishment to come here. But I see you are stubborn—'

'I'm not stubborn,' I said indignantly. 'I just—'

'It's fine.' She pulled her shawl over her shoulders. 'I have said what I came to say. And now I must go.'

She pushed past me, walking slowly to the trees that marked the beginning of the ascent up the hill. As she reached the small wood, she turned, smiling sadly back at me.

'I wish you luck,' she called. 'Believe me, you will need it.' And then she moved into the trees and I lost sight of her.

I stood for a while, staring. Feeling scared all of a sudden. It had to mean something that Dalya had risked so much to come here and warn me, but I still couldn't believe or trust that Luca's motives were anything but self-serving. It would be very convenient if Evan was bad for me.

I got back to the house, finally. I had sat for hours, watching the clump of trees where Dalya had disappeared, experiencing regret for being so short with her, so disbelieving. I turned everything over in my head. Why did the thought of Luca being right make me feel angry and defensive? If I didn't believe him – if I really thought it was nonsense – then why had it riled me like it did?

Because I wasn't sure. I had heard everything Evan had to say about his past, and it explained a lot, but there was something . . . something I couldn't put my finger on, that wasn't quite right.

So I stayed, sitting on the grass as it grew damp with dew beneath me, staring at some unremarkable trees as though they would untangle my thoughts and create a solution.

Eventually the moon's gauziness turned to opaque white and the sky surrounding it darkened. I got to my feet, rubbing the goosebumps on my arms, and I ran up the hill, up the track, arriving at our back door, feeling comforted by the light on in the kitchen, and the figure of my mother washing dishes in the sink. She looked out of the window at the sound of my tread and I smiled at her, glad to be home. But she didn't smile; she seemed to look through me.

I felt a lurch in my chest. Sensed something was wrong.

I took off my shoes in the hall and shut the back door. The television was on in the living room – a talent show – and I heard Dot laughing at what my dad was saying. Something smelled good and I realised I was starving.

'What's for dinner?' I said, walking through into the kitchen. Mum had her back to me, but I noticed where her eyes were looking – in the reflection in the window. Straight at me.

'Mum?' I put one hand on the back of the kitchen chair. 'What's the matter?'

She didn't answer, but she took her hands out of the sink and wiped them on a tea towel. And then she turned, putting her hands behind her as she leaned back against the sink.

'Where have you been?' she said quietly.

'Nowhere,' I said, watching her. 'Well . . . nowhere in particular. Just walking, you know. How was—'

'You've been there,' she cut in abruptly. 'My God. Why didn't I know this was going to happen . . . ?' She dropped her head then, looking down at the floor. 'I mean, there is no reason why . . . But they told me it was unfinished, that it wasn't over.'

'Who?' I frowned as though confused, but my grip on the chair tightened. 'What's unfinished?'

'Stop being obtuse.' She looked straight into my eyes. 'Pretending.' She shook her head. 'You've been pretending for months, I see now.'

I opened my mouth, but words refused to come. I stood, waiting for her to say something else. But she just watched me. Her eyes boring into my soul, or that's what it felt like. I always thought that was a stupid, meaningless expression. Until that moment.

'Mum, you're freaking me out. What are you talking about?'

'It's happening to you . . .' she faltered. 'It happened to me, too. I had the dreams, I had the longing. And out of nowhere I suddenly had everything I wanted.'

My eyes widened. 'Wait a minute . . . Are you—'

'Nissilum.' She shook her head. 'I've been there, too.'

I sat down with a thump on the kitchen chair.

'Oh my God,' I said, putting my hands up to my face. 'It's almost a relief . . .' I looked up at her. 'I had these dreams. So intense. Every night. Just before my birthday . . .'

She sucked in her breath, sharply, fearfully, but she didn't speak.

'And this boy . . .' I went on.

'Who?' she said sharply. 'Which boy?'

'He's . . . he's called Luca. He's . . . I don't know where to begin . . . He's like my best friend.'

She nodded. 'Yes. But *what* is he?'

'A . . . well, he's part human . . . part wolf,' I said, feeling stupidly ridiculous.

She shut her eyes. 'I fell in love with someone on Nissilum,' she told me. 'Utterly and completely. I have never felt so happy, and so ill, at the same time.'

Suddenly something fell into place.

'You wrote a journal,' I whispered.

'The one hidden in your chest of drawers,' she said. 'Yes.'

I felt like everything was closing in on me.

Mum moved closer and pulled out a chair next to me. Her face was strained. And something else clicked inside me.

'Gabriel,' I said in shock, as the truth struck home. 'It was Gabriel you fell in love with.'

I saw pain in her face. Her eyes clouding over with memory.

'So many years ago . . .' she said tearfully. 'It all came back when I read what I'd written. So intense. So painful . . .'

'Mum.' I took a step closer. 'It's OK.'

Her head snapped upright and this time her expression was clear defiance.

'You have no idea,' she said curtly, her eyes scanning my face. 'I knew this would come back to get me. I knew there would be consequences.'

I shut my eyes quickly then opened them again. 'OK.' I tried to sound together, calm. Inside I was panicking. I had never seen her like this. 'I've got it under control. It's . . . it's over in fact.'

'Is it?' She held my gaze. 'I didn't want to face up to it, when I heard you moving about at night . . .'

She got up suddenly and walked over to the counter, opening a drawer and pulling out the familiar shabby cover. She pressed the book to her chest. 'I was tidying up your room . . . I nearly had a heart attack.'

'Luca found it. He knew it was connected to me. Neither of us knew why.'

Mum stroked the cover of the book.

'Such a long time ago. I didn't think . . .' Her eyes flickered to the door. 'Your dad . . . he doesn't know . . . he thinks—'

'That some guy broke your heart,' I cut in. 'Some ordinary mortal.'

She nodded and her eyes glistened. 'How could I tell him the truth? That I fell in love with an angel, from a world beyond his comprehension?'

'Tell me about it.' We looked at each other and a small smile crept on to her face. She was soft again.

'Poor Janey,' she said, in a voice I hadn't heard since I was five years old. 'You're in love with him.'

'It's not what you think, Mum,' I said firmly. 'He's my friend. Just my . . . my very good friend.'

'Your soulmate.'

'Yes.' I nodded. 'Like he knows me inside and out . . . and he's always going to be there for me.'

She smiled properly then. 'That's not love? That's just friends?'

'Evan is my boyfriend,' I said feebly.

She took a step closer to me and held out her arms. 'Sweetheart,' she said quietly, 'come here.'

I didn't move, because I was too old for hugs. I'd never been a huggy kind of girl. But those arms looked inviting. I felt my body giving in and I moved towards her, letting her wrap me up.

'It's awful, isn't it?' she said. 'It's exactly how I felt . . . I mean, I didn't have anyone else in my life, but for a while I told myself that I didn't have those kind of feelings for Gabriel. I wouldn't let myself.'

'But I *don't* have those feelings for Luca,' I protested. 'I want Evan.'

'Does he know about Luca?'

I shook my head. 'It doesn't matter now. Luca has gone.'

'Your decision?'

'No.' I wriggled and she dropped her hands. 'I didn't have to make a choice like you did . . . Luca knows about you and Gabriel. You're legendary. Mortal females are bad news.'

'I didn't choose . . .' She looked confused and changed the subject. 'And what about Gabriel? Is he well? He must have his own children by now.'

I looked away. 'Mum . . . He had children. But . . . he's gone . . . died, or disappeared or something.' It sounded brutal but there was no other way to say it.

'Gabriel,' she whispered, her face so pale all of a sudden. 'How . . . ?'

'Nobody really knows, but they said a broken heart.'

She looked stricken. 'I never knew.' She looked anxiously at me. 'You know you must be careful,' she said. 'It's intoxicating, that world. Everything so intense. You get drawn in, but you will never be accepted . . .'

'Mum,' I pleaded. 'It is over. I will never see Luca again. And we didn't fall in love.'

'Just because you tell yourself that, doesn't make it real,' she said. 'How do you feel about never seeing that boy again? Tell me.'

'I feel . . .' I stopped. 'I haven't let myself . . .'

'See? You *are* pretending.'

'I'm not you, Mother,' I said angrily. 'This is not your story. It's mine. And it's different.'

I backed away towards the door. Towards the sound of my normal little sister and my dad. 'Just because you messed up, don't put it on me.' I turned away from her, not wanting her to see my fear. My panic.

I knew what I had to do.

I ran until I thought my heart would burst through my chest and my lungs hurt. All the way back to the patch of trees. And it was dark – pitch black – except there was the moon, full and bright, looking down benevolently at me standing, hugging myself at the entrance to the thicket. I didn't feel afraid. I knew now that everything was real. It had been the same for my mother. I couldn't pretend to myself any more.

I watched the little wood, dark shapes flapping gracefully around the branches. Small birds. I craned my neck to see further in and concentrated on that tall, slender boy with milky skin and moss-green eyes. I had to see him, if only one more time.

When an owl called softly I turned my face up to the sky, gaining strength from it. Tiny, bright stars winked encouragingly – and then I felt the faintest breeze, like sweet breath on my neck, and then, as I stood perfectly still, the breeze became warmer. And closer.

'Is this the end?' he whispered.

I didn't turn, I waited.

He put his hand on my shoulder and the feel of his fingertips was like home. I stretched my own hand up and put it over his, touching the fine hairs on his wrist. Finally I found my voice.

'That girl . . .' I began, faltering, 'in the notebook . . . She's my mother. It was her. She knows about us. Everything. Whatever happened to her . . . to make her see your world . . . it has come to me.'

He said nothing, but he rested his chin in the curve of my shoulder. Like a human jigsaw. We felt like the perfect fit.

I took a breath before going on. 'Luca . . . It won't work. How can we be friends? It's doomed . . . Just as it was with my mother and Gabriel. I don't want you to be harmed in any way.'

'But we are not in love,' he spoke at last. 'It's not the same.' His words sounded hollow, though, without conviction.

'I should be with someone whose life does not hinge on the decision I make.' I hardly believed how mature I sounded.

'Evan?' Luca sighed.

I turned to face him. 'Dalya came. Came to warn me off him, too.' I smiled wryly. 'Just what is it about him that worries you?'

He looked thoughtful for a moment. 'I need to show you . . . There is something I have found back home. It may be nothing . . . It may be a coincidence. But I don't think so.'

'What?' I closed my fingers around his wrist. 'Tell me now.'

'You need to see it for yourself. You won't believe me otherwise.'

Back to Nissilum.

'But I can't go back,' I told him. 'You said—'

'I know. But there is no other way. We will

302

just need to be careful.'

I looked back up the hill at my house. It must be dinner time. I needed to get back.

'Maybe tomorrow,' I said, thinking that my mum would be on her guard now. 'She's going to be watching my every move.'

'Jane.' Luca was firm. 'She will understand . . . And I promise you I will get you back here so quickly you will hardly have been gone.'

I still hesitated. Was that just because of my mother? Or was it the thought of what Luca would show me in Nissilum? I couldn't not go. A part of me wanted to. Wanted to still be connected to it all. And there was only one way to reassure Luca that Evan was a good guy. Not the shady character he was making him out to be.

'OK.' I sighed, with resignation. 'Let's go.'

Luca didn't return my smile. The anxiety in his eyes was still there. He took hold of my arms and pressed his forehead to mine.

'I'm sorry,' he said. 'Know that.'

I frowned, not understanding. 'Don't worry about it,' I said. 'You're just looking out for me.'

We arrived, oddly, in a place I didn't recognise at first. I had expected the soothing river of the Water Path, and had also expected night-time. But it was daylight still, and we were crouched by a pale stone wall.

'I had to use all my willpower and it is a little rusty,' whispered Luca. He made a gesture for me to keep silent and got cautiously to his feet, gripping the wall and peering over it.

He looked down and gave me his hand. 'Come on,' he said. 'We are at the palace. It has been in my thoughts, lately, and so I suppose that's why I have brought myself – us – here.'

I stood too, and looked over the wall to see the palace gleaming in the sunlight. A myriad of colourful roses packed the flowerbeds. Immaculate garden furniture was positioned in the middle of the well-kept lawn.

I looked questioningly at Luca.

'We need to get into the palace.' He looked me up and down. 'But you can't go in like that . . . Dalya is bringing you something to wear.'

I looked down at my clothes. Scruffy jeans with a giant hole in one knee and an *I Heart NY* T-shirt Grandma Ellen had brought me back from a holiday in America a couple of years ago. I would stick out like the veritable sore thumb.

As if on cue, Dalya appeared through a gate in the wall further down. Seeing me, she gave me an *I knew you'd be back* kind of look and swung a canvas bag back and forth as she walked quickly towards us. When she reached Luca, she dropped it at his feet.

'I took a uniform,' she said, shrugging at him. 'One of Amelia's. It will be a little big,' she said, staring blatantly at my chest, 'but it will do. And some slippers for her.'

'Thank you.' Luca smiled at her. 'You are a good sister.'

'Hmmm.' Dalya gave me a sidelong look, but her eyes were friendly. 'Well, be careful. You know Lowe is having sport with his gruesome friends. You'd better be quick.'

Luca glanced at me. 'She's right.' He rubbed my shoulder. 'Don't worry. It will be all right. You just need to get dressed.'

I looked around me for somewhere more private to change. But there was nothing except acres of fields. The palace land stretched out for miles in front of us.

'I'll turn my back.' Luca nodded at Dalya. 'And you'd better go home. Tell Henora I will be back in time for the evening meal.'

A flicker of concern passed over Dalya's normally confident expression, but she touched his arm lightly and turned to walk back to the gate.

'She will go back through the palace,' Luca said, his

back to me. 'She's friendly with the servants. No one will think anything of it.'

I picked up the canvas bag and lifted out the heavy, white uniform. 'But won't the servants know I'm an imposter?'

'They will all be in the kitchen,' Luca said. 'Cooking, idling, joking. They will be busy in there for an hour at least.'

I quickly took off my plimsolls and jeans, though I kept my T-shirt on. I'd need the extra padding from the looks of the dress. I pulled it up and buttoned it, feeling it loose and unflattering on me.

'Don't you dare laugh at me,' I said, pushing the slippers on to my feet. 'I look hideous.'

Luca turned, his lips twitching. 'That is not possible,' he said, catching hold of my hair, which hung loose. 'But you need to put this up. I'll help you.'

Before I could protest I felt him gently gather up my hair and twist it into a knot at my neck. His fingers brushing my skin made me close my eyes as I tingled at his touch.

'There,' he said quietly. 'That's better.' As I turned to face him, I had the urge to hold him and never let go. But the sooner this was done, the sooner the drama would be over.

I was convinced that whatever Luca felt compelled to show me would turn out to be insignificant. I couldn't think what it would be. But it was surely not anything to do with Evan.

I felt almost completely sure of that.

I stuffed my own clothes into the canvas bag.

'Here.' He took the bag from me and pushed it into a convenient enclave in the wall. 'It'll be safe here.'

I felt in a dreamlike state. As though I was preparing to act in a period drama. This whole place, the Celestial Palace, was like one of those stately homes plumped in the middle of the English countryside. At any moment a busy-body in a bonnet would appear.

'Jane.' Luca cut into my thoughts. 'This won't take long. You'll be back home before you know it.'

'Yes.' I felt the finality in his words. 'I know.'

He took my hand and we walked casually to the gate.

'Keep a few paces behind me,' he instructed, as he turned the metal handle to walk through to the garden. 'Look as though you have some purpose.'

'Yes, sir.' I smiled. 'Whatever you say, sir.'

He grinned, then stepped ahead of me and we walked through the tranquil space in front of the house, where I spotted a familiar door. It was where we had left last time. After Luca had turned.

I shivered, remembering Vanya. I hoped she was nowhere in the vicinity.

Quietly we moved inside the palace. Down the dark corridor and through to the hall. Ahead of us was the grand staircase, flanked by the family portrait paintings.

'Up here,' Luca whispered. 'If we come across anyone, keep your eyes down.'

Two steps at a time we climbed up, and up, finally stepping inside the spectacular grand room at the top, with its imposing window and the view of endless green fields that seemed to stretch to the ends of the earth. Which perhaps they did.

Inside the room, Luca went quickly to the dark wood chest on top of which was the abundance of photographs. He opened a drawer on the left hand side, and bent down, riffling as quietly as he could through the contents.

I stood by the door, listening for footsteps outside. I watched as he drew out a large book. It looked like one of the scrapbooks I played with when I was little. Newspaper clippings jutted from the pages.

Luca glanced at the anonymous-looking cover before tucking it under his arm and closing the drawer. He looked over at me.

'We have to get out of here,' he said. 'Back the way we came.'

As we hurried down the stairs, a shape flitted across the hall and Luca stopped, drawing me back behind him. The figure carried on, not noticing us where we stood with our hearts in our mouths, and disappeared through the door we were headed for.

Luca frowned. 'We'll have to go out of the front,' he said. 'It's very quiet. Celeste and Cadmium will be sitting in their private rooms. No one will take any notice of us.'

I followed him out through the hall and, to my relief, saw that the door was already open. We moved through it, towards the guarded gates.

Luca went ahead and spoke to the man waiting there, who glanced at me before nodding and gesturing for us to go through.

Finally, when we were some way from the gates and out of sight of the palace itself, I released my breath and stopped.

'That was an experience I never want to repeat,' I said. I glanced at the scrapbook, which Luca still had under his arm. 'Is this the incriminating evidence?'

He looked down at it. 'Let's go back and collect your clothes. And then I will show you.'

Once we had collected the canvas bag, we walked to the Water Path, and only when I had changed back into my clothes and we were perched on the rocks, the water gurgling beside us, did Luca place the book on his lap.

It looked so nondescript. I couldn't believe it could contain anything shocking. Luca opened it to some blank card pages, until he came to the middle where a few newspaper cuttings where stuck, higgledy-piggledy.

'You have newspapers?' I said, twisting my head to look at one of the cuttings.

Luca put his arm over it, obscuring my view. He looked up at me.

'We don't,' he said. 'Which is sort of the point.'

'Luca! Stop talking in riddles.'

Luca held my gaze for seconds longer before he drew his arm away and looked down.

'Celeste found this . . . I heard her talking to one of the servants when I was here yesterday. She thought it belonged to her . . . She'd found it on Raphael's bed. Just lying there . . .'

I raised an eyebrow and he went on quickly. 'I was curious. So when Etta – the maid – was cleaning the hall, I asked her about it. And after some persuasion she told me she had no idea what it was, but that she had put it in a drawer in the room at the top of the stairs until she could have a proper look at it.' He grimaced. 'I immediately went to look myself, and when I started reading these reports, it all fell into place.'

I felt my chest tighten when he said that, and when I glanced at what was stuffed into the scrapbook, my heart nearly rushed through my mouth.

I had seen these reports before.

'Let me look,' I said, breathlessly, grabbing hold of the book.

'Jane,' Luca said anxiously, 'don't make yourself overwrought.'

I ignored him. Instead I frantically scanned what was in front of me. Newspaper cuttings about a kid who'd won a surfing championship. A grainy black-and-white picture of him smiling in his wetsuit, his sun-streaked blond hair flopping over his face.

Another cutting talked of the same boy. Sporty, living with his single-parent mother. A boy who kept himself to himself . . . Who suffered from long periods of depression. Who'd been in trouble with the law. *A TRAGIC WASTE OF YOUTH AND TALENT* ran one caption.

I read on, each cutting about the same boy. The boy with so much potential. Good-looking and devoted to his mum. The boy who'd disappeared. The boy called Evan Daniel Forrest. And then about an unidentified body that had been found, strangled on the beach a year before. And there, underneath the others, the face of the girl who'd seen the boy attacked.

I kept my head down. The blood seemed to have drained from my face, and I scratched helplessly at the card page on which cuttings – photocopies all of them – had been stuck, unable to get my head around what I was looking at.

Eventually, Luca spoke. 'It could be just a coincidence,' I heard him say quietly, without conviction.

I lifted my head.

'No.' I shook my head. 'It's not.'

I heard Luca catch his breath. 'I'm sorry, Jane . . . I didn't want this to be true. Those pictures I kept getting . . . I didn't want you to be in danger.' He knelt down and put his arm around me. The feel of it, solid, protective made me stronger somehow.

'It's fine,' I said blankly. 'Maybe I've known all along. Deep down. Something wasn't right.'

Luca said nothing, just listened.

'I knew it was too good to be true,' I went on. 'That a boy like that could want me. It seemed so . . . ridiculous.'

'What?' I turned to see Luca bewildered, his eyes wide. 'You can't possibly mean that? This is not about you, Jane. Can't you see that? You know what's been going on, don't you?'

I looked back at the scrapbook. 'Yes. Evan Forrest is dead. Which means that the Evan I know is not him.'

'No,' said Luca. 'The Evan you know is Raphael.'

I put my hand to my mouth, a jolt of realisation hitting me. Of course! Evan had taken the photo of Raphael that day. And that meant that he knew about me too. He knew I had been here, to Nissilum.

'Why is he doing this? Why did he go after me?' I looked over at Luca, whose face was twisted in anguish. He reached out for me, but I didn't respond, I felt disconnected from emotion. Kind of numb.

'I think . . .' he said slowly, 'I think it has something to do with Gabriel.' He shook his head. 'Raphael started behaving strangely when Gabriel slipped away. He was so angry. Nobody could console him. He's been looking for someone to blame. I knew there was something dangerous about Evan. I kept getting these . . . horrible flashes of you scared and his presence always there. But I had nothing substantial. It was only today, when I found the book, and all this stuff about Evan going missing, and then the discovery of the unidentified body, that I knew the danger was real.'

I started to get up, panicked. 'Luca . . . this is all about my mother . . .' I paced the grass. 'He wants to get at her through me . . . I have to get back now. She isn't safe.'

I shut my eyes. This was all my fault.

Luca read my thoughts. 'It isn't your fault, Jane, none

of it. How could you have known?'

'Oh God.' I got to my feet, shaking, and Luca grabbed hold of me, pulling me in to him.

'I will not let him hurt you,' he said emphatically. 'Or your family.'

'Luca?' A voice somewhere behind him made me pull away. My heart sank to see Lowe standing, scowling at us through the trees.

Luca turned to his brother. 'Lowe, this is not your business. Leave us.'

Lowe shook his head. 'She should leave. Henora and Ulfred are on their way as I speak. Dalya gave herself away, sneaking around the palace. I had no choice but to inform them.' He smiled almost gently at Luca. 'It is for your own good. You'll see. Some time in the palace cellars will keep you out of danger.'

An angry shadow fell over Luca's face. 'You stupid boy. I can take care of myself, take my own risks and deal with the consequences. And Jane is in danger.'

'Well, she'll have to deal with that by herself.' Lowe's tone was supercilious. I had the urge to slap him.

Luca had not let go of me and I was thankful for his protection. More than that, I felt desperate that he would stay and I would have to go back on my own.

'Lowe,' Luca pleaded. 'After this I will stay. But I have

to go back with Jane. One more time.'

I tried not to dwell on the miserable reality of that last sentence. I had to get home.

'It's all right.' I tightened my hold on Luca. 'I can do this.'

But as Luca pulled away to respond, I saw two horses; astride one was Ulfred, on the other sat Henora, and behind her a stricken-looking Dalya.

'Hell,' Luca whispered. He glared at his brother. 'I will not forgive you for this.'

'You were warned once, brother,' Lowe replied, 'and you promised to abandon mortal Earth. And Jane. Forever.'

'Sometimes life is too complicated to keep promises,' snapped Luca.

'Ah.' Henora stepped ahead of her husband and stood studying her elder son with disappointment. 'I had hoped this was some elaborate story of Lowe's. I am sorry to find you here.' Her glance fell to me, though she avoided eye contact.

'Mother, please. You taught me to be kind, to help others in distress.' Luca begged her. 'Let me help Jane.'

'I'm sorry, boy,' Ulfred put in. 'But you know the rules. And you have disobeyed us twice. Lied to us. We have no choice now but to confine you. Just for a while. So that you can contemplate your actions. And learn obedience.'

I looked at them all. Henora and Ulfred, stern-faced; Dalya, sighing heavily next to them; Lowe looking a little too pleased with himself – and Luca. Luca, torn between his loyalty to his family and to a girl who had caused him nothing but trouble.

'I'm so sorry,' I said. 'None of this is Luca's fault. He has only ever tried to help me. You must believe he is a good son. The kindest, most honourable son you could wish for.'

Henora finally looked me in the eyes.

'I'm sure you mean well, child,' she said coolly, 'but the standards we have here as a family on Nissilum are somewhat different to those mortals abide by. Honour is entirely bound up with family, with breed. I cannot expect you to understand. But you too have lied to us. Forgive me if I hold your words in little esteem.'

Indignation rose inside me, but I held my tongue. Luca was silent now. It was clearly a mistake to challenge Henora. I saw properly how formidable she was.

'Come, Luca.' Ulfred took his son's arm. 'This will not be a pleasant experience. Better to begin your term of confinement now and the sooner it will be over.'

'Father,' Dalya said miserably, 'is this really necessary?'

'Be quiet!' snapped Henora. She looked harshly at

Lowe and Dalya. 'You two get yourselves home. This is not a show for an audience.'

She grabbed at both their hands and pulled them with her as she marched back to the horses. Dalya threw a sad, apologetic smile back at me, while Lowe retained his familiar smirk.

Henora climbed up on to her horse, while Lowe took charge of the other. Reluctantly Dalya got up behind him. 'Goodbye,' she called as Henora led them all out of the forest. 'Good luck.'

Luca tried to look reassuringly at me, but there was no mistaking the fear in his eyes. 'Remember, Jane. Think hard of where you want to be. And you will be there,' he said, as Ulfred shook his head.

'Luca,' he warned, tugging at his arm. 'Let's go. This is not easy for any of us.'

'I will be with you,' Luca called, allowing himself to be led away. 'Somehow.'

'Boy!' growled his father. 'Enough.' He pushed Luca in front of him, blocking my view as they walked away. Luca would be kept in the palace cellar. I shuddered. It was medieval. And cruel.

Luca finally turned his back to me and I gulped back a mixture of fear and intense sadness.

'Goodbye, Luca,' I whispered.

CHAPTER TWENTY-THREE

I sat back down by the river, knowing I should act now, but feeling briefly frozen. I shut my eyes and focussed my mind on home – the voice in my head began to chant it, over and over again. But I was still aware of the pure air of Nissilum and heard the rustle of the leaves in the cool breeze. I tried again, but willing myself not to panic interfered with my greater wish. To be back in my home, to see my mother there, safe. It was all I wanted. Yet somehow, nothing was happening. My body was tensing, frustrated. So when I felt cool hands grabbing hold of mine, my eyes flew open.

'Vanya?'

'Sssh,' she said. 'Mortal girl. I can help you home. No need for all this telekinetic rubbish.' She screwed up her nose. 'It is so unreliable . . . The more you force it, the harder it becomes.'

'I don't need your help,' I said abruptly, adding more nicely, 'Thank you,' in case she cast some kind of spell on me then and there.

She pouted. 'Don't be tiresome, girl.'

Warily, I realised I needed to keep her on side.

'Another time,' I said quickly. 'There'll be another time.'

'I doubt that,' Vanya purred, brushing her black mane out of her eyes. Her face was almost blue it was so pale. And in the daylight she looked older, her face creasing in places it hadn't before.

'Let's get out of this grim light,' she said, pulling at me.

My energy was draining out of me. It was not just the events of the past couple of hours here, it was Vanya's presence. Luca had warned me about her. I struggled not to succumb.

'I have to go,' I said vaguely. 'There's something I have to do.'

'But I want to apologise,' she said in a syrupy tone. 'Staying a little longer won't harm, surely? Come, let me take you home and we can think of a plan to thwart those insufferably self-righteous wolves.' She winced. 'Soon, though. I don't fare well with the sun.'

I squinted into the shard of light coming through the

trees, my head was fuzzy.

'They are a bit self-righteous,' I found myself saying. 'And they've taken him somewhere. They'll lock him up to punish him.'

Vanya cocked her head. 'Who darling? Who have they taken?'

'No one. Nothing. I must go now.'

Vanya moved swiftly to me. One manicured hand just touching my arm.

'We got off rather on the wrong foot at the ball . . .' she flashed a smile, 'as your people would put it. I apologise. It is hard to shed certain innate needs . . .' She examined my face almost kindly. 'It was an aberration. A moment of weakness. I hope you understand.'

I stared at her. 'Weakness is human. I understand weakness. I just don't understand evil.'

Vanya's eyes widened innocently. 'Oh, but I'm not evil. I would not be allowed to reside here in this hell-forsaken world if I were evil.' She pulled back her shoulders and seemed to tower above me imposingly. 'And I would like to help you.'

'You can't help.' I shook my head. 'This needs to be dealt with without tricks and . . . and bloodshed.'

'Oh,' she said, in exaggerated disappointment. 'How boring.'

The sun went behind the trees and I realised how vulnerable I was, standing alone with a vampire.

'Sweet girl,' she said, 'once upon a time I was innocent. Untainted.' She looked sorrowfully down at the water. 'But one can't turn back time . . . One just has to get by . . . somehow.'

She took a step closer and I moved back.

'Just think,' she said, holding eye contact, 'if, hypothetically speaking of course, I were to turn you, then your troubles would be over. You would be free to stay here . . . you would be one of us.'

It was true. I could be here. Everything would be all right. I would belong. It would only take a minute.

'Vanya,' I said, shivering with temptation but forcing myself to think straight, 'I have a home.'

'Ah. Home,' she said wistfully. 'Surely home is where you feel you belong?'

Oh, she was good.

'And leaving that poor smitten boy to pine and . . . wither away. Can you really live with that?'

'I'll have to.' She seemed to glide closer. 'I don't want to be one of you.'

'But what have you got to return to? Betrayal. Loneliness.'

The truth of her words stung, but I knew she was

trying to lull me with her lilting, sympathetic voice. I had to battle the tears that threatened. I felt suddenly drained of strength, my thoughts growing fuzzier by the minute.

'Here you can live forever.' Her voice was distant. 'Just think of that.'

Clouds in my head obscured my thoughts and I tried to clear them. Tried to think. There was something I had to do. Someone I had to stop.

'Raphael,' I said abruptly. 'He betrayed me. My mother is in danger. I have to stop him.'

I felt Vanya's mouth against my ear. 'It is too late for that . . . There is nothing you can do. Wait here, and Raphael will return . . . eventually.'

I came to my senses then. 'You know what he did?'

'Not exactly,' she said. 'But it doesn't surprise me in the least. He's unhinged . . . Of course the angels see no harm in the boy. But he's a psychopath. You mark my words.' She gripped me around the waist. 'And you need me on your side . . . now that Luca is indisposed.'

The gallop of hooves startled us both and hope flared inside me.

'Leave her,' said the rider, glaring at Vanya as she dismounted her horse. 'Just let her go.'

Vanya pulled away from me as I felt the sky, the trees, everything blurring.

'Thank God,' I said, and felt myself falling.

'You really are as green as a goose,' said Dalya, shaking her head as she looked down on me. 'But that woman is powerful. Even us immortals need to be on our guard.'

I sat up on my elbows and realised that the river had gone, and the canopy of leaves. We weren't at the Water Path. We were back on Earth.

Dalya had brought me back home.

She thrust my plimsolls at me, wrinkling her nose. 'You nearly left these behind.'

'Thank you for helping me.' I took the funny little slippers off my feet and replaced them with my trusty plimsolls.

Dalya sighed, sinking down into the grass. 'Luca is my dearest brother. And his wish is my command,' she said solemnly, though there was a flash of humour in her eyes. 'And if he wishes you well . . . then so do I.'

What else did Luca wish? I felt sadness tugging at me. Did he wish he'd never found me in the first place?

'So here you are, and I must be away,' she said lightly, getting back up on her feet. 'Henora and Ulfred may be getting suspicious. It is the early hours of the morning by now.' She puffed out her cheeks. 'Dratted mortal time.'

It was hard to imagine I would never see her again either. And horrible.

'Tell Luca I'm sorry,' I said. 'For everything. And that I will never forget him.'

Dalya gave me an uncharacteristic tender look in return.

'The feeling will be mutual,' she reassured me, and I could have hugged her, had either of us been that kind of girl. 'And be strong. You have the power to outwit Raphael. Just gather it to you and hold it there.'

I nodded, hoping, but not really believing she was right.

CHAPTER TWENTY-FOUR

I trod carefully up the track to the house and arrived to see the back door open. But there was a curious silence. A lack of life about the place that filled me with foreboding. I told myself that my family were home. Of course they were. It was dark. They would be in the living room watching TV. My mum always turned the lights out in the kitchen after dinner.

But my dad always locked the back door.

I took one cautious step further.

'Mum?' I called. 'Dad?'

The house still stood silent in the dark-blue sky. Up above me the moon shone full and white.

I gathered all my strength and walked purposefully towards the back door, through the corridor, round into the hall. There was no noise at all and everything was in darkness.

I switched on the light, swallowing fear. And the clock in the kitchen ticked noisily.

Then saw the dark shape on the kitchen floor.

'Bobby!' I dropped down frantically to the dog, sprawled, motionless. I put my head to his chest and to my relief he was still breathing. But he was more than asleep. I knew that. Looking up I saw the keys to my dad's truck on the table. They couldn't get anywhere at this time of night on foot. They wouldn't. I got to my feet and, without hesitating, I picked up the keys and ran back out of the house to the truck.

I didn't know where I was going to go. I just thought if I drove around for enough time, I'd see something. Find something.

I put the key in the ignition and went through the same motions I had seen my dad go through. After that, I would have to rely on my few driving lessons with Evan.

As I put my foot on the accelerator, I glanced up into the mirror and shunted forward, cautiously down the rough track, turning on to the clear mountain road. I breathed out, relaxing slightly and checked the fuel gauge. Just as the engine started to sputter.

'Damn,' I hissed, keeping pressure on the accelerator. But I was out of gas. And the truck wouldn't move.

I stopped the engine and leaned back, my breath

coming heavily. I must not panic. Or lose it. I had to keep calm. I was safe inside the truck. No one could hurt me in the truck.

I stared uncomfortably at the shapes of the trees lining the road, which were rocking slightly in the night breeze.

And then I saw the figure, trudging towards me. Male, broad-shouldered. I thought for a minute it was Dad . . . but no, this shape was taller, younger . . .

Evan.

I put my hand out to make sure the door was locked and tried to slide further down in my seat, but the figure had seen me, was looking straight at me and crossing the road, heading for the truck.

Quickly I composed myself. Pretend everything is fine, I told myself. Everything is completely normal.

He arrived at my window, bending to peer inside. I smiled as convincingly as I could and he smiled back.

'What happened?' he asked, craning his head to look at the dashboard.

I wound down the window, slowly.

'I thought I'd do some practice. Ran out of fuel.'

'At this time of night?' Evan raised an eyebrow.

'Everyone's gone out,' I said, shrugging. 'I was bored.'

He held my gaze, though I couldn't tell whether he was suspicious, and then he thumped the car door lightly.

'Your dad probably keeps a spare can of fuel in the back,' he said then. 'I'll go and check.'

Without asking for the keys he moved to the back of the truck and I heard him moving things around, looking for Dad's secret stash.

In minutes he was back, waving a familiar-looking, large, plastic watering can. 'Got it. I'll fill her up.'

I sat waiting, thrown by his kindness. But then why wouldn't he be kind? He didn't know I knew . . . He was still play-acting. In that case, so was I.

I unlocked the doors.

Finally Evan finished. He opened the driver's door. 'Shift over,' he said good-naturedly. 'Better if I take it from here.'

I had no choice and shuffled over to the other side as Evan got in.

'So,' he said, his hand on the ignition keys, 'where shall we go?'

'Maybe we should just go home now,' I said, keeping my voice steady. 'Mum and Dad will be back soon and Dad will freak out if he sees the truck's gone.'

Evan gave me a sidelong look. 'I'm sure we've got time for a little drive,' he said. 'It'll be OK.'

He seemed pretty sure about that. I tried not to swallow. Instead I managed a casual kind of shrug.

'OK then . . .'

'Hey.' He put his hand on my leg. 'You seem a little jumpy tonight, Janey . . . Relax.' He moved his hand up my thigh. But the tingling feeling I had was not from excitement this time.

'I was coming up to see you,' Evan said, as he started the engine and the truck continued its descent down the mountain road. 'You did one of your disappearing acts.'

Before I could stop myself I shot him a look. 'Disappearing acts?'

Evan was looking ahead at the road. 'Yeah . . . I called your house. Your mum said you'd gone off somewhere.' He changed gear. 'She sounded a little anxious to be honest. I thought I might run into you if I took myself off for a walk.'

'It's late for a walk. Why didn't you drive?'

Evan hesitated only for a second. 'My dad needed the car for something . . . And I felt like some air.' He turned to smile at me. 'You know the feeling?'

Did he know?

I nodded, wondering if there was some other meaning to his words.

'Where are you taking me?' I tried to sound light. 'I don't want to go far.'

'You'll see,' he said, pressing down on the accelerator

so the truck sped up.

As we rushed through Bale, heading for the other side, anxiety gathered like a little storm inside me. When we left the town and joined unfamiliar winding roads, I felt myself beginning to panic. But that wouldn't help me. I had to stay as calm as possible. I snuck a look at Evan's profile as he drove. His mouth was set in a determined, aggressive kind of way, and his hands gripping the steering wheel were anything but relaxed.

I closed my eyes, pretending to doze. I should never have agreed to come for a drive. I should have insisted on going home. But then again, he would only have come back with me, and then we would have been alone.

In my empty, eerie house.

With my eyes shut, I heard him switch on the radio and the music grew louder. Dad's favourite station. It should have comforted me – instead it just made me, and my family, feel kind of violated. Evan was acting like it was his truck, to do what he liked with.

Evan stopped and I opened my eyes. The truck was parked at the gate to the training ground, which sat gloomy and unwelcoming. I could just make out the curved corrugated roofs of those horrible Nissen huts.

'What are we doing here?' I said, unable to keep the fear out of my voice. 'I don't like it here.'

Evan leaned across and kissed me roughly on the cheek, his stubble scratching me, and I tried not to jerk away. I felt repelled.

'Don't be such a baby,' he said, his hand now on my leg. 'It really is time you grew up.' His breath was heavy, his good-looks masked by that mean, intent expression on his face, in his eyes.

'Evan,' I said, my own breath coming quick and short, 'it's late, and I want to go home.'

Slowly I moved one hand to the door handle, gently pressing down on it. I shifted, as though I was getting more comfortable in my seat.

Evan reached out and traced a line down my cheek, while his other hand moved between my legs. I clamped them together instinctively. 'Get off me,' I said, and this time there was no mistaking the revulsion in my voice.

Before I could blink, his hand shot up and slapped me hard on the face and I screamed, releasing my hold on the door handle. Evan glared at me and locked the door, and I slumped against the window, too shocked to cry, or make any sound at all.

CHAPTER TWENTY-FIVE

'You're not going anywhere.' He pressed his face to mine, and I could actually hear the pulse in his neck. I did as he said, I didn't turn, I just stared straight ahead, focusing on the treetops in the darkness, looking at the moon, full in the sky.

All I could hear was the intense pounding of my heart.

'What a treacherous little witch you are.' His voice came out in an acid whisper. 'Just like your whore of a mother.'

I turned and we stared at each other. I could smell his familiar smell, but otherwise I didn't recognise him. He looked . . . ugly.

He gave a nasty, twisted kind of smile. 'Now that I know what you've been up to I feel even less guilty . . .' He sighed. 'I was going to give it a little more time. Properly ingratiate myself with your family. Your mother would have begun to think of me as the son she never had . . .' He paused. 'Except she would always have looked at me and seen my birthmark, and been reminded . . . wondered if it really was just a coincidence.'

I was confused for a second but then my eyes fell to his neck, where the crescent-shaped scar seemed more prominent now.

'My father's was almost identical, except his was on his back. It's all I have left of him.'

'Sorry,' I said tonelessly. His eyes swept over me, contemptuous.

'I hear you've been tampering with my world,' he said calmly changing the subject. 'You and that pathetic wolf-boy, Luca . . .' He shook his head. 'He always was spineless. Even when we were small. A disgrace to his family.'

I kept silent, figuring it was the best policy.

'You were playing us off against each other.' Evan laughed nastily. 'And here was me priding myself on my deceit.' He pinched my cheek painfully. 'Sly little minx, aren't you, Jane?'

I shook my head.

'Actually,' he went on. 'I apologise. It isn't your fault. Really . . . it has nothing to do with you.' There was a pause before he continued. 'But on the other hand, it has everything to do with you.' I flinched at how cold he sounded. Worse than cold, his voice was flat and emotionless.

'How?' I said quietly. 'I don't understand . . .'

'Because she is your mother. Your flesh and blood. And I know you have inherited the bond with Nissilum . . . you and Luca.' He relaxed his grip a little. 'You mortals pretend innocence. You appear passive . . . But you are so dangerous. So indecisive. So weak.'

'You used me,' I said numbly. 'Everything was just . . . an act.'

Evan pouted. 'Don't look so sad, Janey. You didn't really want me either . . . did you?'

'I . . . did. At first I did.'

'That's what I thought,' he said, in a mock-sad voice. 'I thought I had you so smitten. I mean, I know you wanted me. You can't fake that. And everything was going so well. Just the right amount of attentive and loving, just the right amount of moody and unavailable. It's pathetic how easy it is to get a girl interested.'

'You wanted to break my heart. Make me feel that pain.'

'Something like that.'

'But it broke her heart,' I said, my voice seemed

to crack a little. 'My mum. It was the hardest thing she ever did.'

'Really?' he said, icily. 'Harder than watching your father disintegrate. Fade away in front of your eyes. Punished because of her.'

Evan was insane. I needed to choose my words carefully.

'It must have been terrible for you.'

'You have no idea,' Evan said with more feeling.

The curved roofs of the abandoned Nissen huts were suddenly bathed in light from the moon glowing above us. The cawing sound, the crows, was louder than ever. I felt sick with fear.

'But it was his choice, too?' I ventured dangerously. 'He had free will.'

Evan didn't speak but his grip tightened again. I looked furtively down at his hands, saw the veins standing out with the effort of holding so tight.

'They both took a risk—'

'What do you know about it, freak!' hissed Evan into my ear, and the nausea became worse. I kept my mouth shut, though I wanted to both scream and vomit at the same time.

'You're so naïve. So green. You fell for the first enigmatic sweet-talker that walked into town.'

A tear slid, unstoppable, down my cheek.

'When I walked into your house and saw your mother for the first time, it took all I had not to scream in her face. There she was, happy, carrying on her life like nothing had happened. Talking all that crap about being in love. Not being able to eat! I nearly slapped her. Heaven knows how I kept my cool.'

I remembered that day. I thought Evan had been quiet, thinking about his family.

He turned to me. 'There is so much you don't know.'

'What?' I said, feigning ignorance. In a macabre kind of way I wanted him to tell me about what I'd already found out.

'I can . . . I suppose you'd call it "shapeshift".' He sighed, as though the explanation was boring him. 'There was an Evan Forrest. Everyone thought he went missing, but he died in an "accident". Body unidentified. He was strangled. I believe.' Evan looked directly into my eyes, enjoying the fear he saw there. 'But the killer was never caught. Just disappeared.'

'Until he came here,' I said. 'You killed Evan.' I dug my nails into my palm, feeling drops of sweat on the back of my neck.

'Well, how else was I going to take on his form?' Evan chewed his lip casually.

'But why him?' I found myself asking. 'Why go all the way to Australia?'

'Easier to cover my tracks,' Evan replied evenly. 'No awkward questions.' He shifted, looking at me with indifference, as though he was confessing into a police tape recorder. 'It meant I could teach myself to drive, get myself a good tan, become the rugged outdoors type . . . and I could reinvent Evan a little . . . And then I could turn up here, knowing my dad would welcome me with open arms.'

'All that stuff about your mother . . .' I murmured in disbelief. 'Her depression and the neglect . . .'

Evan grinned. 'Good, wasn't it? Considering I made it all up on the spot.' He paused. 'I almost believed it myself.'

'She doesn't even know her son is dead,' I breathed. 'Her real son.'

He shrugged. 'A few "civilian casualties" were inevitable. It couldn't be helped.'

He truly was a monster. Or mentally ill. I didn't know which I was more scared of.

'How long have you been planning this?' I shrank from him.

'Years. Since my father passed away.'

'I don't get it. He died of a broken heart?'

Evan's eyes glinted sharply then. 'I told you. Falling in love is dangerous. In my father's case, it was fatal.'

'But he married your mother, had children . . . He moved on.'

'Obviously not,' Evan said in a voice laden with sarcasm.

'You really think my mother is to blame?' I shook my head. 'That's insane.'

'Your mother is a foolish, cold-hearted woman. She walked away and now she has everything.'

'It wasn't like that.' I felt tears pricking. 'She was torn apart.' I thought of the notebook. 'She wrote it all down and she hid it.'

Evan turned abruptly. 'What?'

She wrote down all her feelings, what was happening . . . Her mum – my grandmother – was very ill, she needed to take care of her. She tried to explain.'

His lip curled into a sneer. 'A convenient excuse maybe—'

'No!' I wrenched myself out of his grip. 'You don't have the monopoly on suffering, Evan. Neither did your dad. Shit happens. Deal with it!' I realised I was shaking, but I was less afraid now. I was angry.

Evan stared hard at me, he made no move to touch me. Instead he ran his hands, maddeningly slowly, through his hair.

'Oh, I'm dealing with it, Jane,' he said coldly. 'Just you wait and see.'

CHAPTER TWENTY-SIX

Luca kicked the bolts on the door one more time. His low growl of frustration sent a mouse skittering to its hiding place between two wooden benches. He closed his eyes and sank back down on to the floor.

'Please, brother . . .' he whispered into his hands. 'Understand.'

But outside, in the depths of the palace, there was just silence.

He sat for what seemed hours, staring at a spot on the floor, trying to stop the tumult of thoughts in his head. If he focused on any one of them he would start to rage and cry . . . Perhaps he would disintegrate? Perhaps he would deserve to. The sound of a door opening some distance away made him look up. Then footsteps, light, childlike, approaching the door to his prison, stopping just outside.

'Brother,' he heard a voice whisper loudly, 'I have the keys.'

His heart shot up into his mouth and adrenaline made his body bounce up and stand, then run to the door.

He pressed his ear against it.

'Quickly,' he told his sister. 'I have to get out of here right now.'

'I know, I know,' she grumbled, and he heard the jangle of keys. She had stolen the large master bunch from the palace cellar and was sorting through them.

'What are you doing, girl?' he hissed, exasperated.

'Trying to find the right key,' she told him, witheringly. He would have smiled to himself had his mind not been wholly on what he had to do.

Eventually the key turned in the lock and she stood before him, a small triumphant smile on her face.

'Good work,' he said, briefly touching the top of her head before pushing past her towards the stairs.

'Wait,' she grabbed his arm. 'I found something.' She took a letter out of her pocket.

Luca frowned. 'Dalya, there is no time.'

'Read it.' She thrust it at him. 'It could be your only hope.'

He opened the folded letter and scanned the contents. His sister watched his eyes widen as he read. When he was finished he stared at the words in front of him, eventually looking up at the girl.

'How can I take this with me? We will have to convince him of its existence.'

She nodded. 'I'll keep it in a safe place. For when you return.'

They looked at each other, neither knowing whether he would come back at all.

'I have to go,' he said. 'Time is running out.'

The two of them ran nimbly up the stairs, her breathing was heavy behind him.

He turned at the top. 'This is as far as you go,' he told her. 'You know that.'

She pouted, but waved her hand. 'Go, then,' she sighed. 'Be careful.'

'You are a good sister,' he said, feeling it. 'And I will be back.'

Pulling up his hood he ran at the speed of a puma across the servant's courtyard and through the back gate.

Watching him disappear out of sight, she closed her eyes, allowing anxiety to come.

CHAPTER TWENTY-SEVEN

I stopped the engine and I stared across the lake. Bird Lake. That's what I had called it when I was little. Years before – I must have been about five or six – my dad had brought me here. When we'd walked down to the water's edge, I'd put my hands up to my face. Two white swans had floated, dead and bloody, on the surface of the water.

White-faced and shocked, Dad had pulled me away, picking me up and holding me close, taking big anxious strides away from the scene of the crime.

I'd screamed all the way back to where Dad had parked the truck, and I hadn't stopped until I fell asleep, cried-out and exhausted. Nightmares had come for months. My mother sent Dad to the doghouse. She was furious with him.

'How was I to know we'd find savaged swans!' I heard him say guiltily when I listened outside the living room door one night. 'Jesus, Anna. Must have been a wild dog of some kind.'

Since then, since the nightmares had stopped, I hadn't been back. And after time, I had stopped thinking about it. Blocked it out I suppose.

But now I was here again. Looking over the grey-green, reed-covered expanse of water, nausea rising in the pit of my stomach.

Evan's voice was casual, thoughtful. 'Creepy, isn't it?'

I said nothing, concentrating on not shaking. Not vomiting.

'I call this place Death Lake,' he went on. 'Everything dies here.'

A sharp noise cut through my thoughts, like a knife slicing through my brain, and a hissing sound, turning from a sound to words.

'*I'm coming*,' said a voice. '*Don't be afraid.*'

I didn't dare believe it. Evan was playing tricks on me. But when I lifted my eyes to see his face, his mouth was set, silent.

'So, you're going to kill me then?' I said. 'Just get it over with.'

He turned to look at me, began to smile. 'But that's not the point, Jane.' His eyes danced, teasing. 'Where's the fun in that?'

I felt bile again. Part of me wanted to spit all of it out on to his face. But I restrained myself. He wanted me to react, I realised. Start screaming, or try and escape. I wasn't going to give him that.

In the middle of the lake, an unwitting bird swooped, circling, interested. I watched as it hovered, its beak pecking tentatively at a piece of sodden driftwood. I focused on the creature's investigation, ignoring the darkening sky above me. I felt colder than I had ever done in my life.

Hold on.

I jerked in response to the voice and, somewhere inside, hope stirred. Luca was coming. Luca would make it all right.

'I heard you were the talk of the Great Ball,' Evan said, conversationally. 'Such a pretty little mortal.'

My head snapped round to face him. 'How did you . . . ?'

He was smiling unpleasantly. 'Did you really think I wouldn't find out about that?' Shaking his head, he picked up a slender stick and began prodding at the ground. 'There are some voracious gossips in Nissilum,' he went on. 'The witches can't help themselves.'

Tilly.

I said nothing, I wanted to hear every detail of what he

knew. In a sick kind of way, him talking about the ball made me feel close to Luca. I gulped to keep myself from crying.

'And when I saw that photograph in your room . . .' His tone darkened. 'I suppose it just speeded up the inevitable.'

I remembered that. Remembered his weirdness. He'd said it was something he'd seen out of the window. But he'd seen the photograph.

'That boy is you,' I said then. 'Of course.'

'That boy was innocent, trusting, full of love . . .' He paused. 'But your mother destroyed everything.'

I wasn't going to contradict him again. There was no point.

'Where is my family?' I said.

His mouth twisted into an ugly smile. 'They are still alive, if that's what you're worried about.'

Still alive. Was he going to kill us all?

'Please . . .' I thought of my little sister. Confused and frightened. Of my dad, who knew nothing of my mum's dark secret. They didn't deserve to be punished. Neither did she.

'Do what you want to me,' I told him, sounding a lot braver than I felt. 'But don't hurt them.'

'Loyalty,' he said quietly. 'I like that . . . Unfortunately for you, not enough to reconsider.' He scratched at his chin, thoughtfully. 'But what's the hurry? I'm enjoying our little chat.'

If it bought me more time, I was grateful. It began to sink in that there would be no happy ending. I tried to bring Luca's face into my mind. I could see his eyes and I focused on them.

Keep him there, he told me, clear as a bell. *Just keep him there.*

CHAPTER TWENTY-EIGHT

Luca leaped over the palace walls; lithe and strong, his cheekbones narrowing, his face changing shape. It was the full moon and the time for turning had never been more right.

He was conscious of someone behind him, but he had no time to stop and look. He was about to do something he had never attempted before. To turn in one world and jump to another.

His heart was speeding up and his skin grew tauter, then more elastic as it prepared itself for its cataclysmic change. Soon his organs would grow and his heart would enlarge to twice its size. His hair would turn thicker and the blood vessels in his eyes would explode with pressure.

He was familiar with this. He knew this. What he didn't know was if he could save the girl he loved.

'Luca!'

He heard the scream as he vaulted through the fields and he shook his head as he ran, wondering if she was calling for help. If Raphael had already . . .

'Luca!'

The voice was close now, right behind him, and he turned to see his sister. A smaller neater, prettier version of him.

Dalya was wolf.

He stood up on his hind legs, which shook with the shock.

'Brother, you can't do this alone,' she half panted, half growled, and then she lost her voice. Her slender jaws snapped together.

He met her gaze full on, silently communicating gratitude, and she pawed the ground, ready to run with him.

And as the moon held court above them, brother and sister bounded forward, heading for the Water Path.

CHAPTER TWENTY-NINE

It would be light soon, I thought, not knowing whether this would make things better or worse. I was both exhausted and wired; I didn't dare drop my guard.

Evan was pitching stones into the filthy, stagnant water. I used the time to look around me, wondering how, if, I could possibly escape this.

Through some trees, I could see Dad's truck, which Evan had made me drive, enjoying watching me as I'd nervously navigated the narrow roads. It had been one hell of a way to lose my learner plates. I didn't think I would ever be able to drive again.

That was, if I didn't die before I got the chance.

I tried to think of where my parents and Dot might be. Where he would have taken them. He had driven us to that creepy abandoned army training ground . . . He could have put them in one of those rusting old Nissen huts.

He could have put them anywhere.

'What is it with you and that place?' I said to his back. 'That army training ground?'

His arm was lifted, poised to cast another stone into the water, but he paused, turning part way back to me.

'I like it,' he said, then. 'So cold and abandoned and bleak . . .' He turned all the way to face me. 'It feels like a place I belong. Somewhere a person could stay for years . . . and no one would find them. Not a soul.'

He turned back and hurled the stone aggressively forward. It didn't even cause a ripple, it just landed on some rotting reeds.

'But you haven't been abandoned,' I said quietly. 'You have a family that . . . loves you.'

'I don't care,' he snarled, and I jumped a little in fright.

He walked back towards me and grabbed my arm, leaning into me, his mouth next to my ear. 'Let me show you what it means to be truly afraid,' he said, 'because really . . . you have no idea.'

I tried to control my breath, which was coming heavily, and allowed myself to be dragged over to the truck.

'Get in,' he said roughly, opening the door.

I climbed into the passenger seat and Evan started the engine, ignoring his seatbelt. I didn't dare reach for mine,

351

I just stared straight in front of me, feeling sweat forming on my body, even though it was the middle of the night and chilly. Evan drove fast, winding around the roads, scaring night-time creatures and birds.

There was no mistaking where the vehicle was headed. In spite of the speed I saw a sign, a familiar sign.

We were going back there.

The place was dank. Evan drove straight through the closed wooden gate and I put my hand to my mouth as it splintered apart and wood flew into the surrounding bushes.

'Please,' I heard myself gibber, 'stop this.'

'Shut up!' he snapped, and the truck screeched to a halt. He opened the door roughly and I sat where I was, unable to move.

'Get out.' He pulled open the passenger door, and I somehow managed to get down on to the grass, though my legs were like jelly.

It was raining now. Nasty, spitting rain, and the grass was wet. Across from us, the eerie huts stood, as though waiting to receive us.

I didn't care, I just wanted to see my family alive.

CHAPTER THIRTY

Luca wrestled in the darkness. His whole body in pain, stretched and distorted, he opened his jaws and howled, pawing angrily at the ground.

Behind him, Dalya panted, looking to him for instructions.

Slowly he wound his way through the trees, shaking rain off his head, and she dutifully followed.

The sky was gradually getting paler, soon the moon would disappear. He growled, sniffing the ground, trying to find her scent. Jane's scent.

They were near her house. Their silhouettes were shadows against the back wall and something made him stop, putting his snout to the ground again.

He could smell her.

Now all they had to do was get there in time.

He turned to Dalya and silently spoke to her, and she let out a low whine in understanding.

Together, the animals ran down the rough track towards the mountain road, headed for the other side of town.

CHAPTER THIRTY-ONE

The entrance to the hut was hung with rusting bits of metal, hostile and creaking as they swung slightly back and forth.

I screwed up my eyes to see the back of the hut, but there was nothing there except shadows.

'Mum!' I called, my voice coming out as a sob. 'Dad!'

Beside me, Evan laughed humourlessly.

'They can't hear you. Don't waste your breath.'

'Where are they, you bastard?' I tore into his chest, hitting him as hard as I could. 'You evil—!'

'Calm down,' he said, amused. 'They're safe . . . for now. They're knocked out.' He scratched his chin. 'Your mum and the kid were easy enough, but your dad . . .' He shook his head. 'That required a bit more effort.'

'Are they here somewhere?' I said desperately, pushing past him.

He grabbed my arm, which hurt. I winced in pain.

'Careful, Jane,' he whispered. 'Not so fast.'

'You'd better not have touched them,' I said. 'Dot . . .' I put my hand to my mouth, not wanting to think about what he'd do to my little sister.

'Calm down.' Evan sounded bored now. 'They're not far. You'll all be together soon.' He smiled nastily. 'They're incapacitated, that's all.'

'What did you do to them?' I was shivering uncontrollably.

'Tilly has her uses,' he said mildy. 'Irritating little wretch most of the time, but she mixes up a highly effective sedative. Strong enough to put a horse to sleep for six months.'

I gaped at him, standing so casually. So dismissive of other people's lives.

'So you avenge the death of your father by trying to destroy an entire family,' I said in disbelief. 'Can't you just get the hell over it?'

His face snapped back into a look of pure hatred as his arm shot out and I felt his fingers straddling my neck.

'Watch your mouth, freak,' he said. 'You don't get to judge me.'

He paused, sniffing the air, frowning.

'What are you doing?' I glared at him.

He shrugged. 'Nothing. Shut up for once, would you?'

I flared my nostrils. I felt nothing but hatred for Evan now. His once-beautiful face looked almost haggard. Bitter.

He moved around the hut, kicking bits of old rusting machinery on the ground. A rat scuttled out from beneath a tyre and I shuddered. Were my parents lying with rats?

'How does this compare,' said Evan leaning back against the wall, 'in terms of pure misery, to your schooldays?' He grinned unpleasantly. 'Sarah not quite so bad now I imagine. Just a harmless kid.'

I stared at him. 'You two are made for each other,' I said, icily. 'I mean . . . she knew all about this, right?'

'Clever.' He tapped his head patronisingly.

I felt disgusted. 'You really are a piece of work.'

'Thank you.' He crossed his arms. 'She was only too happy to help. Bored, spoiled . . . She was just itching to liven things up in her life. I studied her for some time before getting in touch.'

'How?'

'I spoke to her . . . in her dreams.' He raised one eyebrow. 'Does that ring any bells?'

'Wait . . . You can do that, too?'

'We all can . . . If we want to enough. It just takes a

willing accomplice . . . You know what I mean?'

I turned from him. He'd told her to torment me. He wanted to make all of our lives hell.

Ironic, coming from an angel. I opened my mouth to ask another question, but shut it again. What did it matter any more?

'So what are you going to do with us?' I said instead, not wanting to know, still listening – but there was only silence in the hut.

'Hmmm.' He narrowed his eyes. 'I had wanted to drown you, one by one – but lifting those bodies . . . I am sure I can make use of some of these mortal weapons lying around here.' He studied an old saw, lethally sharp and rusting.

I had no defence against him. I was all alone. Luca wasn't coming. We were all going to die here. I let out a small sob.

Thunder suddenly rippled across the sky and we both jerked, startled, looking out to see a white fork split the darkness. It lit up the whole of the field outside, and for a second I saw the dark shape, moving across the grass. Two dark shapes . . . dogs, or . . .

It couldn't be. Could it? My heart did a silent, hopeful cheer.

I forced myself not to react outwardly, and not to hope,

but the animals were picking up speed and heading straight for us.

Evan pulled me roughly to him, putting an arm around my neck, pressing against my throat.

The dogs slowed and stood panting at the entrance. The bigger one's eyes flashed at me.

Green eyes.

A little bit of fear left me.

Luca snarled, revealing his sharp teeth, his ears back, ready for attack.

'I'm not afraid of you,' Evan hissed at him, still pinning me to him. 'Why would I be afraid of you?'

Luca rolled his head, pawing angrily at the ground. The hanging metal jangled in vibration.

'Get back to your family . . .' Evan spoke to him, tightening his grip on my neck and I whimpered slightly.

Luca shot forward, his jaws snapping, brushing aside the hanging metal as though it were nothing more substantial than a net curtain. He rocked his head from side to side, frustrated, but Evan didn't even flinch.

'Luca,' I said, reaching out to stroke his nose and he nuzzled against me briefly, before turning to stare Evan headlong in the face. Behind me I felt Evan reaching for something in his pocket with his free hand and I wrenched myself out of his grasp, turning to see that it was a bottle.

'Luca,' I said warningly, but he was ahead of me. Rolling his head he quickly lunged at the bottle, which smashed on to the floor.

'My friend,' said Evan softly. 'You wouldn't hurt me . . . Remember, Luca. You would never even swat at a fly.'

'Don't listen to him,' I bleated.

Luca shook his head and I saw that his body was contracting, shrinking.

I looked back at the wolf standing guard at the entrance, whose eyes glinted anxiously over at Luca.

'Dalya?' I said. 'Is it you?'

She whined in answer.

'You can't hurt me.' Evan shook his head at Luca. 'You know that.'

Luca's bodily hair was disappearing and he moved to stand upright. With a start I realised he would be naked once the process was complete. I wrenched off my jacket, wrapping it gently around Luca's waist. He licked his lips and I saw those familiar pale cheekbones appearing.

'How sweet,' Evan sneered at us. 'Enjoy your last moments together.'

'Evan, this is not what Gabriel would want,' Luca spoke at last, and his voice, low and calm sent ripples of relief through me. Relief . . . and something else I was starting to get used to.

'What would you know?' Evan's face twisted with contempt. 'You have no idea what I've been through. Gabriel would still be here if it wasn't for her mother. And look at you . . . you're destined for the same fate.'

'Gabriel didn't die of a broken heart.' Luca said softly.

'He didn't.' A voice at the entrance to the hut made us all start. Turning, I saw my mother standing behind Dalya. Her hair soaking wet, hugging herself.

'Mum.' I backed away from Evan, practically tripping over all the stuff on the floor. But Mum held her hand up to stop me.

Evan looked shocked, and outraged.

'How did you get out?' he snarled. 'I'm warning you—'

'Listen to me.' She cut through him, her voice firm and authoritative. The adult amongst us. We were silent, waiting for her to go on.

'I didn't break your father's heart,' she said more wearily. 'He broke mine. He didn't love me. He told me so. Told me to go and never come back.'

I frowned. What was she saying?

'Liar.' Evan spat at the ground.

'But I didn't want to believe it,' she went on. 'I deluded myself that it was my decision. My mother was sick . . . I was human. It would never work.' She shook her head. 'I even wrote it all down. I thought if I wrote it down, it would become the truth.'

'You expect me to believe that?' He scowled.

'It's the truth.' She looked straight at him. 'I am not a liar.'

There was a pointed silence as she stared him out.

Luca cleared his throat then. 'Evan, would you believe it, if you saw it written down . . . by your own father?' he asked.

I looked from one to the other, confused.

'What?' Evan snapped.

'Your father wrote a letter,' Luca said quietly, 'addressed to you and Dorcas. Dalya found it, in the palace. In Gabriel's bureau drawer.'

Dalya, who by now was her familiar dark-haired self and wearing my mother's jacket, nodded, shaking a little from the cold.

'I didn't mean to pry,' she said demurely, 'but I thought there might be some clue . . .'

'Enough!' Evan looked furious, but a little uncertain too. He backed away and leaned against the wall. 'Where is this letter then?'

'Nissilum,' said Luca patiently. 'We could hardly bring it with us as werewolves.'

'No,' Evan said, darkly sarcastic.

My mother stepped forward then. Her jeans and shirt were clinging to her. She was wet through. And she looked younger somehow than I'd ever seen her.

'Listen,' she said. 'Your father was a good, strong man. He dreamed of having his own family. Living a peaceful life. Guided by morality . . .' She glanced quickly at me before continuing. 'He knew he could never have that with me. And he wanted it.' I watched as tears gathered in her eyes. 'He wanted your mother, and you. More than anything.'

There was a silence as Evan digested her words. He was obviously struggling to hide any emotion other than sheer contempt. Hatred even.

'He would never have left us if it hadn't been for you,' he began, his voice catching slightly. 'Whatever you tell yourself. If you had never existed he would never have been tempted to—'

'Evan,' she said, exasperated. 'Part of being a man is accepting responsibility.' I glanced at my mother with admiration, then at Evan, whose face twisted with frustrated rage. That really got to him. For the first time what was written in his eyes was real.

'How dare you—' he spat out at last, unable to articulate anything beyond that, as he clenched and unclenched his fingers.

'Life presents many challenges,' Mum went on, fearlessly. 'Temptation is one of them.' She reached out then and took hold of my hand. 'And free will governs us all. We have the power to choose.'

I held my breath, waiting for Evan to explode, but he seemed frozen to the spot by Mum's words. Lifting my head, I met Luca's eyes. He didn't look away, but held my gaze. The sound of the rain seemed the perfect backdrop to what we were facing up to.

'Jane,' Mum said quietly. 'Nothing is simple. Particularly not love. You must trust what your instincts tell you.'

Was she warning me or giving me some kind of blessing? When I saw Luca looking at me in a way that I could no longer describe as just 'friendly' I hoped it was a bit of both.

From behind us, Dalya broke the spell. Clutching my mother's jacket to her, she sighed heavily, then spoke to Evan.

'I can show you the letter,' she said, her voice wobbling slightly. 'Back home.'

'Bring the letter to me,' he snapped, his eyes down. 'Then I will decide.'

Dalya looked to Luca for guidance. He hesitated, before replying.

'Go and fetch it.' He spoke to Dalya, though his eyes were on Evan. 'I will stay.'

Dalya nodded and turned to leave, when she stopped, with her back to us. We saw another shape approaching. I held my breath, hoping it wasn't Ulfred or Henora come after their errant children.

But it was worse than that. My heart sank as Lowe came clearly into view. I heard Luca groan slightly, while Evan looked amused.

'Excellent,' he said. 'Another interfering do-gooder come to talk me round.'

Lowe ignored me, simply put his hand into his pocket and drew something out. 'You forgot this,' he said, thrusting a piece of paper at Dalya.

Confused, I glanced at Luca as a smile replaced the frown on his face. My mother's hold on my hand tightened protectively.

Luca stepped across to his brother and embraced him. Over his shoulder Lowe's eyes met mine, but this time there was no malice, just a weird kind of acceptance.

Dalya handed what I now saw was a folded letter or note to Evan.

'Here,' she said kindly. 'This is from your father.'

Evan's hand shook as he unfolded the letter, and to my surprise, he cleared his throat, now looking more like a boy than a monster, he began to read out loud:

My dearest Dorcas and Raphael
I am slipping away. It is not my body, it is my mind. I
know neither of you will understand. But I cannot go on
living as one of the Seraphim, one who is supposed to
guide and protect his family and the population of
Nissilum – I can't go on knowing what I did many years
ago. It was a moment of foolishness, of rare human
weakness, but I became infatuated with a mortal girl.

She was beautiful and strong and brave and she lived
a life that I could only dream of. One where human error
is tolerated, sometimes embraced. I wanted to be part of
that. I was just a boy. I dreamed of her, and I misused all
my power to get her. And she fell in love with me. I
thought I felt the same way. But I realised after time, that
she could never give me what I truly wanted and what
Celeste and Cadmium wanted, a wife and children who
were untainted by human, mortal blood. I did not treat
her well. I left her and though I knew she travelled to see
me, I didn't go to her. I felt such guilt, I confided in my
sister, who took my pain to be the pain of heartbreak,
and so I let it be believed. Because I knew what I had
done was callous and cruel. Anna did not deserve it.

The guilt I feel now is partly to do with that, how I

treated Anna, but partly with tainting my family with
that brief, adolescent crush. I am not pure. I do not
deserve my position here. Or my life.

I love you both more than I can say. And Raffy, the
thought of leaving you brings me more pain than you
can ever imagine. Go carefully, boy. Rein in your
emotional nature, become what I am not able to become.
A true leader, a role model to all on Nissilum. I am so
proud of what I know you will become.

Gabriel.

Glancing up I saw my mother's face was wet with tears.
And across from me, Evan stood, suddenly smaller and
vulnerable, though doing everything he could not to
show it.

'I'm sick of you,' he hissed at Luca and me. 'Just make
sure I never have to see you again.'

We were speechless. Relieved. Hardly daring to move.

Evan pushed past us, his elbow digging into me as he
went. I could hardly believe that only a few days before he
had been my adoring boyfriend. But I didn't feel hurt. I
didn't even feel surprised. I felt nothing for him.

When Evan reached the entrance to the hut, where
Dalya stood nervously with Lowe, Luca turned to speak to
him. 'You did the right thing,' he told Evan. 'Thank you.'

CHAPTER THIRTY-TWO

'Come, Dalya,' said Lowe, tugging at his sister's arm. 'We should get back before Henora and Ulfred discover we have all disappeared.' He nodded at Luca. 'I will make it right,' he told him. 'They will never know about this.'

'Thank you.' Luca smiled. 'I just need some time . . .'

Lowe fell behind Raphael and, together with Dalya, the three of them walked out into the sodden dark of the early morning.

My mother wiped at her eyes with her hand. 'Now I need to wake up Dot and my husband,' she told Luca, sounding more like her usual brisk self. 'They are heavily sedated in the hut next door. Evan just knocked me out with his fist.'

I looked down at the bottle on the floor.

'Some potion Tilly made up for him . . .'

Luca shook his head. 'Traitorous shrew,' he said. 'But

knowing Tilly, she will have vastly exaggerated the potency of whatever she gave him. Dalya will go back and fetch a remedy,' he told my mother. 'They will be back to normal in no time.'

Luca and I helped Mum put Dot and my dad into the truck. She insisted on driving back home herself, giving me one last thoughtful look before she climbed inside and started the engine. When the truck had pulled out of the field, through the broken gateway, it left Luca and me alone together.

I prepared myself for the fact that this would be the last time.

'Thank you,' I whispered. 'For caring about us.'

'Come here.' Luca held out his arms and I nestled willingly into them, feeling his body still hot, trembling, as I stroked his slender, muscular back. I pressed my face against his chest. He traced down one of my cheeks with his finger. 'They will be back to normal in no time.'

I nodded, though I realised that I too was trembling, unable to look into his eyes. This was the end.

'Jane,' he said after a pause. 'You know what I told you. About never falling in love with you? How dangerous it is? The risk . . .'

I swallowed the disappointment, the pain I knew was coming.

'It's OK,' I said. 'You don't have to say it again.'

He put his arms around my waist, holding me tightly to him.

'You're wrong. I do have to say it,' he murmured, 'and I will say it every day for the rest of our lives.'

I finally raised my head and saw his lips, level with mine. 'Say what?' I said, trying not to dwell on how full and kissable his mouth looked.

'That I love you. And I want you . . . like a boy wants a girl. And I don't think I want that ever to stop. However much of a risk it is.'

He stroked my hair away from my face as I gazed up at him.

'We'll find a way to do this,' he whispered. 'If it means we have to be apart sometimes, then so be it.'

'Luca.' I smiled. 'Can this really work?'

He laid his head on top of mine as my fingers felt the soft strength of his body, his long torso, breathing in his familiar woody smell.

'Our hearts are bound together,' he said, 'and I am free to decide who I love. And what I want. Nothing – not the pressure of my family, or what anyone else thinks – matters.'

And as I pulled free to look up at him, he lowered his head and his lips moved closer to mine, and then, finally, we were kissing. Not softly or tentatively, but hungrily, his mouth moving across to my neck and then to my lips again, pushing away my hair, and letting his hands explore my arched back.

I knew then that whatever I had felt with Evan was just a fraction of what I was feeling now. I was scared. But this time I loved being scared.

'You've no idea how often I have wanted to do this,' Luca said in between kisses, his breath quick and heavy. 'And how much I have wanted to touch you. Every inch of you.'

'I don't know why I didn't see it,' I said softly. 'And now that I do see it, I don't think I can stand being without it . . . Without you.'

Luca tilted my chin up gently. 'I promise I will do everything I can,' he said. 'I have a few battles to fight. With my parents. With Celeste and the angels . . . They trust me. And who knows what Raphael will say or do next . . . He has stepped so far into the darkness now I don't know if he will ever properly come back . . . But what I feel for you is far too much to let you go.'

He kissed me quickly and firmly on the mouth, causing sparks to dance around my heart.

371

'I can wait,' I said, hoping that I really could. That time and practicality and other people wouldn't get in the way.

'I will wait.'

Not alive. Not dead. Somewhere in between
lie the Beautiful Dead.

A stunning series that will leave you restless.

Books 1-4
OUT NOW

Sisters Red

'The wolf opened its long jaws, rows of teeth stretching for her. A thought locked itself in Scarlett's mind: I am the only one left to fight, so now, I must kill you …'

An action-packed, paranormal thriller in a gritty urban setting, with a charming love story and unexpected twist that leaves you wanting more!

Sign up to the mailing list to find out about the latest releases from Jackson Pearce

theVampire
Diaries

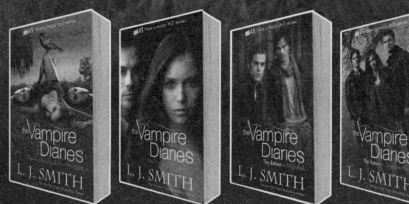